SECOND ACTIVATION

OTHER TITLES BY THE AUTHORS

Fast Forward by Darren Wearmouth

Critical Dawn by Darren Wearmouth and Colin F. Barnes

Critical Path by Darren Wearmouth and Colin F. Barnes

Sixth Cycle by Darren Wearmouth and Carl Sinclair

Eximus by Marcus Wearmouth

First Activation by Darren and Marcus Wearmouth

SECOND ACTIVATION

Darren and Marcus Wearmouth

47N🔆RTH

Published by 47North, Seattle

www.apub.com

Amazon, the Amazon logo, and 47North are trademarks of Amazon.com, Inc., or its affiliates.

ISBN-13: 978-1477828588
ISBN-10: 1477828583

Cover design by Jason Gurley

Library of Congress Control Number: 2014955282

Printed in the United States of America

SECOND ACTIVATION

1

In my peripheral vision, I saw Jack's arm rise to meet Ron's handshake. As it carried on in an upward motion past the height of Ron's chest, I turned to look.

Jack pulled the trigger.

At the ear-splitting crack of the Ruger, I blinked hard and focused back on Ron.

He tried to speak. His lips quivered and his mouth erratically opened and closed. He looked up at the ceiling. A thin stream of blood, running from the forehead entry wound, momentarily pooled in his twitching left eye before rolling down his cheek.

Ron's legs buckled. He collapsed lifelessly to the ground. His head slammed with a dull thud onto the tiles at my feet, and his left leg twitched.

Jack stood motionless. A wisp of smoke curled from his pistol, still raised and pointing at a now blood-spattered cupboard. Lea stared open-mouthed.

I looked down at Ron. The round had blown out a fist-sized chunk of skull as it exited, confirming he wouldn't be getting backup, even though it appeared that he was still breathing.

Twisting toward the kitchen door, I waited for the inevitable sound of gunfire that would accompany the guards when they burst through.

"What the hell have you done?" Lea asked.

She rushed over to Ron and knelt over his body. I edged over to Jack and grabbed him by the shoulder. "Are you okay? Jack?"

He lowered the pistol and stared into my eyes. "Sorry, I couldn't . . ."

"It's done Jack. We were never leaving here anyway."

Lea stood and slowly shook her head. I unhooked a bunch of keys off Ron's chinos, identified the long, thin one for the cuffs, and freed her wrists. She caressed the red marks and inhaled sharply.

Perhaps the goons were circling and coming in slow. I strained to hear any sound outside the kitchen but couldn't detect anything. Jack looked quizzically at me. He gestured with his head toward a back entrance.

I scrambled to the window. A neatly manicured grassed area, a couple of old tires in the corner, and a chain-link fence that formed the boundary to the rear of the property, but crucially, no guards.

"What's beyond the fence, Lea?" I asked.

"Oh my God. Martina's gonna think I killed Ron. I need to speak to her," she said.

"You'll never see her again if we can't get out of this mess. Concentrate: What's the ground like beyond Ron's garden? Can we get out that way?"

"There's a marsh that leads to the river. It's open country. Why aren't they here yet?"

"We can't escape through the back door," Jack said. "With machine guns at both ends of the road, they'll easily cut us down in the open."

He took up a firing position and aimed his pistol at the interior entrance. "They'll be coming. Mark my words."

I rummaged through the kitchen drawers, pulled out a carving knife, and positioned myself against the wall, out of sight to anyone who approached via the front door.

"Is that all we have?" Lea asked.

"No guns in Ron's house—you should know that," Jack said.

We waited silently and braced for the expected assault or a shout to drop our weapons. I tried to imagine what was happening outside. Our chances of survival hung on the general incompetence of the enemy. So far, they'd proven to be far from Special Forces material.

"We need to create a diversion. Any ideas?" I asked. "Quickly—the Genesis Alliance goons are probably sealing off the perimeter or planning a house clearance."

I watched the digital clock on Ron's wall flicker and change to 11:02. My hand cramped from squeezing the knife, and I loosened my grip. The longer we failed to act, the less were our chances of survival. I was sure of that.

"We could pretend we've taken Ron hostage," Lea said.

"That won't work. They'll want to see him alive."

"What if I stagger out, pretending I've been shot?" Jack said. "You could say Ron wants me to go for treatment?"

"They won't fall for that. We'd be instantly heavily outnumbered and outgunned. Besides, after what Ron said about his house rules . . ."

Ron's retro control panel clicked, and an internal fan started to whir inside it. Its speaker crackled and squelched. I ran over to inspect the panel, brushing my hand over the buttons and switches, but pulled it away at the thought of accidentally triggering a second activation.

"You think they've frozen?" Jack said.

"It's possible, or they're laying siege."

Jack edged toward the internal door and looked around it. "It's now or never. We need to move."

I decided to take the initiative in case something bigger and badder than the goons outside was on its way. "Wait here until I call out; I'm going to take a look."

"Look where?" Lea asked.

"There's none at the back, so they must be out front. I'll try and find out their positions. At the moment I can't think of any other plan."

"I'll watch the back," Jack said. "If you see any danger, come straight back. If we're going down, we'll do it here."

"This is crazy, guys. We need to give ourselves up. We're surrounded," Lea said.

Jack put his finger to his lips. I ignored Lea and gently pushed open the door to get a view of the living area. The room remained exactly as we had left it.

I turned to shake my head at Jack, then leopard-crawled across the lush cream carpet to the front window. Below the window, with my back against the wall, I listened. After hearing no sounds, I raised my head and peered through the sheer curtain.

The immediate vicinity looked deserted apart from the Range Rover we'd arrived in, still parked at an angle opposite the house. I raised the curtain from the bottom and glanced up and down the street. There appeared to be no threat in either direction as far as my angle of vision would allow me to see.

"Jack, Lea—get over here quickly!" I shouted.

Both came through the living-room entrance in a crouching run and joined me, ducking below the window, with their backs against the wall.

"What's going on?" Jack asked.

I gestured toward the street. "No idea—take a look."

He pulled the curtain to one side and craned his neck. "I can't see anyone. Do you think they've taken cover?"

"An ambush?" Lea said.

It didn't make sense. The guards had been all over us less than ten minutes ago. I knew the Genesis Alliance members we'd previously come across weren't trained soldiers, but the ones around the house appeared more experienced or better trained. Their inconsistent nature meant I couldn't tell what to expect. A potential opportunity presented itself, and I decided to take it with both hands.

"I'm going to scout outside," I said. "Jack, you search the house for anything useful. If we're clear, we make a break for the Range Rover. There's no way I'm waiting in this house like a sitting duck. Our best chance is to make a run for it."

Jack immediately ran to an adjacent door in the hallway.

"What about me?" Lea asked.

"Keep looking through the window. If you see any movement—anything—shout. If I draw fire, try to ascertain the location."

She feverishly nodded and raised the curtain.

I crept toward the front entrance, keeping down to avoid throwing a silhouette in front of the frosted glass door panel. The brass handle turned easily, and I twisted the latch.

I took a deep breath, mentally counted to three, and pulled the door open a few inches. The noise of a reversing engine echoed in the distance. I sprang out and hugged the exterior wall.

Toward the west end of Oak Street, I caught a brief glimpse of a black Range Rover turning and disappearing to the right.

I scanned the quiet tree lined street again in both directions, clutching the knife in my hand, trying to work out what was going on. Both cutoff groups and the previously circling guards had disappeared.

We had to take advantage. I sprinted to the Range Rover, expecting shots to split the air at any moment. None came.

The keys were still in the ignition, and the engine instantly roared into life. I clicked the vehicle into reverse, accelerated hard, and turned the wheel. The Rover shot backward, crashing through Ron's white picket fence. I hit the brake hard, skidding to an abrupt halt inches from the front door. Jack appeared from the entrance and yanked open the passenger door.

"All clear at the back. Where the fuck are they?" he asked.

"I caught a glimpse of them leaving. Come on—get in. They might be regrouping."

He climbed into the passenger seat and slammed the door. Lea jumped in the back and lay across the seat.

A burst of automatic gunfire rattled in the distance, followed by several single shots in rapid succession. The firing appeared to be close, maybe only a street away, where the other Range Rover had turned.

"There's something else going on here," Jack said. "They could be getting attacked from the Army or government. Maybe the cavalry's arrived?"

"Doubt it's the cavalry," I said and turned back to Lea. "Is there another way out of Monroe?"

She poked her head between the front seats. "Turn left. Where do you want to go?"

"Back to the Toyota we left on the outskirts of town. Hopefully, the rifle's still there."

Jack kicked his door open. "Wait here a minute."

"Christ, Jack. We've just had a break here," I said.

He ignored me, jumped out of the Rover, and ran back inside the house. My eyes darted to either end of the street as we waited. I wondered what could be so important as to stall our escape.

A minute later, he returned and buckled up. "Right, let's go."

I shoved the Rover into drive. "What were you doing?"

"Set fire to the house. If activations are controlled from there, it might stall them for a day or two until we figure out what—"

"Martina's going to kill me," Lea said.

"She's the least of our worries," Jack said. "She might not even be alive."

"She's the least of yours. I know she's alive."

I detected more than a hint of anger in Lea's reply. I wasn't sure what she expected us to do, and I wasn't prepared to risk my life for a woman that seemed to be neck deep in Genesis Alliance. To be clear of the building, in a vehicle, was more than we could have hoped for twenty minutes ago.

Tires screeched against the road surface at the right end of Oak Street. A light-blue Mustang skidded around the corner, then came to a sudden halt around two hundred yards from us. The engine revved several times. Puffs of white smoke came from the wheels as they started to spin.

"Go left— *now!*" Lea shouted.

I punched the accelerator hard and felt the wheels rip out chunks of turf from Ron's lawn. The Rover gained traction, and we sprang back onto the road.

"Right here—that's Clark Street."

The Mustang disappeared from the rearview mirror as we turned and sped along.

"Right at the end of Wood Street, then take the first left. I'm taking us a different way out of town."

I kept the pedal to the metal, and the Rover gathered speed along Wood Street.

The blue Mustang tore out of the side street. It skidded to a halt diagonally across the road, blocking our path.

"Ram it," Jack said.

I had no other option and aimed at the side of the Mustang, bracing for impact. With a thunderous crash of metal and breaking glass, the vehicles collided, and I was thrown forward, then backward, in my seat.

The scene outside whizzed past in a blur. The Rover spun out of control, and I slammed on the brakes. The car came to a juddering halt facing the critically damaged Mustang. Its front left panel and lights were crushed.

Inside the vehicle, Jerry looked dazed while Anthony glared out of the window and his face contorted in anger. He shook Jerry, and they both reached backward.

I shoved Jack's shoulder. "They're going for weapons, Jack—shoot the buggers!"

He pressed a button on the door, and his window lowered with an electric whine. "Where the hell did they come from?" he asked.

Both men in the Mustang struggled with the doors. Jerry elbowed out parts of smashed glass on the driver's side and thrust out a rifle with a single hand.

Jack aimed the Ruger and fired twice at the Mustang's windshield. Both rounds punctured holes through the middle, and it splintered and cracked. Jerry dropped his rifle and ducked down. Anthony struggled to open his door.

I pressed the accelerator and rammed the vehicle again, turning it backward and creating a gap to squeeze past and keep going. As we raced away, I spotted Anthony in the rearview mirror. He kicked the car door open and lay down flat on the road in a textbook prone firing position.

"Get down!" I said.

Two rounds hit our Rover. One shot went high through the rear window, and the other sounded like it ricocheted off the underside of the vehicle. As I turned right at the end of the street, two tracer rounds streaked over the hood. Seconds later, we were out of Anthony's line of sight.

"That guy's skilled with a rifle," Jack said. "I thought he was totally useless."

Anthony had showed no signs of lethal competence when we ambushed him in Hermitage and captured him with his pants down. Perhaps that incident pushed him into action. Whatever the cause, I was glad to be out of range. I glanced at Lea. She hugged herself and quivered as if she'd just climbed out of a pool of freezing water. I hoped she wasn't going into shock.

"Where now, Lea? Take us the quickest way out of town," I said.

"We'll be on Hull Road in a few minutes. We can shoot straight to the southern edge. There're a couple of farms and a few houses—that's about it."

Open fields concerned me. The lack of cover would leave us painfully exposed, but our options were limited. I screeched around a corner, and we hit a main road. Jack had two rounds left in the Ruger and maintained aim out of his open window as cool spring air rushed inside, giving my arms goose bumps.

"Think of a couple of alternatives in case we come across GA," I said. "If we're blocked off, we'll have to go on foot."

As we passed a large lake to our right on Hull Road, speed started to drain from the vehicle. A burning aroma flooded through the vents, accompanied by wisps of white smoke from under the hood. I pumped the accelerator but received no response.

"You've got to be kidding me," Jack said flatly in disbelief.

The Rover lost all power and coasted to a hissing halt.

"Damn," I shouted and slammed my hand against the steering wheel. "Everybody out."

A train track ran along our right side, with thick, impenetrable vegetation on the rising ground behind it. To our left, small white bungalows with generous yards and long driveways dotted into the distance along a tree lined road. This wasn't the most affluent of areas, but America had the luxury of space compared to England.

Jack gazed along the line of houses. "Garden hopping?"

"Sounds like a plan," I said. "Gives us a bit of cover at least."

Without the advantage of speed, being off the road seemed a sensible option. Garden hopping was an activity Jack and I used to carry out as youngsters. It involved running through strangers' gardens and avoiding capture by an angry resident. Prestigious estates and larger houses were prime targets. We'd only been caught once—and gotten dragged home by our ears.

Lea's eyes darted from side to side. "Can you hear that?"

I crouched and listened to a confusing mixture of faint noises coming from the direction we had driven. Smoke towered into the darkening late spring sky—Ron's house probably burning to the ground. The breeze dropped. I picked out the sound of dogs barking, some muffled shouting, and the roar of engines.

"It sounds like Anthony or Jerry is organizing a hunt," Jack said.

I glanced across to the closest bungalow. "Let's get the Rover off the road."

"Lea, you get in and steer, and we'll push," Jack said.

We both grunted as we shoved the vehicle across the road and down a driveway. The Rover gained momentum down a slight incline. Lea steered around a rusty red pickup onto a neatly trimmed lawn at the rear of the house; the grass had probably been cut a day or two before the activation.

Jack and I took a few moments. I leaned against the filthy white wooden boarding on the side of the house and sucked in oxygen.

The distant engine noises slowly grew louder. The dual tone suggested more than one vehicle, but they weren't rapidly approaching. They didn't know our exact location and were, ominously, taking their time to hunt us down.

"Stay back," I said.

I peered around the corner wall. Jack looked over my shoulder. Voices became clearer, shouting over the noise of the engines. A man appeared on the road and aimed along the tracks on the opposite side. He swung around to face the houses. I edged back.

A minute later, a pickup truck rolled along the street, with two men aiming rifles out of the back. Five more armed, competent-looking guards, all dressed in black, swarmed around the truck, focusing on each side of the road.

I listened for any slight change in the engine tone or for approaching footsteps. One of the men raised his rifle to his shoulder and casually fired twice into the house next door. A window shattered. He continued after the truck.

The short procession rumbled away, and the noise gradually receded.

"Those guys look like they mean business," Jack said. "Not like the clowns we met on our way here."

"Why let us shoot Ron and escape, and then chase us?" I wondered aloud. "Lea, how many people did you say were on the payroll?"

"A couple thousand, but they could've been distributing the money to others. I transferred hundreds of thousands of bucks on a monthly basis."

"Maybe we've only seen the tip of the iceberg?" Jack said.

"If I can find Martina, I'll get you more info."

"Forget about that for now. Let's concentrate on getting out of here," I said.

The more I got to know about GA, the bigger the significance they seemed to take on. There was no way in the world that Ron and his goons ran the operation or even had a prominent role in the higher echelons. The events were too vast and far-reaching to be carried out by group of gun-toting amateurs. I had little doubt that we were dealing with the bottom feeders, but they still posed a significant threat.

"What do you think that gunfire earlier was all about?" I asked.

Jack shook his head. "No idea, but I'm pretty sure we're not the only ones pissed off around here."

I took a few paces forward and gazed along the road. The GA team rounded a bend about a half a mile away. "Looks like they've got a game plan now. Lea, is there a cross-country route to that big pile of cars?"

"Fields for a mile or two." She pointed to her right. "Or we cut through that neighborhood to the South Dixie Highway."

"Whichever," Jack shrugged. "Let's stay off the roads till we're clear of Monroe."

"Let's stop talking and get moving before they seal the whole area off," I said.

We could have followed our noses toward the jumble of cars that had greeted us on arrival at Monroe. A large pit lay next to the mangled, bloodstained wrecks, roughly the size of a football field, filled with corpses. A light southerly breeze gave us intermittent blasts of deathly decay, but for the time being, the stench acted as our homing beacon.

We wound our way around neat flower gardens, kiddie pools with dead bugs floating in the tepid water, and piles of children's bicycles and swing sets; we stayed away from streets, jumping over wooden and metal garden fences. We were still a mile away from the South Dixie Highway, which led to the first cars in the group of abandoned vehicles.

Jack dived for cover behind a hedge. "Get down!"

Lea and I followed.

Three black Rovers roared along the South Dixie Highway in tight convoy. They stopped just short of their occupants' self-constructed roadblock.

"That's the rifle out of the window," Jack said as he peered through the leaves. "We'll never get past that lot without being spotted."

I swept a branch to one side. A man exited the front Rover and swept the area through his rifle sights. "There're plenty of good places to hide among those vehicles. If they park there, it'll be the last place they'll expect us to go."

Lea hadn't said a word since leaving the back of the house on Hull Road. She closed her eyes and clenched her hands tightly together.

I placed my hand on her shoulder. "Are you okay?"

She groaned and rolled to face me. "I'm going back."

"What?" Jack said.

"We're not going back there, Lea—they'll kill us," I said. "You can't have forgotten Jerry and Anthony already?"

"I'll find Martina and explain. Ron was alive, and he would have kept her alive too; she was all he had." She paused and waited for a reaction. I was speechless. "I'll create a diversion in town to help you get away," she said.

I looked back at the stationary Rovers. Six small figures jumped out of them and wandered across the tree line ahead of us—not in our direction, but if they carried on, our cover would be blown, and we'd be in range of a crack shot.

"We'll get you back in later," I said. "Give us chance to shake the immediate danger and regroup first."

"You don't have to risk your lives for me. When it's safe, I'll come and find you."

"No way, Lea. I can't allow it," I said. "We know there're other survivors in New York. If we can persuade them—"

She shook her head and looked despondent. "What if there's a Second Activation? You can't outrun the effects of the devices."

"It's not our priority at the moment, and I don't think there'll be one anytime soon. Not after what's happened here."

Jack tried to put a reassuring hand on her shoulder. "Come on, Lea?"

She brushed it off and scowled at him. "Whatever. I'm coming."

A roll of thunder echoed above. The guards continued along the tree line, almost level with our hedge. I found it hard to believe how Lea turned from titanium to putty when she thought she was in close proximity to Martina, and how she contemplated taking a suicidal chance to see her.

"Track back and cut across to the highway," Jack said.

We moved at a crouching run over an open field. I glanced intermittently across to the men in the distance, who seemed preoccupied with something in the opposite direction. With this momentary diversion, I sped up, over a mixture of soft soil and grassed areas, until we came across a group of cows that appeared interested in our sudden appearance.

"Do they normally walk toward humans?" Jack asked.

Lea staggered by his side and dismissively waved her hand. "Some do, some don't. Who cares?"

"Keep moving and hope they don't start making any loud noises," I said.

The closest cow stood in our path. I jumped to its side and gave its rump a powerful slap to move it along. The cow snorted and trotted away. I vaulted over a timber fence and landed with a squelch on the other side; then I paused to take a breather, obscured from the view of any prying GA eyes.

Jack wiped sweat from his brow with his forearm. "Do you think cows were affected by the activation?"

"I doubt it. How do you tell a cow to kill someone?" I said.

"Or commit suicide," Lea added.

We jogged across one more muddy field, peppered with hoofprints and cow pies, to the edge of the highway. I would describe it as a dual carriageway. It had two lanes in either direction, and motorways in England had three. A mix of larger residential, business, and industrial properties lined the route, giving it a cluttered mishmash feel.

I ran for the closest property. A big, two-story, gingerbread-style house, painted light green, with a fenced-off garden at the back. I always preferred to live away from main roads but would have made an exception for this place, sheltered by trees and set back around fifty yards.

Somebody had loved the back garden. Lush dark-green ferns and light shrubs stuffed the borders. Daffodils and tulips proudly stood in the neat circular rockeries dotted around the smooth lawn. I would have been proud of producing this myself.

Jack's hand snapped up, and he aimed the Ruger toward the back fence. I ducked behind a wooden chair on the patio.

He lowered it, let out a deep breath, and clutched his chest. "Jesus Christ."

I visually swept the garden.

"What is it?" Lea asked.

He pointed to where he'd aimed. "I think GA missed someone during their cleanup operation. By the buttonbush."

"The what?"

"That shrub over there," I said.

She aligned her vision with my pointing finger and gasped.

Since leaving the Army, Jack and I had taken up gardening and were adept at identifying objects by orienting them to the nearest tree or plant. It had almost become second nature.

A discolored, naked corpse lay under the shrub. I'd initially assumed, with a casual glance, that it was another rockery or garden decoration. On closer inspection, it looked as though an animal had feasted on various parts.

"I think I'm going to be sick," Lea said.

"We've seen worse—get a grip on yourself," Jack snapped. I think he still felt irritated by her wanting to go back to Monroe while we were in immediate danger.

The stench from the pit wafted over on a light gust of wind, and I pulled the sweater over the bridge of my nose. Thunder rolled again overhead. I yanked a small chopping axe out of a tree stump and ran my finger along the blade. It wasn't very sharp, but it was better than nothing.

After negotiating our way through two more or less attractive gardens and sprinting across a derelict office car park, we arrived at the edge of a field with a small wooded area on the opposite side.

We were only forty yards from the Rovers. I studied the tree line in the direction the goons headed, but couldn't detect any signs of movement.

I knelt by a thick tree trunk. "Wait here for a few minutes. Make sure the coast's clear before making our move."

"Why don't we take a Rover?" Lea said.

"And drive where? Back to Monroe?" Jack said.

She turned away from him and sighed. He looked at me and raised his eyebrows.

We crouched in silence, observing for the next two minutes. Flocks of crows swept down and landed in large clusters. Individual birds of prey, recognizable by their broad wings, soared overhead. I guessed they'd been attracted by the human dumping ground, an unlimited supply of food, but it made our movements dangerous. If we startled a group of them, they could give away our location from a reasonable distance.

"Run for the cars. Once between them, we keep low and move quickly, got it?"

Jack nodded and checked the Ruger. "Got it."

Lea vacantly stared toward Monroe. I reached over and shook her shoulder.

"Got it, Lea?"

She rolled her eyes. "For Pete's sake. I heard you. We move through the cars."

"We need to work as a team and move quickly if we're going to get out of this in one piece," I said, attempting to hide my frustration at her flippant attitude. "Drop all thoughts of Martina until we're clear and have time to come up with a plan."

She moved to within inches of my face. "Do you think it was easy for Martina and me? She's the one shining light in this mess, my hope. You get that, right?"

I didn't return her icy stare; instead, I squeezed her shoulder and tried to look sympathetic. Internally, her loss of focus concerned me. Our full concentration had to be on our escape, and nothing else.

Another rumble of thunder banged in the sky, followed by a flash of lightning. Rain pattered against the trees around us, lightly at first, but within a minute it bucketed down.

"Those guards could be back here at any minute," I said. *"Now!"*

I set off at a sprint through the field, past the Range Rovers. After quickly reaching the first few cars, I ducked into a small triangular-shaped clearing and waited for the other two. Jack and Lea followed, and we hunched together between three damaged vehicles. I carried out a quick inspection of the closest, which had taken a side impact. Small sections of dried bloody handprints flaked off the door as raindrops hit the paintwork.

"How far do you think this stretches?" Jack said.

"Hopefully, right up to where we parked at the end of Otter Creek Road," I said.

Vehicles had been parked in rows of six across the highway, sometimes five where trucks or large SUVs were positioned. I couldn't see the end as the massive parking lot disappeared around a shallow bend in the distance. I reasoned that we wouldn't have far to go. GA didn't have unlimited resources, and this job alone must have taken them hours, if not a couple of days.

Two hawks circled high to my right, above the death pit we saw from Otter Creek Road, which confirmed my theory. Luckily, the rain kept the full force of the stench at bay.

I gestured to a foot-wide gap ahead. "Jack, lead the way. Lea, you follow and I'll bring up the rear."

"No, Harry, I'll take the rear," Lea said. "If we come across anyone, you've got an axe."

"Okay, keep checking our rear. We don't want any nasty surprises," I said.

I wanted Lea to feel like an active part of the group and not just a passenger, mainly to take her mind off Martina. I edged in front and followed Jack as he crawled forward on all fours. The deeper we penetrated, the more tangled the obstacles became. Jack managed to find just enough space for us to crawl between the gaps or underneath larger vehicles for the first few hundred yards, and we made good progress.

He stopped abruptly and turned back. "We'll have to slide over the front of this one."

A green Chrysler with flat tires was parked at a slight angle in front of him. Not enough room to go underneath or around.

"Crack on," I said. "We'll be right behind you."

Jack slid over the hood, and his boots crunched against ground on the other side. He leaned under the chassis. "All clear this side."

I crawled over the hood on my belly and noticed a large circular hole in the windshield, about the size of a golf ball. Dried streaks of blood stained the cream leather passenger seat.

While elevated, I glanced around at the trees, the scruffy rows of vehicles, and back to the Rovers before easing myself down onto the other side. Rain continued to fall, and my clothes started clinging to me, but the noise of the weather came as a welcome bonus to aid our escape.

Jack sat with his back against the Chrysler and ruffled water out of his hair. His buzz cut had grown to the length of a number four and had efficiently collected droplets. I did the same and felt the water spray through my fingers.

I glanced at my watch. Just past two o' clock in the afternoon. I wondered how relevant time would be in our future. Just over a week ago, it ran everyone's lives; now it seemed like an old passenger that kept ticking along but wouldn't be noticed if it slipped away.

Jack stooped toward the ground. "Lea, come on—hurry up."

We looked at each other. I looked through the Chrysler's windows to the opposite side. Nothing.

He scrambled to the ground and looked underneath. "Shit. I think she's gone."

I slid back over the hood. My left ankle twisted on landing, and I nearly lost my balance but managed to stop myself going ass-over-tit by grabbing the wing mirror of a rusting Dodge.

Lea must have gone as soon as our eyes were off her—the reason she wanted to bring up the rear. I searched through windows and along the narrow gaps. "She's not here, Jack."

"We need to keep moving."

I strained to see or hear any movement. The faint sound of barking dogs and distant shouting from the direction of the Range Rovers told me where Lea might have gone. I crawled back to Jack with a resigned looked on my face.

"Do you think she's given herself up?" he said.

"Looks like it, but I'm not that surprised. You saw how upset she was about Martina."

If Lea was Superwoman, Martina was her kryptonite. I wondered what kind of person she might be, to have a vicelike grip and weakening effect on such a strong-willed woman.

Jack shook his head. "She could have told us."

"I think she tried. Didn't want us risking our lives to help her."

A voice called out in the distance, "You take the left side."

I dropped to one knee. "We've got no choice—come on."

Lea could have gone in three different directions. We had little option but to push south. To our north, Genesis Alliance goons were closing in. An area of thinly populated woodland that would be useless for cover stretched along our western flank. The pit lay to our east. The Toyota provided our means of escape and a rifle for defense. By my reckoning, we were only around one hundred yards away.

The downpour increased and battered vehicle roofs. Jack crawled forward with more urgency, wriggling below trucks, squeezing through gaps, and tumbling over twisted wreckage. My arm caught on a jagged piece of windshield that ripped flesh open just below my elbow. I dropped my axe, clasped my hand over the wound to stem the flow of blood, and continued to follow.

Jack rolled over a Nissan, and I heard a loud pop as he reached the other side.

"Are you okay?"

"Nothing to worry about."

I rolled over the Nissan and saw groceries spilling out of the car's passenger door. Jack had landed on a large bag of chips and it had burst open around his boots. I took the opportunity to stuff my pockets with chocolate and a small bottle of water.

"Over there," a voice called out.

We both froze on our hands and knees in an oily puddle. I looked at Jack. "That came from in front of us. They're covering both ends."

"We're trapped," Jack said and clutched the Ruger to his chest.

He scrambled underneath an SUV and gave me a nervous look.

I leaned toward him. "We've only got one option: the last place they'd ever suspect."

"I know. I was going to suggest it, but . . ."

I dropped to my belly and crawled eastward, toward the pit.

2

We left the formation of vehicles and moved through a low hedge on the opposite side of the highway. The rain eased off as I crawled across a small grassy area toward the pit's verge. Hundreds of bodies were stacked close to the brim. Thousands of flies buzzed an incessant drone. A rat, startled by our appearance, disappeared into a hole. Birds perched indifferently on corpses, sporadically pecking at the exposed rotting flesh. A large yellow mechanical backhoe was parked to the left. A pair of blue-and-white-checked golf trousers hung limply from the toothed bucket.

The distant shouting from the road continued. Had they captured Lea? I'd heard no gunshots since she split, so that was at least one positive sign.

Jack grabbed my arm. "Are we going in?"

"We can't stay here—they'll spot us immediately. Just in the edge and cover ourselves with clothes. As soon as it's dark . . ."

I covered my nose with my sweater and tried to block my mind from the fact that human life had been treated beyond contempt, dumped like last week's garbage and left to rot. I'd seen a mass grave during a tour of the Balkans and had nightmares about it, but never imagined I'd confront something on this scale. Genesis Alliance's atrocities even put the Nazis to shame. They were truly evil and had to be stopped. Adrenaline pumped through my body as I braced to descend. I vowed to find a way to effectively fight back and make them pay.

"There's going to be some scores to settle after this," Jack said.

I knew he would be thinking along similar lines. Our fight for survival had transformed into a mission for justice and revenge.

I dropped three feet, and my boots landed with a squelch on the back of a large man. I pushed up, aghast at the bouncy bloated feel and smell of him; maggots wriggled around a wound on his temple.

Jack jumped down and retched after his hand went straight through the chest cavity of a lady. He lurched up but couldn't stop himself from vomiting a little.

He spat to his side and licked his lips. "This is bloody horrible."

"Just remember, it's saving our lives. Let's get covered up."

I reached toward a body wearing an unbuttoned, short-sleeved shirt and attempted to yank it off his green torso. As my elbow sank into his stomach, a gargle and hiss came from his innards and escaped from his neck and mouth. The noxious gas made me reflexively vomit. I thrust my head up in an attempt to breathe in fresh air.

My mouth filled with watery saliva. I swallowed hard, trying not to breathe in through my nose. Remembering the water in my pocket, I fished it out, carefully unscrewed the lid, and took a few gulps. I passed the bottle to Jack, focused back on the shirt, and managed to rip it free.

The shouting from the road sounded more distant, but we still couldn't take any chances.

Jack finished the water, cast the bottle to one side, and tugged at a purple blazer. He tried to force the arm of the garment over the owner's swollen hand.

"For God's sake, get off," he muttered.

Jack gritted his teeth, pulled hard, and toppled backward as the blazer came free. He landed back on the exposed chest cavity. The corpse let out a strange yawning sound.

"I'm desperate for dusk," I said. "The place will be riddled with disease, and I'm not sure how much longer I can take."

"Me neither. How long till dark?"

"Three or four hours. Get covered and keep still."

Jack pulled the blazer over his chest and face. I pushed my legs under a body and lay back, covering my head and arms with the mottled shirt. Conscious of my recently acquired wound, and the diseases that would be rife around me, I dragged my arm through my sleeve and protected it against my body.

Our pursuers' voices had faded to nothing over the last twenty minutes. The only noises I could hear were from in and around the pit: the constant hum of flies and a strange low crackling sound from the corpses as they slowly decayed while maggots, birds, and rats fed. Something scurried onto my chest. I punched it through the shirt, and it quickly fled.

For an hour, I thought about New York and the possibilities of creating a force to take GA down. I hoped Morgan and his group had survived, which would instantly boost our numbers.

Two animals approached the edge of the pit, both rapidly panting. I slowly raised the shirt and peeked through the gap. Two stray dogs surveyed the area. One of them spotted my movement, tilting its head and staring with curiosity. I slowly lowered the shirt and prayed that it wouldn't bark. They hung around for a few minutes before scampering away.

"I've been thinking about things," Jack said.

"What things?"

"The flight, New York, and home. I can't decide whether we were lucky or doomed for getting into all this. I've never told you, but I was kicked out of the Army for punching a major."

23

"Why are you telling me this? It hardly matters now."

Jack sighed. "It's something I've wanted to get off my chest for a while. I don't want you thinking—"

"Why don't you tell this lot? I'm sure they're bothered."

Typical Jack. He'd never had a sense of timing. The incident probably weighed heavy on his mind, and he would have stewed over telling me. Lying in a pit of dead bodies, it was the least of my concerns. The major probably deserved it.

He raised the blazer a few inches and looked at me. "I suppose you're right. Our history is irrelevant now."

"Remember northern England, Jack. We've still got a glimmer of hope."

Jerry had told us during his interrogation in Montgomery that the activation had failed in northern England. Ron's reaction had seemed to back it up, but I'd refused to let myself get carried away. Killers could easily spread from the southern end of the island, Scotland, and Wales. Besides that, our priority remained immediate survival.

Jack gasped.

"What's up?" I asked.

"I think a rat bit my finger. I'm going to move toward you. I can't stop myself from sinking here."

I heard a moist crunching sound and a twiglike snap as he shuffled across. "Don't even think about telling me what that was."

"Don't worry. I'm not looking."

I reached out and patted him on the shoulder. "We'll be all right. If we can get through this, we can get through anything they throw at us."

He grunted. "We'll see."

For the next hour and a half, we lay in still silence. A Genesis Alliance goon could arrive at any time to scan the area. Signs of movement would be easy to spot. Corpses don't scratch themselves, cough, or flinch if a bird lands on their head.

Eventually, the light began to fade, and we still hadn't experienced any live human contact.

"What's the plan?" Jack mumbled through the blazer.

"I'm still trying to decide. The way I see it, we've got three options. Option one: We go cross-country, away from Monroe, and pick up a vehicle on the southbound highway. Option two: If the coast is clear, we sneak back and get the rifle to give us a bit more protection, then either take the Toyota or revert to option one . . ."

"And the third?"

"We try and find Lea, but I—"

"No way, Harry. I've already thought about that. She sneaked away from us, and we have no idea how to find her. A betting man would put money on her being in Monroe, dead or alive. You know she went back to find Martina. It's too dangerous."

"I kind of agree. We don't owe her our lives. I think that's why she did what she did, to save us making a difficult decision."

"We could always come back for her with a small army."

"Do you want to go back there?"

"No."

"What's your preferred option?" I asked.

I felt regret about leaving Lea behind, but she had made her own move and taken the decision out of our hands. The first mission had to be getting out of this stinking pit at nightfall; the second, to move away from danger and come up with a plan. The longer I spent in the place, the more rage bubbled inside me about Genesis Alliance and their actions. They were pushing me to prioritize revenge over survival.

Jack peeled the blazer away from his face. "I say we recover the rifle, hunt a goon, and gather some intel. What do you reckon?"

I thought about it for a moment. Although it initially seemed an unnecessary risk, we needed to know about the prospect of a second activation. "Give it another half an hour. We'll crawl along the hedge and sneak through the cars again. If we can't find a goon before midnight, we go."

"Two would be perfect. I'm stiff and cold. We could both use some dry clothes."

I fully removed the shirt from my face, and rain spattered against it. I used the last few minutes of the fading light to gain my night vision and check our immediate surroundings. Without seeing any danger signs, I sat up, stretched my limbs, and shivered before rubbing my arms and legs to get the circulation going. If GA had fanned around the perimeter of Monroe, they wouldn't be expecting what we were planning.

I rolled to the edge of the pit. "Leopard-crawling all the way unless the shit hits the fan."

The Army had taught me to lose my silhouette in the background and not to expose it to the skyline. We only had a short distance to travel, and I was conscious that we wouldn't last long in a firefight.

I balanced my boot on top of a human head, hoping for a solid platform to haul myself out of the mass grave. I thrust upward and my sole slipped on the hair below it. My boot slid down the face and twisted the jaw into an unnatural position with a crunch. I composed myself, stood on the side of the same face, and successfully hoisted myself out. I'd never felt happier to be lying on wet grass.

Jack clambered out a couple of feet to my left. He raised a thumb and crawled toward the hedge. He wriggled through the gap, and I followed him through, back among the clutter of cars.

He held the Ruger forward in his right hand. Rain tinkled off the vehicles, and a slight breeze created background noise as the trees rustled on our right. Under the cover of the wet darkness, we snaked through the tangle and cleared the mass obstacle within minutes.

My clothes were soaked. The sweater seemed to be very efficient at absorbing moisture, but I was glad of anything that might dilute the stink of the pit that we had brought with us.

Jack crouched behind a stray vehicle at the end of the mass and pointed his Ruger. "Over there. Can you see it?"

I squinted into the dark and picked out the shape of our Toyota, still in it's original position. We had fifty yards to cover. Other vehicles, indiscriminately parked at angles on the road, were clustered around it, most likely from a continuing cleanup operation.

We edged closer, ducking between cars. I caught sight of a red glow in my peripheral vision and grabbed Jack's arm.

He spun to face me. "What is it?"

I held up two fingers and pointed ahead. Jack looked toward eleven o'clock from his position. The glow illuminated at regular intervals from inside one of the vehicles close to the Toyota. We shuffled behind an SUV.

"Somebody's having a smoke in there," Jack said.

I peered over the SUV's hood to confirm. "It must be one of them. Who else is gonna be out here tonight?"

"Okay, let's take it."

"Check it out first. If it's one person, we jump straight in. If it's full, we leave it." I glanced over again but couldn't see inside the dark, rain-covered windows. "If the doors are locked, make sure they don't get a chance to pull a gun."

Jack held up the Ruger. "If the doors are locked, I'm not fucking about."

Dark shapes of single-story houses ran along the right side of the road. Perfect for sneaking—level with the car for a quick assault. "Right flanking maneuver. Take them from behind."

I ran for the closest property, trying to stay light on my feet. At the back, I climbed over a six-foot fence, landed in a neighboring property's back garden, and clattered into a child's swing.

Jack passed me and slapped my shoulder. "We'll be heading away in no time. I can't wait to get those heaters on."

We crossed one more garden and passed through an open ornate iron gate at the side of the house. I crept to the front and glanced around the corner. Our route had taken us around the occupied car, now around thirty yards away.

I waved Jack forward and he crept toward an Audi, halfway to our target. He stooped by the driver's door and glanced over the hood.

Cigarette smoke drifted over on the breeze. The occupant took another drag, illuminating the interior. At this range, it looked like only one person in the car, unless they had a partner having a nap on the back seat.

I moved across to Jack and crouched. "Go for it. They don't exactly look vigilant to me."

"You go to the driver's side; I'll take the other."

He darted across the road and crouched by the rear of the vehicle. I edged toward the driver's door. Ten yards away, an arm flopped out of the window, cupping a cigarette from the rain, and tapped ash to the ground.

Before the smoker could react, I sprinted to the open window and thrust my arms through it, wrapping my hands around the driver's mouth and windpipe. Jack ripped open the passenger door and held his pistol to the side of the driver's head.

Two small hands grabbed my left arm and weakly struggled. This person smelled far too sweet to be a man; smoke aside, the long flowing hair and small shoulders were also a giveaway. Her wide eyes shot from side to side, and she tried to suck in through my hand and blew hard out of her nose.

Jack leaned to her right ear. "Scream and I'll shoot."

The woman rapidly shook her head and tried to say something.

He pulled an AR-15 from between the two front seats with his left hand. "We'll be taking this."

"Are there any other people close by?" I asked.

The woman shook her head and blinked several times.

"Are you sure?"

She nodded rapidly and tried to say something. My hand stifled her response.

"We only want to talk; we're not here to kill you," Jack said.

She nodded again, tears, snot, and saliva moistening my hand. I loosened my grip around her throat. "Pass me the Ruger, Jack."

He sat in the passenger seat and closed the door. I opened up the driver's side, leaned over, and grabbed it from his outstretched hand.

I looked into the woman's eyes. "I'm letting go of your mouth. Shuffle across."

She edged between the two seats and balanced in the middle. I wedged myself in, squeezed the door shut, and raised the electric window. I wasn't a fan of cars that stank of stale smoke, but like most of my previous minor irritations, I didn't care anymore, and it was preferable to where we'd spent our last few hours.

"I won't say a word—take the rifle. Please don't kill me," she stuttered and wiped her mouth. No doubt to rid herself of the foul taste of death on my hands.

"What are you doing out here?" Jack said.

"Watching our southern flank . . . The radio on the dash—I'm supposed to use it if I see anything."

She wore a black jumpsuit, spoke with a southern drawl, had short sandy hair in a side parting, and looked around thirty years old.

"They sent you out on your own?" I asked. "What time's your change of shift?"

She wiped tears from her eyes and sniffed. "I'm supposed to do a radio check every ten minutes. I'm here for another hour."

"Radio who—Jerry and Anthony?" Jack snapped.

"They're as much of a threat to me as you are . . ."

29

Jack frowned. "Why are they a threat to you? Do you know how many GA are looking for us?"

She pulled a folded piece of paper towel from her pocket and blew her nose. "They're both psychos. I'm not sure how many of the local team are here—maybe forty."

"Were you outside Ron's house today?" I asked.

"I wasn't, but Brett was; he's on the other end of the radio. We won't say anything."

"It doesn't matter what you say," Jack replied. "We've seen what you've done."

She shuddered and reached for a packet of cigarettes perched in a cupholder. "I'm not like those guys. We're all from the Technology Department—not the local one. Let me call in Brett. He'll tell you."

"No, you're not calling anyone or lighting a smoke," Jack said.

"Not local? Technology Department? What are you talking about?" I said.

"It's all gone to shit here. The local team is late with the processing. We want to make sure we're not tied to it all."

"You're not making any sense. C'mon, we need more than that . . ." Jack said.

I felt like we were starting to get under the hood of Genesis Alliance and didn't want to waste the opportunity. We also had some temporary cover from the rain. The woman glanced at Jack, then me.

"Let me call Brett; he'll talk to you. He can neutralize you—he's a good guy."

"Good guy." I laughed. "You can't be serious?"

"He's a techy geek, like me, not a murderer. Do you think we knew what was going to happen?"

"Yeah, I do. How couldn't you know?" Jack said.

The only danger nerds had posed to me in the past was the threat of being bored to death. We wouldn't have a problem getting information and escaping from this scenario.

She bowed her head and closed her eyes. "We were just following orders, working on our own little parts of the design."

"Whatever," Jack said. "They said the same at the Nuremburg trials. Was this your version of the final solution?"

"You don't know what you're dealing with, trust me. Brett is your best chance to avoid processing; he'll let you go."

"Why would he do that?" I asked.

"He's one of the only ones who suspected what was happening early enough to try and get out. They threatened to kill his wife and kids. He's only here now to keep them alive. I've seen him help others to escape from this."

Jack snorted. "Sounds like bullshit."

"Look, just go and I won't say anything."

"What happens if we do and the second activation happens?" I said.

"You'll be processed, and trust me, you two guys don't want to be processed in Monroe. Brett told me the local guys had some medieval plans for you."

Jack leaned close to her face. "Like what?"

She wiped more tears from her face with a trembling hand. "None of this is me. I don't even know how to use a rifle. You can hold me at gunpoint if you want. He won't do anything."

Who would offer herself as hostage, unless she was confident of the result? Maybe Brett or another one of the Technology team had the ability of a crack sniper, maybe she thought we would fold against numbers, or maybe she was telling the truth. The chance to find out more and possibly avoid the effects of any future activation proved a tempting offer, but signaling more of their team would be a gamble. I decided to test her confidence in whatever scenario she had in mind.

"What do you reckon, Jack?"

"Sounds like we can drive right out of here, like now."

"We could always let her get in touch with Brett and tell him to come on his own. Then we take the radio and hide. If she moves, you give her a shower with that AR-15. If Brett brings others, it's the same treatment. If he comes on his own, unarmed, and can neutralize us—whatever that is—we can talk."

"You do realize that he'll be shitting in his own mess tin if he comes on his own and tries anything?" Jack said.

The woman gave Jack a confused look. "He'll do what?"

"Pissing on his own bonfire, raining on his own parade, cutting off—"

"I get it. Jeez, it'll be cool."

"I wouldn't call it 'cool,'" I said. "But I think you get the picture about what'll happen if things go south?"

"Yeah, I do. I don't wanna die."

She reached for the radio, and I grabbed her arm. "Not so fast. What are you going to say? Is it an open network with the rest of GA?"

"It's on our own net. Relax."

"Don't describe us," I said. "Just in case."

"Do you two think you're important? In the grand scheme of things, you're even more irrelevant than me."

"We killed Ron," Jack said. "I'm sure there's one or two who are slightly irritated."

"Not from the tech team. Like I said, the shit's going to hit the fan because of the slip in schedule. We want to be on the right side."

"The shit's already hit the fan and splattered over everyone," I said. "Tell him we want information and food."

She nodded and picked up the radio. "Echo-zero-Charlie, this is Tango-two, over."

"Echo-zero-Charlie, is everything okay?" a male voice crackled.

"Tango-two, can you come over on your own with the device and food?"

"Echo-zero-Charlie, no worries. Have you found a stray?"

"Tango-two, I've got two here. Come unarmed."

She received no instant reply and transmitted again. "It's fine, Brett, trust me."

"Okay, I'll be right over. But I'm not coming unarmed; it's too risky."

They didn't use the call signs for the last part of the conversation. I wondered if it was because they had no military experience, were simply paying the procedures lip service, or if it was a sign that all was not well. From what we had seen so far, I doubted the latter. We still had the upper hand in this situation and could easily flee into the dark if they tried an ambush.

"I'll take that," Jack said and grabbed the radio.

The rain eased to spits. Jack beckoned the woman out of the car and kept his rifle trained on her. I searched the vehicle for any communications devices or weapon but found nothing. With the car clean, I waved her back into the driver's seat before twisting the keys out of the ignition to stop any attempts to flee.

"How long till he gets here?" Jack asked.

"Probably five minutes if he drives; the farm's just off Laplaisance Road."

"We'll be behind the fence over here," I said, pointing at a waist-high brick wall in front of a white bungalow with a hipped roof. "You know the drill?"

She nodded and I backed away from the car. We crouched behind the wall, keeping a good view along the road, close to a potential escape route back around the houses. It would be difficult to approach our location on foot without making a noise, because the rain had stopped.

After a couple of minutes, the rumble of an engine rose in the distance. A pair of dazzling headlights rounded a bend in the road and approached. I looked across to the woman, who sat facing away from the oncoming vehicle. She hesitantly raised her arms in the air.

"Rifle's got a full mag," Jack said. "First sign of trouble, and I'll fill them with lead."

"She won't give us up. She was shitting herself," I said. "If they're a bunch of techy geeks, the last thing they'll want to do is have a firefight in the dark."

Jack gazed down the rifle sights at the headlights. "I hope for her sake they don't."

The vehicle slowed as it neared her car. It abruptly halted twenty yards from it, engine still rumbling and headlights illuminating the road. I kept one eye closed to try to maintain my night vision.

A man got out of the car and held a rifle above his head. He walked five yards forward, placed the weapon by his feet, and held up his arms. "I've come on my own."

"Kill the lights and stay by the car," Jack yelled.

He quickly returned to the vehicle, put his hand through the open window, and switched the lights off.

"Are you sure there's nobody else?" I called.

"It's just me, Brett. I've got a device in the back and some sandwiches," he said with a heavy New Zealand twang.

I put my arm on Jack's shoulder, listening for any sounds around us. Without hearing anything suspicious, I nudged him in the back.

Jack moved forward with the rifle on his shoulder. "Put your hands behind the back of your head, and keep still."

He kept his rifle trained on the new arrival. I approached through the gloom and patted Brett down. He had the look of a slightly over-the-hill surfer, with straggled short blonde hair and a healthy tanned face.

I picked up his rifle and took a step back. "Brett, is it? I'm Harry and that's Jack."

"Look, I know who you are, but you need to get away from here. Anthony's named Jerry as his number two. He's taken control of operations and focused the entire organization here on finding you—"

"Hold on," Jack interrupted. "We're severely pissed off with you and Genesis Alliance, so don't bloody tell us what we have and haven't got to do. If I had it my way, you would be on your knees, about to kiss your life good-bye."

He jabbed his muzzle in the direction of Brett's head. I understood Jack's fury. We had only been out of the pit a short time, and I'd already experienced several vomit-inducing flashbacks.

"Like he says, Brett," I said while glancing at his black clothing, "wearing that uniform means you don't get to call the shots."

Brett looked toward Monroe. "We need to get away from here. There're patrols all over looking for you. Jerry thinks you're hiding in Monroe. They're searching houses and burning the whole bloody town to the ground."

Through the trees, I noticed a red glow hanging over areas of Monroe. I didn't care if Jerry wasted his time burning down the whole place. It wasn't our problem and would give us time to get clear.

"So if you aren't with Jerry, who are you?" Jack said.

"I was seconded to Monroe by Genesis Alliance to work on the technical side of the operation. None of us knew exactly what was going to happen, but we didn't expect this."

"Your girlfriend told us the same. Are we supposed to feel sorry for you?" Jack asked.

"Look, mate, they have my wife and kids locked up somewhere—what was I supposed to do? I'm here to neutralize you and help you get out of here."

"Why should we trust you?" I said.

He narrowed his eyes. "Do you think I'd lie about my wife and kids?"

Brett was either a convincing actor, or he was telling the truth. He ran his hand through his hair and sighed. The woman walked to his side and gripped his arm. He turned to her. "Are you all right, Kate?"

She shuffled closer to him. "I'm fine. A little shaken but . . ."

"Where's the rest of your team?" I asked.

"We're holed up at a farm a couple of miles away," Brett said. "If we go there now, we'll have some safety for the rest of the night. Jerry's boys won't get near without us knowing."

I considered our options. Spending time in the pit and thinking about the state of the world, I'd realized I needed to know more about GA, the enemy we needed to confront. Brett seemed to be different from others we had come across. On the flip side, he could be leading us into a trap set by Jerry or Anthony. The need for information proved to be a stronger pull, and we both had rifles.

"Okay, Brett, I'm going to trust you this far. We go in your car. I'll drive with you in the passenger seat, and Jack will be in the rear. You can imagine what Jack will do should there be any monkey business. Once back at your place, you talk."

Brett lowered his arms. "I've nothing to hide. Kate, you wait here and get ready to bug out if you see anyone coming this way."

She nodded and returned to her a car. I heard an electronic lighter click three times.

Brett headed back to the driver's side of his car.

"The passenger seat, Chief," I said.

He raised a hand and walked around to the other side, ducked in, and slammed the door. Jack closely tracked him with the rifle. He looked over the roof at me. "Are you sure about this?"

"Let's play out our hand. He seems genuine. We need some food, water, and clean clothes," I said.

36

"We're going into the enemy's camp. If I suspect a single thing . . . I'll take him out."

"Jack, no more shooting unless we face a confrontation. We got away from Ron's, God knows how. Don't put us in that position again unless it's absolutely necessary."

He shrugged. "I'm just saying it's an option."

Jack climbed into the rear directly behind Brett. I familiarized myself with the controls, flicked on the lights, and turned the car around.

"Which way, Brett?" I asked.

"Straight on. I'll tell you when to turn."

Nobody spoke as we traveled the short distance to a deserted farmhouse. Brett used his radio to confirm his arrival and directed me to park at the side of the property.

"It's a walk from here," he said.

We headed away from the farmhouse and across a sodden field. I could see the logic: park the cars at one place, then continue on foot to the real location. Brett carefully slogged through the mud. It wasn't a concern for Jack and me; our filthy clothes and boots couldn't get any dirtier.

After scrambling through a hedge, I could see a dim outline of a building in the distance, flanked on both sides by trees. Brett stopped and clicked his radio. "About to arrive with our two guests."

A red laser appeared on my chest. I looked across at Jack, who also noticed, and we both instinctively dived for cover.

"Don't worry, guys—it's a laser pointer. On nights like this, it's a handy way of avoiding the swamp to our left. Come on—we need to get inside."

Brett continued forward. I followed a few yards behind, trying to position Brett between the thin red line and myself. If a sniper had us in his sights, the game was up anyway. When we got within a few yards of the two-story house, its front door creaked open. Brett wiped his boots on the mat outside and entered without saying a word. Jack and I followed into the gloom. All rooms appeared to be in total darkness.

Two figures moved out of the shadows. I tensed and curled my finger around the rifle's trigger.

"This way," a male voice said.

We thumped over creaking wooden floorboards, along a narrow hallway, to an internal trapdoor at the end of it. Steps led down into further darkness. I held my hand against the rough brick wall for guidance as I descended. Flecks of old paint cracked and flicked off it as I swept my hand down.

A light flared into life, causing me to squint and peer half-lidded into a musty-smelling room. The basement wasn't decorated like a hidden emergency bunker. Rusting bicycle frames and farm implements were stacked against the right side, next to old boxes and tools. A table with six chairs and three silver suitcases sat in the middle. At the back, four mattresses with sheets scruffily pulled over them lined the wall.

"This is our crash location," Brett said. "There's a small kitchen and store through that door on the right."

"How many of you are here?" I said.

"There's six out on guard and four in the house, including me."

I swept back my greasy hair and received a sharp reminder from my wounded arm. "Don't suppose you've got a first-aid kit?"

"I'll see what I can do."

He disappeared into the storeroom and returned with a roll of crisp white cloth, bottled water, and prepackaged burritos, and sat at the table. Jack and I joined him, and he pushed the items across.

"Get cleaned up and have a bite to eat, guys," he said. "It's the best I can do."

I poured water over my arm and wrapped the cloth around it. A crimson pool immediately formed on the cloth, so I wound another three layers around the cut.

We probably smelled revolting, but I didn't feel a shred of guilt about that. Jack and I hungrily demolished the snacks and drained the bottles of water. Brett watched and forced a smile. Now that I had the chance of getting more information on GA and the next activation, I wasn't going to let it slip. I decided to try the soft approach.

"What's your story?" I asked. "You seem like a decent guy. How did you end up getting involved?"

"I worked on a network planning project in the UK. It was coming to an end so I made my CV available on the CommServe website."

"CommServe?" Jack asked.

"It's a specialist website for IT developers. A bloke called Steve from Fairfax Industries e-mailed me the next day and asked if I was interested in meeting him in London. I googled them and found they had a huge renewable energy division that stretched all over the world."

"Renewable energy?" I said. "I don't get the link."

"Who would? They were big, interested, and offered a decent daily rate on an extended contract for a position on their technology team. I popped a few champagne corks at simply having an opportunity to speak with them and looked forward to the meeting."

Jack frowned. "What's this got to do with anything?"

Brett's face dropped, and he glowered at Jack. "Everything. Steve e-mailed again with directions to their London office on Euston Road. I turned up in my best suit, feeling confident after doing plenty of research on Fairfax Industries. He guided me very politely into a small office with a single chair and a plasma screen on the wall. I thought it must be some kind of orientation."

In a dark corner of the basement, a man bitterly laughed. "You had it easy compared to me."

Brett rolled his eyes and continued. "A video started playing, showing my wife and kids on a street, being bundled into the back of a black Range Rover. It cut to a close-up of my wife's crying face. She said, 'Brett, if you do as they say, they've promised to let us go. They're watching you all the time, and if you speak about this to anyone, we'll be executed.'"

Jack sat back in his chair. "Fuck me, are you serious?"

"You couldn't make this shit up," Brett said. "The screen went black, and I looked around the room in complete shock. I jumped out of the chair and tried to leave, but the door was locked. They left me there for an hour. Steve eventually opened the door; he was flanked by two large men and simply said, 'You can go now, be ready to start work in a week.'"

"Christ, what happened after that?" I asked.

"Before I left, they showed me photos of a dead man with a woman and child, riddled with bullets in a shallow grave. The man apparently told the authorities about GA. They didn't believe him. You can guess the rest. I felt scared and drained. What could I do? I left the building and went straight home. The organization seemed to be so big and slick that it would be like an ant trying to fight a shoe."

"The more I hear about these people . . ." I trailed off. Just as I thought GA couldn't get any worse, I found out they press-ganged poor buggers into working for them too.

"A week later, they couriered tickets to my house, and I traveled to Estonia. They picked me up at the airport and whisked me to a compound just outside Tallinn. The workers called it 'Doctor Death's Military Academy.' Most of us were in similar situations, and no one dared disobey orders. We had a simple goal of bringing a global communications network online. To effectively activate all the devices simultaneously."

Brett held his head in his hands. I considered what I'd do in his situation and concluded I would probably act in a similar way. Although as a part of the technology team, he couldn't have been completely blind to the ultimate solution. "Hold on, if GA is activating these gizmos simultaneously, why the need for local controllers like Jerry?"

He rubbed his face and looked up. "The devices are individual so local areas can adjust the frequency and method of operation. Basically, when all devices go live, the head of each region inputs the activation codes to send out the required signal instructions."

"Is Ron head of this region?" I said.

"He was . . . Monroe controlled a big area."

"Do you know the codes?" Jack asked.

"No, I've haven't got access to the activation codes and didn't get near any devices until coming here a few weeks ago."

Brett left the table and returned with two more bottles of water and a package of cookies. He dropped them in front of us. "Do you have any more questions? I need to get back to my post, and you need to get clear of here."

Jack opened the package and stuffed two cookies in his mouth. I unscrewed the cap on the water bottle and had another drink. I think we both wanted to make the most of our free supplies.

"Why did you come to Monroe?" I said.

"It's a key place to the strategy, apparently. It's not like I could argue," Brett said.

"What happened when you got here?" Jack said, spitting crumbs across the table. "Did you work with Jerry or Anthony?"

"Ron greeted me at the airport and told me I would be shortly reunited with my family. He said I should be grateful that I was a chosen one."

"Chosen one? Some choice," I said.

Brett grunted a sarcastic laugh. "Just before the first activation, we were all taken to a bunker close to Lake Michigan and stayed there for three days."

"Why three days?" Jack asked.

"That was supposed to be the time span for the activation effects."

"Supposed to be?" I asked.

"I'll get to that in a minute. We were given training on survival techniques and procedures for the new world and a whole load of information that was impossible to remember. We were also issued personal weapons and radios."

"So who's behind it all?" Jack asked.

"The last morning, before being released, everyone gathered to watch a video presentation by an old guy I immediately recognized as Henry Fairfax."

"Fairfax Industries? I thought that was renewable energy," I said. "Is he the one running the show?"

"Yeah, he proclaimed a new world order and said we'd been chosen to rebuild humanity."

"Why did he do it?" Jack said.

"He mentioned religion, politics, and fossil fuels. I can't remember exactly, but it was all kinds of crazy shit. When we came out, the whole world was a complete fucking mess. Ron said he'd received orders that we were to stay here and assist with the cleanup operation in Monroe. He held daily meetings to reassure us that our families were okay, and said there was a lot of work to do in getting the rest of the surviving population back on its feet."

"How many are left alive?" I asked.

He leaned back and puffed out his cheeks. "No idea. The plan for the second activation was to bring in survivors for processing. But you two torturing Jerry and Anthony sent Ron into a tailspin. The activation got delayed, procedures were thrown out, and we were all told to wait for you to get here so they could have revenge—"

Jack banged his fist on the table. "I knew he was full of shit."

42

Brett paused, eying us both, as if waiting for one of us to speak. I didn't know about Jack, but I was consumed by his story and wanted to know more. Brett continued, "Ron ordered us to report communications problems to Headquarters. They could tell we were hiding something. My team started to get nervous. We didn't want to poke the hornet's nest. Ron said if the local operation was shut down, our families would be butchered like pigs."

"Does he have the authority to do that?" I said.

"I doubt it." He leaned toward us and lowered his voice. "When you shot him, we heard Jerry screaming down the radio for the guards to stand down. They wanted to kill you themselves. Jerry and Anthony appeared in a Mustang and started blaming everyone for letting you take a weapon into the house. They shot up our last vehicle. Those were the guys who were supposed to frisk you outside."

"I tucked the pistol down the front of my pants. People don't tend to search there," Jack said.

"I wondered where everyone went," I said. "Where did those other GA goons come from?"

"Jerry's order caused massive confusion over the radio. Nobody knew what the hell was going on. All of a sudden this guy turns up, barking orders, and rumors are flying around that Ron's dead. My team isn't trained for this. I'd already scouted this location as a fallback position. The way we see it, if local GA are going down, we didn't want to be part of it."

"We thought something weird was happening," I said. "Couldn't believe it when I looked out of Ron's window."

Brett cracked a smile. "We're a techy team. The last thing we wanted to do was to come charging in. Jerry's order was a relief. What did you do to those guys to get them so pissed?"

"We tortured information out of Jerry," Jack said.

The voice from the gloomy corner of the room said, "You did us all a favor. Shame you didn't kill the bastard."

"What about Anthony?" Brett said. "He's the one you really need to be worried about."

"We sprayed mace in his face and put a plastic bag over his head," Jack said. "After that, we burnt his house down and left him tied up in his vehicle with a dog bowl full of canned peaches."

Brett appeared to take some pleasure from hearing about our run-ins. "I heard him say on the radio that he wanted your heads put on spikes. I can see why."

"It's not like we wanted to do any of it," I said. "Jerry had our friend Bernie killed, and we found a device in his barn. He also led us to Anthony. What would you do in our shoes? They were partly responsible, and I suppose . . ."

I trailed off, not wanting to blame Brett. He was a victim of cruel circumstance, and I suspected most of the others in his team had suffered the same kind of treatment.

"Why's Anthony more dangerous?" Jack asked. "Jerry seemed the more evil of the two."

"Jerry's a fool, not necessarily a harmless one, but he's more dislikeable than dangerous. I got the impression that he was a loser in his previous life and is reveling in his newly found importance. Anthony is on a whole other level. He was fiercely loyal to Ron, is completely at ease with what's happening, and the bastard had one of my team executed."

"Bloody hell, what did he do?" I asked.

"One of our guys tried to argue with Ron in the bunker. Anthony lined us up for a parade and beat his brains out with a baseball bat. I told Ron I'd be reporting the incident to Headquarters. He gave me two options. First, he could send Anthony back to Hermitage in exchange for my silence. The second option was me reporting the incident. He said he couldn't protect me from Anthony or the team. Basically, I was a dead man if I said anything."

"Why didn't you guys take them out?" Jack said. "If most were recruited like you, there must be a lot of pissed-off people."

Brett shrugged. "You'd be surprised. Anyway, they're all experienced with weapons. It's not exactly my area of expertise, and I have my family to think about."

I looked around the room again at the forlorn shapes in the shadows. An air of resignation and depression infested the place. It was bad enough to live through our own experiences, I would have hated being forced to take part.

"Can you stop us from getting activated?" Jack asked.

"The devices are activated, you are just signaled," Brett said.

Jack leaned forward. "Don't get all techy on me—can you do it or not?"

"I'll take care of you. You can't take the neutralization tool, though. We've only got two, and Headquarters will check when they arrive. If I lose this, I lose everything."

"They're coming here?" I said.

"I managed to get in touch with a friendly colleague a few hours ago, using our satcom. They've already sent a force to deal with Monroe, and he told me to make sure I wasn't with the local team. They're docking in Boston. I know they own a warehouse there, filled with weapons and armored vehicles."

"Do the local goons know about it?"

"They suspect. That's what's thrown them into a meltdown. They're all shitting their pants."

"HQ is coming from the UK? You're kidding me?" Jack said.

Brett sighed. "Why would I joke? He said they sent a ship filled with choppers and troops."

"How long does that take?" I asked and tried to roughly calculate it in my head, remembering the distance to be just over three thousand miles from the airplane computer. "Eight days?"

"I doubt they're coming over on a pleasure cruiser," Brett said. "Maybe four, and they left yesterday."

"If they're after the local team, and you've been attached, what happens to you?" Jack asked.

"GA needs the techs a lot more than Ron's rednecks. I might be okay."

He led us to a small enclave and picked up something that looked like a silver Ping-Pong paddle. Brett depressed a button on the side, and a single red light started blinking on the handle. The object made a quiet whirring noise. The light stopped blinking, changed to green, and the device let out a small beep.

Brett held it toward us. "Who's first?"

Jack stepped forward. "Are you sure it'll work? You're not going to turn me into a killer are you?"

"A killer? . . . Oh, I see what you mean. No, just relax. You'll feel a bit of pressure in your head for a second."

He held the device against the back of Jack's head, thumbed a button, and the object beeped three times. Jack winced and hunched his shoulders.

"That's it, you're done," Brett said.

Jack ruffled the back of his hair. "Am I supposed to feel any different?"

"No. You're lucky you avoided the first activation. HQ is putting it down to software problems. It hasn't gone exactly as planned."

"What do you mean?" I asked. "Do you know the plan?"

"They won't tell the likes of me. Stay away from people—that's all I'm saying. We've had some crazy reports in."

"What kind of reports? At least give us an idea," Jack said.

"It's too random to give you anything concrete. Sorry if that sounds like I'm hiding something, but the truth is, I don't know and wouldn't want any innocent people dying because of my bad advice."

The red light stopped blinking again and turned green. I switched positions with Jack, and Brett carried out the same procedure. For a second, I felt like I'd just woken up with a horrible hangover, but the pain quickly receded. I palmed my greasy hair flat against my head.

"Can you tell us, in simple terms, a bit more about how the technology works? If we decide we want to do something about it, where's the best place to strike?" Jack said.

Brett placed his weird implement on the table, turned, and gave Jack a stern glare. "Listen to me. It's not going to be pretty when HQ shows up. The best thing you can do is to get as far away from here as possible."

"Come with us. Stop this thing from happening again," Jack said.

I had been thinking the same thing. Although I didn't want to suggest to Brett that his family was already dead or that his actions wouldn't change their outcome. GA was ruthless, and from what I'd heard of them so far, he would be viewed as a flea in their big picture.

"You're one of the only people around who knows a piece of how these things work," I said. "Join us and help to locate and destroy the devices. We know of other survivors in New York."

He slumped in his chair and looked away. "You can use a cattle prod. It's unreliable; you'd probably have to do it several times at least. But you'll give people a chance—"

"Brett, come on. Everyone's life is at stake," Jack said.

"Take the bull by the horns, mate," I said. "You only need to take one look at that pit to know what you should do."

"What are your plans—?"

The trapdoor opened and a head appeared in the gap. "There's a Rover heading our way. It might be them."

Brett's eyes widened. He grabbed a pistol from the top of a workbench. "Stay here and keep quiet."

47

He clambered up the stairs and slammed the trapdoor shut. I checked the rifle I took from Brett and shouldered it.

Jack crouched and pointed Kate's rifle. "Caught like rats in a sewer. I don't fucking believe it. He set us up."

"I doubt it," I said. "Keep your cool and we'll be okay."

The voice in the corner of the room said, "Don't start a shootout. We're not going down because he brought you here."

Above us, I heard Brett's muffled voice, probably handing out instructions to his team.

The trapdoor creaked ajar. Brett leaned down. "They're heading across the field. Get under those sheets on the mattress."

The door slammed shut.

"Fuck that," Jack said. "I'm staying here. If they come down, they won't be expecting an ambush."

Through a small cracked window at the top of the room, I heard voices approaching. Boots squelched in the mud outside, getting closer. Somebody thumped on the front door.

More mumbling overhead. The echo of a bolt scratching along its rail. Then a latch being twisted, followed by creaking hinges as the door opened. I could hear every detail through the old floorboards. Perhaps amplified as my adrenalin levels rose.

Loud footsteps clattered in the room above. Frantic voices, occasionally raised. It sounded like an argument, although a loud laugh kept punctuating the debate. Somebody mentioned our names.

The trapdoor creaked open.

"Get ready," Jack whispered.

Somebody climbed down a couple of steps and cleared his throat.

The instantly recognizable voice of Jerry shouted, "Get out there and start looking for those two murdering assholes!"

A man appeared from a dingy corner of the basement. He walked to the foot of the basement stairs, glancing at me as he passed. "We'll be out in twenty minutes. Just getting some rest after working the last twenty-four hours."

"You're going to need it," Jerry shouted down. "They burnt Ron's place to the ground. We're all heading to Hart Island tomorrow to trigger the second activation."

The man shook his head. "We can't get there and do it tomorrow."

"I know that, you big galoot. I just said we're heading off. We need to get it done before they realize we've missed our cutoff. Who's down there with you?"

Jerry descended another couple of stairs. My heart thumped against my chest. I prepared to fire.

The man took a couple of paces forward, blocking the basement entrance. "Just me, Terry, and Jim. We're all pretty beat."

"What have you got down here? A secret hideout? Did Ron know about this?"

"It's where we keep our supplies and test kit. Do you want me bring you one of the cases and show it to you?"

Jerry snorted. "Just get your ass out and start looking. I want those two dead by the morning."

"We'll be out soon. Give us a chance to get ready."

Jack edged back. His boot crunched against something. A dry leaf, empty snail shell, or a chip.

Jerry dropped another couple of steps. "Did the rest of you hear what I said?"

"I hear you," a voice called from the kitchen area.

"We can't afford screw-ups on Hart Island. Just make sure you've got your shit together."

He clunked back upstairs. The trapdoor slammed shut.

A conversation continued upstairs. I peered around the corner. The man turned to face me. "I didn't do that for your benefit. That psycho would've killed us all."

"Thanks, we appreciate it," I said and gave him a single firm nod.

"Whatever. He might come back," he said and shuffled back into the gloom. Mattress springs groaned. He clearly didn't take Jerry's orders too seriously.

Footsteps left the room above. The front door closed, and a bolt scratched across.

"I can't believe he was here," Jack said.

I let out a deep breath and shook my head. "Let's just hope he's gone."

We waited in silence in case any of the recent arrivals had stayed. A minute later, the trapdoor opened again. Brett came running down the stairs with a grim look on his face.

He rested his hands on the table and closed his eyes. "They killed Kate and they're coming back to sweep the area. Anthony wants us to help form an extended line across the countryside."

"Why did they kill her?" I asked.

"Anthony started tracking you. He found your vehicle and traced your footprints to where they put the cars during the cleanup operation. His hands were covered in blood. He claimed it was from trying to stem the flow from her throat. Said that meant you must still be in the local area."

Jack pulled out a chair and sat opposite Brett. "That sly bastard. We should've killed him in Hermitage."

"I suppose he thought it would get us to cooperate with hunting you down. It might have worked if we hadn't already met you."

"Can we take your car?" I asked.

Brett paced around the table and rubbed his chin. He stopped in front of me. "I'm coming with you."

"You're not serious—" the man on the mattress said.

"You're welcome to stay here and wait it out, Stan. But after what just happened, there's no way I'm risking my life by being anywhere near those crazy bastards."

Stan sat forward. "What do I tell Anthony? What about your family?"

"Just say I went missing. That's what they'll probably say about Kate. For all we know, our families might be in a big pit somewhere in the UK. It's time to stop being GA's bitch."

I stood and faced him. "Why the change of heart?"

"I could handle it pre-activation. It was just a weird blackmail. I never thought they'd go through with it. After leaving the bunker three days ago, seeing all this and talking it through with people who are prepared to fight . . ."

"Grab a rifle and let's get moving," Jack said.

Brett picked one up from the workbench, stuffed three full magazines in his cargo pants pockets, and tossed us the remaining four mags. "We need to beat them to Hart Island. Forget the devices—they're too spread out. If we destroy the control unit, they can't use them."

"Should be easy enough," Jack said. "We burnt the last one."

"Not this unit," Brett said. "It's in protective casing, like the transmission devices. I need to configure it from the console."

"Why didn't they have one like that here?" I asked.

"They were supposed to bring one here and leave the uncovered unit at Hart Island as a backup."

It hardly came as a surprise that the local team had fucked up. They were like the Keystone Cops, but with a lethal edge.

"What about HQ?" I asked.

"We avoid them at all costs. Forget about Boston—we'll end up bringing a shitstorm on ourselves. The local team has roughly three days to try and get things working before the others arrive. We don't want to be around when they meet up."

"You sure about this?" I said.

Brett folded a map into the inside pocket of his blue Gor-Tex jacket. "I'm not sure about anything anymore. But I feel a whole lot better after making this decision."

I respected Brett's courage in the face of his situation. He reminded me of a close friend back in England, not only in looks but also attitude. My English friend faced different kinds of problems from Brett's: an alcoholic brother and a cheating wife. Eventually, he made a brave decision and faced down both problems by helping his brother get dry and getting a divorce.

"One question: Where's Hart Island?" Jack asked.

"New York, opposite Pelham Bay."

"I think I know it," I said. "And we drove up here from the city."

"No time to lose. Let's get out of here before I change my mind." He ushered us up the basement steps and knocked three times on the trapdoor. It swung open almost immediately.

"All clear, come up," a voice said. "They drove away after leaving the house."

We made our way back along the thin hall.

"Jim, I'm out of here," Brett said. He extended a hand to an overweight silhouette by the door. "I've got a feeling you'll be all right without me."

Jim grasped Brett's hand. "You sure about this?"

"Positive. Good luck. I hope you see your wife and kids again."

Jim gave a resigned nod and opened the front door. "I'll tell them you went back to Ron's to try and salvage some equipment."

"Thanks, man. If I run into HQ, I'll clear you from this shower of shit."

"I doubt it." He sighed. "Got a feeling that we're all going to pay."

Brett clapped Jim's shoulder and nodded before heading out. Jack and I followed without saying a word.

After squelching across the field, we reached his car. He walked around it.

"Aren't we taking it?" I asked.

"No. They'll have the roads guarded. We need to head cross-country for a couple of miles at least. We'll pick something up on the highway."

Automatic fire rattled in the distance. We sprinted south.

3

Our immediate plan consisted of running through open countryside, vaulting fences, and crawling through hedges, getting away from Monroe as quickly as possible. Thankfully, the route stayed clear of any search parties, but if Anthony could successfully track us, only the cover of darkness would conceal our escape.

"I reckon we're close to the highway," Jack said after we stopped for a quick rest.

We pushed through a hedge and emerged onto a road leading away from Monroe. The route seemed to be parallel with the highway, and the solid footing offered us a chance to increase our speed.

Shadows of isolated houses began to loom on our left, and I considered searching them for supplies or a vehicle. We had to create distance from Monroe. Our pace faltered and we now were maintaining a fast walk rather than a run. I kept twisting around every few yards, checking for signs of pursuit.

Brett wheezed alongside me. "You boys know how to run."

"We've had a lot of practice in the last week."

Jack stopped, put his hands on his knees, and vomited. Brett pulled out a water bottle from his jacket, had a quick drink, and passed it to him as he straightened.

"You look like a zombie," Brett said.

Jack took three large gulps, swished the water around his mouth, and spat it on the ground. "I snuggled up with rotting bodies all afternoon. Are you surprised I'm sick?"

Brett turned and peered into the distance. I thought we urgently needed a change of clothing. Who knew what kind of nasty disease had invaded our clothes while we hid among GA's innocent victims. Jack's illness didn't come as a surprise.

"We're getting nowhere fast on foot," I said. "We need to freshen up and get to the highway."

Jack nodded and drained the bottle. I led the way toward the closest property, through the trees, and toward the white façade of a house.

"What the hell are you doing? We can't stop now," Brett said.

"We're not using this place for R&R. We'll grab a change of clothes, scavenge supplies, and find the nearest vehicle," I said. "Don't tell me you can't smell us."

Brett and Jack covered me. I found the front door unlocked, eased it open, and crept inside. Ignoring the stench coming from the adjacent room on the ground floor, I climbed the squeaky staircase and pushed open a bedroom door. Jack followed me inside.

The wardrobes were packed full of adult male clothing. In the dim light, I selected underwear, jeans, T-shirts, and lumberjack shirts. Jack found a decent-sized backpack under the bed.

"Where's Brett?" I asked.

"Searching the kitchen."

"Need to make sure we keep an eye on him, for now."

The jeans were my size but felt loose. I grabbed a belt from a pair of trousers hanging in the wardrobe. I must have lost a reasonable amount of weight since boarding the plane in Manchester. Jack also looked gaunt. I headed to the bathroom and had a quick wash, using some tepid water and a bar of soap, before putting on the rest of my clothes.

I headed downstairs to the kitchen and found Brett rummaging through the cupboards. He piled up bottled drinks and packaged food on a kitchen table. Jack appeared after his wash and put the supplies into the pack. I checked my watch. Half past eleven.

"How are you feeling?" I asked.

"Like I've got an alien in my stomach, but I'll live."

"You can get some rest in a car." I turned to Brett. "Do you think we've come far enough to escape their roadblocks?"

"We've passed where they had them yesterday."

Jack crept to the back of the property and slid open a patio door. We listened for a moment, checking for any suspicious noises, before heading off. I looked forward to chatting with Brett when we were finally clear. He'd given us a lot of info, but I still had plenty of questions. Like how we could expand our operations against GA after spiking their secondary control unit. They had pushed me past a point where I wanted simply to survive.

The brief respite gave me some energy back. The road disappeared behind us as we ran across an open field, toward the highway. Without a hedge line for cover, we were horribly exposed, but we quickly crossed the short distance and dived down on the highway embankment.

I shuffled on my elbows to its ridge, wincing as I received constant reminders of my injury. As long as I kept the wound clean, I felt sure the pain would eventually subside.

Jack and I had learned many years ago to be absolutely still and silent when acclimatizing to the surroundings and before making any move. Lanes on both sides were clear of vehicles in front of us. I could make out a few dark shapes in the distance on the southern lanes.

Something moved on the opposite side of the silent expressway. Possibly animals, rustling about in trees. Two four-legged creatures scampered along the shoulder. An owl hooted.

"Ready to move?" I asked and indicated to my right.

They both nodded. I sprang to my feet, skidded down the slippery grass banking and headed along the inside lane. Without wanting to waste any time, I jogged toward the distant shapes, hoping that one would be a usable vehicle.

I dismissed a big old dirty truck. It had corpses in the cabin, and something smaller would be more suitable when the roads became more cluttered around the built-up areas.

A driver's door on a silver Honda hung open. There were keys in the ignition, and no bodies, so I jumped in and unlocked the passenger doors. Brett slid into the front and Jack took the back seat, checking for any lights to the rear. The Honda's headlights immediately lit up the highway after I turned the key. I unsuccessfully fiddled with the controls, trying to switch them off. After quickly admitting defeat, I jumped out and smashed in both the headlights and taillights with my rifle butt.

"You don't mess around," Brett said.

"It's a different world outside Monroe. I'm sure you know that."

"If I didn't, I'm about to find out."

I crunched the Honda into first gear and pulled away. All our previous rides in America had been in a car with automatic transmission—a blessing when having to concentrate on other things besides simple driving.

——

Heading slowly south, we suffered several minor collisions due to the darkness and state of the road. Our hunters would have the same issue unless they used headlights, which meant we would see them from a distance. As we passed the Luna Pier exit, my thoughts switched to Lea. I wondered if she'd survived. With Jerry and Anthony on the warpath, itching to exact some justice and crapping themselves about HQ's imminent arrival, I hoped she'd met up with Martina and found some protection.

"Christ," I said as the Honda bounced violently off another vehicle, snapping a wing mirror off.

"Bloody hell," Brett said. "You sure there's not an easier way?"

Jack leaned between the front seats. "We'd be better off on bikes."

I swerved around and bumped over more debris on the road. "Our path could be tracked by a child, never mind Anthony. We have to lose the trail."

"Why don't we find a boat at Lunar Pier?" Jack said. "Cut across to Ohio."

I loved the idea and immediately pulled over to the side of the highway, ripped up the handbrake and killed the engine. "Unless they do the same thing, that'll put us ahead of the game. Great thinking, Jack."

"I can drive if we find a suitable model," Brett said.

"Can't be that difficult," I said. "We don't need to be shy about bashing it about."

"We'll see about that."

Jack grabbed the backpack and threw it over his shoulder. He seemed to show no signs of his previous illness, but knowing him, he probably hid his pain to avoid being a burden. When we were kids, he fell off his bike and cut open his thigh. He tried to hide it from our parents by wearing long trousers. They became suspicious when he refused to take them off for bed. The trousers had stuck to his wound, and he'd screamed his head off when our mum and dad pulled them off him.

We slung our rifles and doubled back to the exit on foot. Halfway along Luna Pier Road, I glanced at the house that had provided a temporary refuge the previous night. Yesterday, I hadn't expected to make it out of Monroe alive. Today, I felt vengeful and focused on destroying the Hart Island installation. Brett had given us a mission with a clear, tangible objective, and I felt for the first time that we had an advantage.

At the end of the road, I expected some kind of port, but I couldn't see a single boat. Turning left, we kept level with the water gently lapping against the shore. In the distance, a long dock stretched into the lake.

Our boots thumped along the wooden decking that led to a medium-sized cruiser. It bobbed on the water in silent greeting.

I jumped onto its slippery deck and rattled the cabin door. Locked. With no tools handy, I absently smashed the rifle butt against the sturdy door, only managing to chip the paintwork. I looked back toward an imposing property on the shore.

"We'll search the house. Jack, you keep a lookout."

Jack searched around the deck area, pulling up padded benches, looking for anything of use. Brett followed me back along the dock. He unsuccessfully attempted to open the doors of the house. I tried to slide open the side windows without success and stood there, frustrated.

Picking up a stone, Brett smashed the closest window and knocked away pieces of jagged glass with his rifle. "You coming in or what?"

I liked his style. He reached through, unfastened the window, and jumped inside the house.

"You take upstairs. I'll search down here," I said.

"No worries." He shouldered his rifle and crept to a large open entrance.

I began with the cabinets behind a long leather couch. This had clearly been a boat lovers' place, with related maritime ornaments and pictures on the glass shelves. I wracked my brains, trying to think where they might store keys. I usually put them on the kitchen counter or in my jacket pocket.

"There's a safe here," Brett shouted. I ran up a varnished wooden staircase with an ornate banister and found him sitting on a queen-sized bed, fiddling with a metal box. "It's okay—I can open it."

I lowered my rifle and watched him place his ear close to the safe's door and spin the dial. "I think you've been watching too many films, Brett."

"I just need a drill."

"A drill, seriously? Where are we going to find a fucking drill?" He looked slightly hurt and threw the box to one side. I sat on the bed next to him. "Sorry about that. It's been a long day."

The temptation to lie down and rest almost overwhelmed me.

Brett stood and picked up his rifle. "Let's try next door. I'm not giving up that easily."

Outside, I waved Jack over and we moved along the lake until we reached the next house with a dock. A smaller craft gently rocked at the end of it, but more importantly, it looked fast, like a speedboat.

Brett stayed by the boat and kept watch. I shouldered my rifle and covered Jack as he swung into the house. Two bodies lay on the ground in the front hallway, twisted miserable figures with pasted rotting death masks. I couldn't afford to linger and moved around the bodies into the dining room. After checking the cupboards without success, I heard Jack's gleefully whispered, "Yes!" Meeting me in the hallway, he held up the keys and a pair of binoculars.

I patted his back. "They'll come in handy—good score. Where did you find them?"

"Keys on a hook in the kitchen. The binoculars were on a hat rack in the hall."

We thudded back along the dock. Brett looked over in expectation. Jack rattled the keys and jumped behind the wheel. I untethered a thick, knotted rope from the mooring and hopped aboard before kicking us away. The boat gently floated free. Jack twisted the key in the ignition. The engine spluttered a few times but failed to start.

"Let me check that the fuel line's connected," Brett said.

I leaned by his side and watched him remove the upper casing, check the line, and prime the pump. He looked over his shoulder. "Give it another whirl."

The engine spluttered again, then coughed into life. I felt a rush of excitement over hitting open water and making swift progress away from any chasing goons.

Jack pushed the throttle and we plowed away from the pontoon. I turned to get a view of the lakeside receding in the distance. Lights shone from the highway behind Luna Pier. A beam flashed across the water and positioned on us.

Automatic gunfire rattled in the distance. Brett and I ducked, although our fiberglass hull wouldn't stop an accurate round. He shot me a nervous glance. "Holy shit, Harry. They've found us."

I guessed they were around seven hundred meters away and gaining distance every second. "Don't worry from this range."

Jack increased the throttle, and the boat rhythmically bounced across the surface, leaving a frothing white wake across the black water. We probably weren't identifiable from this range as their quarry, but we were a sign of life.

A window on the side of the boat exploded inward and glass shattered across the small deck. A single loud crack echoed in the distance.

"Shit, that sounded like a high-powered rifle," I said. "Keep your heads down."

As we headed south, more bursts of fire followed. I could just about identify the muzzle flashes sparking around the distant vehicle lights. A couple of tracer rounds whizzed overhead, but we took no more hits and powered around a headland, out of sight.

I joined Jack at the front of the boat. "Great call on the boat. They can't have been far behind."

"Let's hope they don't arrange a welcoming party when we get back to dry land."

"They don't know it's us. We can't be the only people left alive around here."

"Bit of a coincidence, though?" Brett said.

"Unless they get a boat, we'll outstrip them by miles, and they won't know our docking point."

I could understand his paranoia, but our current situation felt relatively safe compared to Bernie's apartment in Queens, a dark highway, or the pit of bodies that I couldn't stop thinking about.

Jack kept the boat a couple hundred yards from shore, and we cut through the water at speed. I breathed in fresh air as wind rushed against my face. A surge of positivity ran through me. For now we had escaped, and I was sure we were ahead of the game.

"We should have killed Anthony when we had the chance," Jack said. "I can't see him backing off any time soon."

"Fuck him. We've a clear focus now. Hart Island. We'll collect Morgan and his gang if they're still alive, and end this thing."

"Who's Morgan?" Brett asked.

"He leads a survivor group in New York," Jack said. "We can gather extra manpower for an assault."

"There's only two GA on the island," Brett said. "If we get there first, I'm sure you can deal with them. I don't think we should waste time finding people we don't need."

Jack glanced across to me and frowned. I knew he wouldn't like Brett trying to dictate proceedings. But Brett had crucial information, and we were all in this mission together. The local team was heading to Hart Island, and more ominously, larger forces were on their way, and would possibly sweep all of us away if they caught us.

"Brett's right," I said. "We waste no time and get there first. After that, we'll round up Morgan's group, if they're still around, and work out how we deal with the rest of GA."

The clouds broke overhead as we continued toward Ohio. Bright moonlight provided good visibility of buildings lining the shore and small islands on the lake. For the first time in days, I felt free from the threat of a surprise attack from around any corner.

I sat next to Brett on the plastic-covered foam bench and leaned forward with my head in my hands, feeling a sudden release of tension. I groggily looked up at Jack, who sat in the control chair, slumped forward resting on his elbows until a wave jerked him upright.

For the next twenty minutes, Brett and I had a nostalgic chat about sport and our former lives. It turned out we both loved football and had been in the same stadium on a few occasions, supporting opposite teams. We even liked the same pubs in London, like the Sherlock Holmes on Northumberland Avenue and The Ship Tavern near Lincoln's Inn Fields. I'd warmed to him since our first meeting on Otter Creek Road and felt pleased we had him on-board.

Brett joined Jack at the front of the boat. I yawned and rested my head on the bench.

———

Jack shoved me awake. I blinked to focus on our surroundings. The boat gently rocked on the water. Brett lay snoozing on the opposite bench.

I sat up and groaned. "Where are we?"

"I've taken us south for the last hour. We might be hitting Ohio soon."

"How about fuel?"

"I think we'll be okay if the gauge is right."

I stood and headed for the wheel. "Get your head down. I'll take over."

Jack nudged past me and collapsed onto the bench. His body entirely relaxed.

I increased the throttle, felt the bite of blades in the water, and we lurched forward. A compass close to the steering wheel showed our heading, and I adjusted the direction to south.

I decided to let both Jack and Brett sleep for as long as possible. Dawn broke just before six in the morning, and they both must have gotten at least two hours. I glanced back at Jack and wondered about his recent actions and temperament.

He stirred in his sleep and raised his arm, like he was weakly fighting off an invisible fly. I hoped he would keep cool with whatever happened now in our bid to trash the local GA operation. The action at Ron's house had shown that when Jack was cornered, he struck back. I needed to channel him in the right way.

In the growing light, only the occasional bird swooping up and down gave any sign of life. The coastline curved ahead of us to the right, and I spotted a small group of islands to our port side.

I angled the boat toward a large island with a prominent landmark, a huge Doric column with a viewing platform at the top, stretching over three hundred feet into the sky. I followed the island's rocky coastline, looking for a suitable place to dock. Jack must have felt a slight variation in course as the water rocked the boat in the stronger current. He yawned, stretched on the bench, and looked around.

"Wasn't the coast to our right?" he said.

"Yeah, but I found an island—might give us a chance for a break and a fuel stop."

He joined me by the wheel and rubbed his eyes. "How long have I been asleep?"

"Couple of hours. I'm thinking we dock the boat somewhere secluded and scavenge for fuel and food."

"Or find a bigger boat. It's the safest I've felt since landing," Jack said.

The coastline began to turn inward in the direction of the huge monument. Jack and I both stared at the structure, gleaming white in the early morning sunshine and surrounded by lush grass. It looked like an inviting place to go ashore.

Our chatter woke Brett. He joined us at the front of the boat and started at the sight of the monument. "What's that?"

"No idea," I said. "But we're going to find out."

I eased down the throttle and approached the rocky shore. Jack shouldered his rifle and scanned the area through the sights. The boat's hull scraped over a rock, and he gripped the side to maintain balance. Brett dropped over the side into waist-high water, gasped, and pulled the boat toward the shore, using the uneven lake bed as leverage. The hull juddered over several more rocks, but we were close enough to dry land.

Jack slung on his pack and splashed into a foot of water. He ran over to a small copse of trees and dropped to one knee, taking up a covering position. I threw Brett his rifle, and he joined Jack, awkwardly hunching into the same position and held his rifle forward, away from his shoulder. I gave him full marks for trying.

I secured the boat's rope to a concrete bollard and visually swept the area of manicured grass surrounding the monument.

"I doubt GA will follow us here," Jack said.

"They haven't got the manpower to search these islands and get Hart Island working at the same time, if they want to do it in three days," Brett said.

His statement reminded me that we couldn't hang around and lose our advantage. I looked toward the distant coastline of the mainland. "I've a feeling Anthony and Jerry won't give up that easily. That monument has a platform at the top. We can have a quick look before heading off."

"What's the plan?" Jack asked.

"Grab fuel and supplies and hit the mainland."

Moving slowly across the grass, I aimed left. A starling burst out of a tree and flew away. Boats gently rocked in their moorings on the other side of the thin section of island, and the rising sun reflected off the lake. Above the monument's grand entrance, a plaque read: "Perry's Monument—South Bass Island." A twisted male corpse lay face down on the grass next to the open entrance.

Jack crouched and glanced to his right. "There're a couple of places through the trees. Try them first for food and drink?"

I spun back toward our boat after hearing a distant cry of anguish. "You two hear that?"

Brett fumbled with his rifle and aimed at the trees, close to where we'd docked. Something or someone wailed.

"It could be an animal," Jack said.

"Sounded more human to me," Brett said.

Jack nodded and we slowly made our way toward a group of cedar trees, rifles ready to fire.

"The one on the right, by the base of the trunk," Jack said.

A shoulder and leg poked out. Somebody sat with his or her back against it.

"Put your hands up and show yourself," I shouted.

An arm jerked out. Fingers spread and trembling.

"Show yourself, now. Don't make us come over there," Jack said.

The figure slowly rose, and a man with a thick mustache, greasy black hair, and bloodstained cream shirt and trousers turned to face us. He clenched his teeth and stared at me with wild, piercing eyes. He mumbled something and staggered toward us as if drunk, clasping a carving knife in his right hand.

"That's far enough—drop the knife," I said.

The man let out a choking sound and jabbed the knife at his own throat. He paused, shook his head, and forced the knife out in front of him with both hands. It looked like he was battling an invisible force.

"What the fuck are you doing?" Jack called.

The man's concentration on the knife broke, and he gazed up. "I've . . . I've killed her. I'm trying to stop me. I can't."

"What the hell are you talking about?" I replied and glanced across to Brett. "Do you know what's up with him?"

Brett shook his head. "I dunno. Is he pissed out of his head?"

The man started tottering away, taking short footsteps, and waved us forward. "Come, come—I'll show you. Come."

I looked at Jack and frowned.

He moved forward and aimed at the man's back. "Just keep a safe distance; he's gone mad."

We followed him, keeping several yards behind. He waddled along a path, whispering unrecognizable gobbledygook, past a couple of Victorian houses, and turned into a driveway, all the while holding the knife and shaking it as if he had two dice in his hands. I detected a faint smell of alcohol.

"Here, here," he said, pointing at an open garage.

The bloated body of a middle-aged woman lay on the concrete floor, surrounded by a purple stain. Her throat had been slit, and she had slash wounds on her exposed arms.

The man stepped toward me and tilted his head. "That's her—that's my wife. He made me do it—it was him."

I edged back. "Stop right where you are."

"Who made you do it?" Jack said.

The man stared into space. "The voice: kill one, kill one, kill one, kill one, kill—"

I turned to Brett. "He's still activated. We need to get out of here."

"I don't think so, mate. He might heard it from someone else."

"Are you sure?" Jack asked. "I don't like the way he can't control the knife."

I wasn't convinced either. He rambled like a madman. What else could it be?

"I killed her?" the man asked.

The stains on his clothing suggested he'd killed something. As he'd led us to the body, it seemed reasonable to assume that he'd killed his wife. I looked over my sights, into his eyes. "Probably, but it's not your fault. We know—"

He shook the knife even more violently and stooped over the blade. The point missed his eye by a whisker. "Me? I did it?"

"Calm down for minute," Jack said. "There's been some crazy shit happening."

The man maniacally smiled through gritted teeth. His jerks became increasingly frantic. "Thank you."

"Wait!" Brett said.

He thrust the knife straight underneath his own chin. His eyes bulged and he sank to his knees, gargling and coughing blood down the front of his shirt.

"Jesus Christ," I said and ran over to him. He let go of the knife and fell to his side.

I went to pull it out but realized it was too late. His eyes fluttered shut, and blood pooled around his head. He let out two wet croaks before his whole body relaxed.

Brett stared, open-mouthed. Jack gazed down with a look of disbelief. "What the fuck?"

I took a couple of steps back to avoid the growing claret pool and tried to rationalize the man's actions. "Remember the guy at the airport needing to confirm a kill? Maybe he thought the voice killed and not him."

"God knows," Jack said. "He's just another poor bastard who died by the handiwork of Genesis Alliance."

"It's not possible," Brett said. "I heard there were problems, but nothing like this. The instructions are quite specific."

"How about you tell us the problems?" I said. "Because at the moment, everything we thought we figured out has gone to shit."

Brett moved away from the drive and stood in the shade on the front lawn. "It was more to do with people not getting activated who were near machinery, or recovering quicker than expected. There's so many parameters to the system, but the message is quite specific."

"Did you program the message?" I said.

"No, I didn't. I worked on inter-device communication and statistics. My side is all commercially available coding. Do you know what they told me it was originally for?"

I slung my rifle and folded my arms. "Try me."

He sighed and leaned against the window ledge. "Marketing. They claimed they would take money from corporations by implanting their products into people's consciences."

I generally didn't believe in conspiracy theories like the moon landings being fake or Elvis still being alive, but I might have been curious about this one. Regardless, I wouldn't have suspected the ultimate aim of the technology.

"How does it work?" Jack said.

"I've told you before, I don't know. I worked on building the inter-device communications, like mobile switching centers in a cell network."

I suspected he was being evasive and stepped toward him. "Don't worry. We're not going to steal the patent. Are you saying there's been no reports of it sending people around the bend?"

He bowed his head. "I heard talk of it but saw nothing in the official reports. Would you question it with your family under threat?"

"Brett, if there's anything you're hiding, now's the time to say," Jack said.

"What do you want to know? The program I developed for monitoring the top ten processes? The statistical reports I created for gathering location updates and memory usage? The signaling protocols and their configurations? You shouldn't overestimate my role. There's nothing I can do to help these poor people."

His last words were heartfelt, although he confused me with his technobabble, which wasn't that hard to do. I reminded myself about his previous openness and the duress that he'd been under, long before the first activation even happened. Perhaps the system had quirks that he didn't know about.

"Forget about it," I said. "We'll have plenty of time to talk things through once we complete our mission."

Jack jerked his rifle to the other side of the road. "Let's raid that house and get out of here."

I followed him and wondered how we could tell if anyone on the ground could be trusted. Brett trudged alongside me. "I'm here to help you and survive. Nothing more, nothing less. It's as simple as that."

"I believe you," I said. "You can't blame us for asking questions."

Jack kicked the door open, leaned against the front entrance, and spun into the light-pink hallway. He glanced back and pressed his finger against his lips. I stepped through the entrance and squatted on the sea grass carpet. A creaking sound came from behind a door, probably the living area.

I aimed over around Jack's side. He thrust the door open with the bottom of his boot and sprang into the room. I immediately followed and swept the area.

A lady, around eighty years old, hung from a beam on the roof. A toppled stool lay beneath her. I looked at her face and immediately turned away. To her right, by an old-fashioned three-bar electric fire, a man of similar age sat in a wheelchair. A knife handle poked out of his chest, and his head rested on the back of the chair, mouth wide open as if he died while screaming.

"Everything all right in there?" Brett called from the hall.

I sighed and peered beyond the couple at a rotting buffet on a wooden coffee table. "Let's find the bathroom and get scrubbed up."

Upstairs, the plumbing in the bathroom still worked and supplied us with cold water. I didn't trust it to drink, unless we found some purification tablets. Jack, Brett, and I took turns stripping off our shirts and cleaning ourselves, using a bar of fragrant soap and a pink sponge from the shower cubicle. I dabbed my stinging arm wound that I'd incurred at the tangle of cars and noticed it becoming increasingly bright red around the edges.

Jack tossed me a small bottle of antibacterial ointment and a bandage from the mirrored cupboard above the sink. "You'll be needing these."

I treated my arm and spotted a disposable razor on the window ledge. "You gonna have a shave?"

"What's the point?" he said and hummed the tune of "When the Saints Go Marching In" while putting his sweater back on and slinging his rifle.

I grabbed a fresh towel from a rack and dried myself. It felt like Jack and I had at last clicked back into gear and were starting to do things automatically. We didn't debate this house clearance— we just did it. I'd feared for his mental health over the last week; it had crumbled on our way to Monroe, causing him to behave erratically. Our new focus and clear mission seemed to be having a positive effect.

In the kitchen, Brett found a sealed box of Belgian chocolates, cans of potatoes and carrots, and a tube of processed cheese. I took a small bottle of sherry from the living area.

"Back to the observation deck," I said. "See if we can spot another boat or place to dock on the mainland."

We arrived back at the monument just before nine on Friday morning. Almost exactly a week since boarding our plane in Manchester. I climbed the stone spiral staircase inside the structure. The smell and buzzing of flies told me that we had obstacles to cross on our way up. Sure enough, I came across a bludgeoned corpse; a bloodstained rock lay a couple of steps above.

"Do you think that bloke outside did this and jumped off the deck?" Jack said.

"It makes sense I suppose," I said. "Although I'm bored with playing *CSI.*"

Brett winced after his trailing leg bumped against the body. I considered telling him that things got easier with time, but I would be lying. The bodies served as a constant reminder of the evil that had to be stopped. If anything, each one hardened my resolve.

I continued upward to the viewing platform. A stone deck gave us a spectacular three-hundred-and-sixty-degree view. I scanned across the quiet, glistening, deep-blue lake and the buildings dotted along the distant Michigan coastline. I shielded my eyes from the sun and looked south, at a small group of islands and the green fields of Ohio, stretching into the horizon.

Brett rested his elbows on the ledge and gazed into the distance. "Great view up here."

Jack pointed over my shoulder. "We'll aim for that peninsula about five miles away. Doesn't look like a built-up area."

"There're plenty of boats in the marina. No point hanging around," I said.

Brett dug the binoculars out of the top of Jack's pack and planted them against his face. He leaned forward.

"Guys, you better come and look at this. We might have company." He handed Jack the binoculars. "A boat. Over there."

Jack pressed them to his eyes and twisted the focus. I searched the water and located a gray speck, heading south.

"It's not heading in our direction. Do you reckon it's GA?" Jack asked.

"Traveling by boat's a good idea for a survivor," I said. "Although we've no idea how GA are spread around the country. Maybe it's the group who shot at us."

"It has to be them, surely," Brett said.

I wasn't ready to believe it yet. My general rule had always been to expect the best, but plan for the worst. If the boat diverted here, we would easily have time to set up an ambush. I hoped it would merrily stay on its current course.

Jack lowered his binoculars. "I think we're good. It's not coming here."

The boat traveled at speed across the water, sweeping between the island and mainland in a southerly direction. I switched my focus to the southwest and inspected the marina for a larger craft for us to use.

I nudged Jack and pointed down to an impressive looking Viking 65 Sports Cruiser. Sleek and white, with a thick blue band running around the hull. "Have a look at the second house, the one with a long dock. Can you see it?"

"Pretty nice boat. I'm sure Brett can get it going."

"Might have all kinds of stuff—" Brett said.

Jack ducked down behind the edge of the wall and gripped his rifle. "Holy shit."

Brett crouched and shot nervous glances at Jack and me. I quickly looked around the quiet marina before kneeling. "What did you see?"

"There's someone in that boat. They stared right at me."

"Give them to me," I said, taking the binoculars.

If we'd already been seen, there seemed little point in hiding. I focused on the windows of the boat. A curtain twitched, followed by the noise of an engine spluttering into life.

A man ran to the back of the boat, released the mooring rope, and vanished back inside.

"Whoever it is, they're out of here," I said.

White water bubbled behind the boat, and it edged forward. Brett peered down. "Why didn't he talk to us? We're not the bad guys around here."

"He probably saw our rifles. What would you do if you were him?"

"Fair point. For all he knows, we're the new occupying force."

"I suppose we are, in a way," Jack said. "He's probably about as trusting as us."

Jack and I had been part of an occupying force during our time in the Army. Although the circumstances were vastly different, this man's behavior didn't surprise me. Even when freeing people from the oppression of local warlords or brutal regimes, we were seen as aggressors and not to be trusted. Despite the fact that we meant no harm and wanted to improve their infrastructure, the bottom line was that we were generally despised. As odd as it sounds, no matter how bad things get, the only change that can be readily accepted by a lot of people is from within, whether that is personal or regional.

The boat noisily plowed out of the bay and picked up speed as it headed in a southeasterly direction.

Jack spun to his right and looked through his binoculars. "For fuck's sake."

I immediately knew his concern. The boat we had previously seen. This person had broken cover and would be easily spotted in open water by anyone observant—or a group on a hunt.

We watched for a few more minutes as the boat made its bid for a smaller island.

"It's turning," Brett said.

Jack kicked the wall. "Bollocks."

I could see with my naked eyes. The other boat headed directly to intercept the smaller craft, which slowed when the skipper probably realized he was being stalked.

The first boat, long and gray, rapidly closed in.

"Can you see who's aboard?" I asked Jack, who continued to observe through the binoculars.

"I think there's one . . . no, two. Dressed in black."

"I think it's safe to assume it's GA." I tracked them through my sights, but had no chance of hitting them from a mile away. "Let's just hope they don't come here."

Jack stuffed the binoculars in his pack. "He could lead them right to us. We need to move."

"We're in a good position here," Brett said. "I think we should wait."

Jack glared across to Brett and clicked the straps on the pack. The silver boat pulled alongside the other. Figures on both stood on the rear decks and appeared to be talking as the vessels gently rocked on the lake.

The man from the island slumped off the side of his boat as the sound of three shots reported across the water.

The two crewmen ran to their cockpit, and the silver boat turned in the direction of our island. White water sprayed around its bow as it powered toward the marina.

"Downstairs, now," I said.

We scrambled down the spiral staircase. I realized that trying to escape on a boat would only expose us. The last thing I wanted was a shootout on the lake.

I reached the entrance and paused for breath. Brett and Jack staggered out shortly after. I gave a crisp indication to a group of trees to the left of the marina. "That's where we set up an ambush. As soon as they're in range . . ."

"We shoot the bastards," Jack said.

4

The marina curved around a small bay. Landings jutted out at regular intervals, with a few small boats tethered. Woodland surrounded the area, interspersed with single-story buildings, mostly boatsheds and shops. I chose the thick copse because of the overall view. We crouched behind two large oaks and waited. My pulse quickened as the faint engine noise grew gradually louder.

"You remember how to use that thing?" I asked Brett and motioned my head toward his rifle.

"Yeah, but don't expect Billy Sing."

"Who?" Jack said.

"Famous Aussie sniper from Gallipoli." He groaned and looked through his sights. "Forget about it."

Footsteps pattered behind me. I spun around and aimed my rifle.

An Alsatian bounded toward me. It stopped a few feet short and barked. Jack approached it, and the dog sat down. He knelt and held out his hand. The dog raised its paw.

"I'm Jack—what's your name, boy?"

The dog rested its front paws on Jack's thighs and licked his hand. I grabbed a can of Spam out of our pack and opened it with the hunting knife.

I turned my back to the dog, chopped the processed meat into small chunks, and threw them in a wide area between the trees. "That should keep her distracted long enough for us to find another place. We can't have barking when those goons show up."

The dog bounded to the closest cluster of chunks and wolfed them down.

Jack stood and brushed pine needles from his knees. "There's a similar spot on the other side of the marina."

The dog sniffed around the woodland carpet for more. We took the opportunity to move and sprinted eighty yards, across grass, past two small wooden boathouses, and took up fresh positions in a copse on the other side of the marina. From here we could still see across the bay and hear an approaching engine.

Jack shuffled around the trunk and pointed his rifle toward the lake. "We need to let them get close. No firefights—just take them straight out."

A silver boat cruised around the corner at the opposite side of the marina, slowed, and came to a stop by the farthest empty landing.

Two men, both with GA standard issue AR-15s, hopped onto the wooden boards. One protected his eyes from the sun and looked at the monument. The other secured their boat with a thick rope. They prowled along the marina, aiming at the monument and edging closer. One paused, took a radio out of his breast pocket, and held it to his mouth.

"That bloody snitch," Brett said.

"Some good it did him," I said.

Jack nudged me. "They'll have no clue if it's us or not. Probably need recognition before the cavalry descends."

The dog bounded out from between two trees halfway between our two locations. It faced the GA guards, wagged its tail, and ran at them.

The first man approached the dog, slung his rifle, dropped to one knee, and started stroking its neck. He took a pistol out of a holster attached to his leg, placed the muzzle into the dog's chest and fired.

The dog yelped and fell to its side. The men continued along the path.

Jack grunted and curled his finger around his trigger. "Those bastards."

"Those *stupid* bastards, you mean," I said. "If there's anyone still activated on the island, we know where they're heading."

The men continued forward, heading further out of our range, and reached the monument entrance. They briefly halted and gazed at the twisted corpse at the foot of the large column. After a quick conversation, they disappeared through the door leading to the staircase.

One of the men shouted, most probably a warning to the people they expected to be on the observation deck. He had a voice like a foghorn.

Shortly afterward, the goons appeared at the top and completed two circuits—the first, slowly; the second time, looking down at the immediate surrounding area.

I pressed my back against the tree to avoid detection. "As soon as they head back down, we move and take them out by the entrance."

Jack didn't respond, but I could see the determination in his face, a look I'd recognized in him since his childhood, when he wouldn't let anything stand in his way. No matter who got hurt. Brett appeared less confident and took slow deep breaths while fidgeting with his charging handle.

"Just stay behind me," I said to Brett. "We need you alive."

He nodded and swallowed hard, no doubt bracing himself for his first taste of real action.

The men spent a few minutes resting their arms on the wall, staring out onto the lake. One spoke into a radio before they disappeared from sight. We waited a few minutes to make sure they weren't just carrying out another circuit.

I tensed and stepped into the open. "Ready?"

Brett moved to my rear.

Jack sprang from around his tree. "Let's go."

We sprinted for the monument's entrance. As I neared the base, a shot split the air. I instinctively looked up before diving for the base. Brett landed next to me and scrambled to his feet. Jack crashed against the wall, and we all stood with our backs against it, out of the platform's view.

Two more shots slammed into the concrete a couple of yards from my feet, creating puffs of dust. Small shards sprayed my shins.

"This has just got a bit more awkward," Jack said.

I ignored his obvious statement and tried to think about a plan.

Something metallic clanked down the internal stairs. I ripped Brett away from entrance. A large blast erupted from inside. More evidence of GA's dangerous stupidity.

"If they had half a brain, they'd have dropped it by our feet," Jack said. "How many more do you think they've got?"

Their radios were my biggest concern. They could confirm our location to a larger force. We were the ones that needed to act, and these two stooges probably knew it.

In my peripheral vision, I detected some movement to our left, and focused in the direction of the houses we previously visited. A figure ducked behind an SUV.

"Guys, we've got more company," I said and jabbed my rifle in the direction of the new arrival. "This is starting to feel like we're up shit creek without a paddle."

Brett flinched as another round slammed by our feet. "Is he wearing black?"

"Civvy, I think," Jack said.

"Give yourselves up," a voice echoed from the top of the staircase.

"You give yourselves up," I shouted.

"We can wait up here all day. Turn yourselves over and we'll spare you."

Jack craned his head around the entrance. "Like you did the man on the boat and the dog?"

After a moment's pause, the voice replied, "Suit yourself. We've radioed in, so you're signing your own death warrant."

"Fuck you!" Jack yelled.

While this hopeless negotiation ensued, I had my eyes glued on the SUV. A bald head rose above the hood.

I decided to fire a warning shot at the SUV to hopefully scare the observer away. The round punctured a hole in the windshield and exited through the driver's window.

A man scurried from behind the vehicle, wearing a pair of khaki trouser shorts and a baggy lime-green T-shirt, and holding what looked like an ornamental sword. He reached within twenty yards and threw himself behind a short, bushy tree.

"Aren't you going to shoot him?" a voice called down the stairs.

"Why should we? We're going to send him up to you," Jack said.

"He'll kill you."

"What do you care?" I said.

The man poked his head around a branch. "I've been waiting for someone to come. Thank God, you're here."

"Take one step closer and I'll shoot," I said.

"Haven't you come to save me?" he asked.

"Don't trust him," Jack said. "Remember the nutter an hour ago."

I took a step in his direction. "We've got enough on our plate here, so do us a favor and fuck off."

"I'll help you," he said. "I saw what they did."

"What?" Jack asked.

He shuffled to the side of the tree. "I've seen the killing and suicides. It's not me."

Jack jerked his rifle to his shoulder. "Stay back."

Another object clanked down from inside the monument.

I held myself flat against the wall. The man put fingers in both ears.

An explosion reverberated through the monument and echoed into the distance, no doubt across the water to the mainland. The place was starting to become a homing beacon for anyone looking for signs of life. I hoped that the handheld radios didn't have the range to communicate with the GA forces on the mainland.

"This is your last chance. Come out with your hands up, or face the consequences," one of the goons shouted.

The man hissed to get my attention. "Let me come over there with you."

"Just get the hell out of here," Jack said.

A round whizzed from above and hit the side of the trunk. Chips of bark sprayed against the man's face. He covered his head with both arms, paused, and made a dash for our position.

Another shot rang out. The man grimaced, slumped to the grass, and clutched his gut. He rolled to face me. "I've been here two weeks. I'm a survivor just like you."

"Holy crap," Brett said. "There's nothing wrong with him."

For a moment I felt speechless and stared into the man's desperate eyes. His quivering hand reached toward me. "Please, help me."

I braced myself to spring out and drag him out of harm's way. Jack unslung his rifle and edged around to me. "I'm gonna grab him."

"Leave it to me," I said. "You step out and give me some suppressive fire."

A third shot thumped down from the top of the monument. The man jolted. A red patch formed on the back of his shirt in the left kidney area. He buried his face in the grass and screamed.

"Now!" I said.

At that moment, a round thudded into the back of the man's head. His body relaxed, and his face flopped toward us, revealing an ugly exit wound on his left cheek.

Jack growled and glanced up. Brett's hands trembled on his rifle. I felt more in tune with Jack's emotions. No matter where we went, GA continued to kick us and take lives.

"You can thank us later," a voice called down.

I ducked around the door. "We know all about Genesis Alliance and that you might have been recruited against your will. Let us go and we won't say a word."

"Show yourselves, and we won't shoot," another higher-pitched voice added.

Jack shook his head. "We can't negotiate with these people."

"I'll talk to them," Brett said. "I think I recognize one of the voices."

"Not an option, Brett. They'll have your guts for garters."

"We've got three options," I said. "Win the firefight and carry out a tactical withdrawal. Wait here and hope their radios aren't in range, or go up and take them out."

"Option one," Jack said. "Pepper-pot out of here and get cover behind the buildings. Find a boat at the far end of the marina."

I heard a hiss of radio static above and quickly made up my mind. "Okay, let's do it. Brett, follow my lead and stay behind me."

Pepper-potting was a fire and movement technique we'd learned in the Army. One part of the team would give covering fire to suppress the enemy, while the other would move. This would happen in small alternating stages until reaching the required ground. It's all well and good being accurate on a range with a rifle, but facing a person who is shooting back is a completely different story. The people at the top of the monument would have to hold their nerve and risk their lives if they wanted a chance of taking us out. The buildings were around a hundred yards away. From there we would have cover to make it to the other end of the marina.

Jack aimed up and prepared to move. "Ready?"

Brett nodded and licked his lips. Anxiety had probably given him a dry mouth.

"I'll throw the buggers off track first." I leaned inside the doorway. "We're coming up. Don't shoot—we just want to talk."

"Take it nice and slow, with your hands up," a voice replied.

Jack ran out ten yards toward the marina buildings and took up a crouching position, aiming at the observation deck. He took his left hand off the rifle stock and held up his thumb.

I grabbed a fistful of Brett's jacket, pulled him twenty yards past Jack, skidded to one knee and aimed. Brett ducked behind me, panting against the back of my neck. No men visible on the platform. They must have been waiting for us by the upper entrance.

"Move," I said.

Jack sprinted past me. A loud boom emanated from monument, which confirmed the goons had no intention of negotiation. Shortly afterward, they appeared at the observation deck. I squeezed my trigger and fired. The bullet smacked against the stone between them. They both ducked.

"Move," Jack said.

I directed Brett to the left of Jack, ensuring we had some width between our positions, thus avoiding being in the same line of sight. Jack fired two more shots.

Twenty yards past Jack, I spun around and aimed. A red spatter sprayed up the deck wall.

"Move," I said.

Jack darted past. "Got one in the shoulder."

A rifle appeared over the top of the wall and fired a few rounds aimlessly in our general direction. A pointless waste of ammo.

"Move," Jack said.

I scrambled to my feet, grabbed Brett, who must have started to feel like a rag doll, and sprinted past Jack to a couple of large trees.

"Move."

Jack hurried past. "I'm going for the building."

A rifle appeared over the wall again and fired another burst. I fired at the arms on the platform, but the men kept their heads down. They'd lost the firefight, and we both knew it. Cool, aimed shots had done the trick. We were fighting amateurs.

Brett and I both rushed behind what was no more than a glorified shed, painted dark red with a white door. Jack bent double behind it, catching his breath.

I felt confident that the goons on the roof would not suddenly grow a pair of balls and start peppering us with accurate fire. They'd wasted their ammo on pointless sprays.

"More could be on the way," I said, not wanting to break our momentum. "Head straight for the boats."

I charged ahead, along thin strips of grass and pavement, between boat sheds, shops, and houses. Three shots rang out from the monument in quick succession just before we reached the trees surrounding the marina. The spring canopy overhead did its job, allowing us to jog slowly between the trunks. From here, they would have to move from their perch to catch us.

Keeping my bearings by using a straight road running parallel to my right, I wondered if the GA guards would follow. Attempting to start a boat might leave us exposed to gunfire, and chugging away from the shore would present an easy target for a marksman.

Jack stopped and checked behind, most likely thinking the same thing.

"Ambush, here—they won't be expecting it," I said.

If they did follow, they had little choice but to directly pursue, based on the land around us being openly exposed. I gestured with two fingers for Jack to cover the arc to our rear.

"We'll cover the left flank, Brett," I said and led him to two large trees. "If they appear, wait for my signal to fire."

"Okay. I can do that."

He leaned around a tree and aimed at our killing ground. I decided to give the goons five minutes to show.

Calming my breathing, I practiced the technique of firing I had almost forgotten: exhaling, relaxing my body, and taking a dummy shot. I half-expected the men to come clumsily crashing through the trees like wild boar running after their prey. Jack looked over to me in expectation.

"That man back at the monument," Brett said. "I think he came to help us."

"Don't think about it," I said. "You're gonna face a lot more of it in the next few days, so try to block things out. That's all you can do."

I realized we'd probably played a part in his death. But who could blame us for a lack of trust after what both Jack and I had been through? If I stewed over every incorrect decision or loss of life we encountered along the way, I would turn into a gibbering wreck. The only solution was to push things to the back of my mind, among all of the other horror Genesis Alliance had imposed on me.

A gentle breeze blew through the woodland, rustling leaves. A wasp landed on my knuckle. I tilted my hand away from the rifle to encourage it away.

A twig snapped in the distance.

Jack peered down his sights and slowly nodded. A figure darted from a building into the woodland and hid behind a tree. He advanced slowly toward us, stopping intermittently to aim forward and observe the area ahead. I had him in my sights, and he presented an easy hundred-yard shot, but I wanted his partner too.

I searched through my sights for his accomplice. He appeared to the rear of the first man, carrying a rifle in his left hand. His right arm hung limply by his side.

I took aim, breathed out, and fired into the chest of the second man. He yelped and collapsed to the ground. Jack fired a split second later. The first man's shoulder jerked backward and he tumbled over, crying out in agony. Brett fired. The man instantly clutched his left thigh. He writhed on the ground and screamed a garbled insult.

Jack sprang up and sprinted toward him. The man shakily held up his bloodstained right hand.

"Let's go," I said to Brett.

We ran to the second man. He lay motionless on the forest floor. I kicked his rifle away from his limp hand. He appeared deathly still and didn't react when I crushed his fingers under my boot.

"Nice shooting, Brett," I said. "We'll make a solider of you yet."

He turned and looked at Jack, who grabbed the other man by his jacket and pulled him to a sitting position. He scrunched his face and took rapid, shallow breaths. I removed the man's weapon sling from around his shoulder and patted him down, finding one full and two empty magazines.

He opened his eyes and sneered. "Who the fuck are you?"

I crouched in front of him. "We're just a couple of landscape gardeners that you've managed to piss off. The guy behind me is one of your former tech geeks. How many of you are in the area?"

He grunted and spat blood down his goatee. "Fuck you."

"Have you called in our position?" I said.

"You'll be dead in half an hour."

"I won't, but you will."

He took a deep raspy breath and grimaced. "Anthony's going to skin you alive when he catches you. Do you realize who you're taking on?"

"From what I hear, they're going to have their hands full with HQ," Jack said.

The man laughed, causing him to cough. "They know they're in the shit. That's why they've broken away from the main group and are coming after you."

"Where are they?" I asked.

He struggled to keep his eyes open. "You're dead men."

Jack shook him. "Where are they? Answer us."

The man exhaled and his eyelids dropped. Jack let go and the man flopped to the dirt. Jack kicked the man in the chest, turned to me, and shook his head.

"Should we hide the bodies?" Brett asked.

Jack scowled at the fresh corpse and wiped his mouth. "I'd throw him in a big pit of Genesis Alliance bodies if I had my way. Fuck him."

I guessed Jack also carried the same mental scars from our experience. I certainly couldn't shake it, and it continued to fuel the fire of anger inside me. I reminded myself that our moves needed to be calculated through logic and not motivated by rage.

"Can they still launch the activation without Anthony and Jerry?" I asked.

"Depends if they've got the codes," Brett said. "As far as I know, only Ron and his niece had a set."

"Martina?" Jack asked.

Brett raised his eyebrows. "How do you know that?"

"Long story," I said. "But we've got bigger things to think about in the next three days. Beating the main group to Hart Island, so you can do your thing. Avoiding nutjobs stalking us, and a bigger group being activated, probably wanting to wipe us all out."

I searched the other man's pockets and found a half-eaten packet of mints and a notebook. I flicked through the pages, scanning each one for anything of interest. He'd written down GA radio voice procedures, listed weapons, and jotted down Ron's address in Monroe. On the back page, he'd drawn a time line. The second activation had yesterday's date. Below it said *"Hart Island—SA/Processing—Next Tuesday."* I doubled-checked the date and time on my watch. Friday the 12th of May, just past eleven.

I held the page up. "Brett, this claims the second activation's in four days time."

"Three was always optimistic. They probably don't want any more fuck-ups."

"What about HQ?" Jack said. "Didn't you say they were arriving on Monday?"

"I estimated, but I do know they're heading for Boston, and the local lot are for the high jump. Trust me, fellas, we need to beat them. The local team I can face; the UK lot . . . they'll be a larger and more clinical force. That's where they stationed all of their elite."

Jack grabbed the notebook and ran his eyes over the page. "We need to get back to the mainland and lose ourselves on the back roads to New York. The earlier we hit that island, the better."

"No arguments here," I said. "Let's move out."

As we jogged toward the marina, I considered this island would have been perfect to visit pre-activation. A lovely bay, monument, manicured gardens to relax around, and fishing on the lake. I scanned the marina and lake for any signs of movement and listened for the sound of distant engines approaching. Without hearing or seeing anything suspicious, I proceeded down a wharf toward several larger boats.

Jack peered along the line. "Which one?"

"Any with keys and fuel," I said. I headed to the closest, a solid-looking launch with tinted windows. "We don't know if those two managed to get in touch with mainland force."

"We're right on the edge of the radio range here. Those GA handhelds are useless," Brett said.

The back doors to the cabin hung slightly open. I quickly boarded and rushed for the cockpit. A flock of startled seagulls burst out of the doorway. I ducked and covered my head as they flapped over me, collectively screaming.

Inside the cabin, two gulls remained, greedily pecking a woman who slumped over a bench next to a small kitchen area. I aimed a kick at the nearest and it attempted to fly, bashing into the ceiling and dropping to the floor. The other perched on her shoulder, gazing at me with its black soulless eyes. I lashed my fist at it, knocking the bird over before stamping on it, collapsing it like a deflated bag.

The cramped cabin stank, but the unease I'd felt at the marina forced me to continue to see if we could use the vessel. I clambered up to the raised cockpit and found keys in the ignition. Jack and Brett flapped around on the deck outside, scaring away a number of inquisitive birds, which flew away in search of an easier food source. Brett took one look inside the cabin, turned, and swore under his breath.

I turned the key and sighed with relief. The engine instantly rumbled to life and steadily hummed while the fuel gauge smoothly raised to almost full.

Brett and Jack carried the body to the dock. Brett placed a tarpaulin sheet over it and crossed himself. I liked his respectful gesture, but he was going to see a lot worse where we were heading. We would have no time to pay our respects to the dead.

Jack untied the boat, and I returned to the wheel. I reversed the boat away with the grace of a drunk driver, turned, and increased the throttle. The engine whined and we picked up speed, slapping over the calm lake in bright sunshine.

Nature would reclaim South Bass Island. I had little doubt about it.

As we sped south toward the mainland, Brett and Jack stood on either side of the cockpit, keeping watch on the port and starboard sides. I rummaged through the drawers for anything of use. I found a chart of the lake and a map of the surrounding area.

I passed the chart to Jack. "Have a look for a decent place to dock."

Jack oriented it to our position and traced a number of options with his finger. "Head southeast to Vermilion. Looks like there's a few quiet spots."

"How far are we talking?" Brett said.

"Just over fifteen miles. Should be there by midday."

I rolled up my shirtsleeve and rubbed the gash on my arm. During the last couple of hours, it had started to throb and sting with growing regularity.

"Probably needs proper attention," Jack said, looking down at my wound. "We'll find a medical center once we dock and grab a decent first-aid kit."

"It'll be fine," I said, but I knew it needed cleaning to stamp out the early signs of infection. "See if you can find a small town near Interstate 80. Best to find a local pharmacy rather than heading into a city."

Jack gave me a curious look. "We're heading back along the main highway?"

"Don't see why not. If we see GA, we can find another route. Speed is the key."

He studied the map and pressed his finger against it. "Elyria looks like a good candidate."

Brett leaned over his shoulder. "Should be a Walgreens there."

"A what?" I asked.

"Local pharmacy. They had one in Monroe, and I've seen them in other towns and cities."

We swept around the coastline, making excellent progress. Brett opened a window to allow a cool breeze to rush through the boat and clear the stench. I kept a safe distance from the sporadically clustered buildings onshore. Only a well-placed marksman could hit us.

———

"This is it," Jack said. "Head for those trees."

I decreased the throttle and gently cruised toward a deserted beach. Trees lined the back of it, partially concealing a row of large residential properties, painted in various light pastel colors. Green seemed a popular choice around here. A set of wooden steps led to a road above.

The boat drifted to a crunching halt several feet away from dry land. I looked over the side at water gently lapping against our hull and could see the bottom of the lake only a yard below the surface.

"You two get out," I said. "I'm sending this back out. We don't want to leave any clues."

Jack strapped on his pack, held his rifle over his head, and swung his legs over the side, splashing into shallow water and wading the short distance to the beach. I passed Brett my rifle, and he clumsily flopped over the side and staggered to shore.

I returned to the cockpit, put the engines in reverse, and turned it one hundred and eighty degrees before thrusting the throttle forward to maximum. I quickly checked the boat's course—straight to the center of the lake—ran to the stern, and jumped. The cold water took my breath away, and I sank until I kicked for land and solid footing. I hauled myself out of the lake and turned to watch the boat powering to the depths of Lake Erie.

Brett passed me my rifle. "Looks like you could do with a set of dry clothes."

"Thanks for stating the obvious." I wiped water from my face and checked to see that my watch still worked. The second hand ticked around, and we'd made it to Ohio minutes before midday.

"Look on the bright side. At least it's not winter," Jack said.

I grunted approval and squelched across the beach to the steps. Pretty colonial-style detached houses lined the street above. One, painted brilliant white, with a spacious porch and huge oak in the front garden, had a red Pontiac Torrent in the driveway.

"Looks like it fits the bill," Brett said.

Jack pulled his rifle into his shoulder and approached the house, aiming at the large ground floor window. My soaked, thick lumberjack shirt restricted my movement. I ripped open the buttons, peeled it off, and dropped it on the road.

Brett covered Jack, who stood at the front door, waiting for me to arrive.

I knelt beside the oak tree. "Go for it."

Jack twisted the handle and shoved the door open with his shoulder. They both entered. I scanned the immediate area for any danger signs and followed.

Both of them were in a farmhouse-style kitchen, rifling through rustic mahogany cupboards and placing cans and packages on top of a large black range. I left them to it and headed upstairs. Brett seemed to be adapting quickly to our situation and I admired his "have a go" attitude, even though he was even more out of his depth than we were.

My luck held in the master bedroom. In the walk-in closet, I found a solid pair of hiking boots, one size too big, but I compensated with a thick pair of walking socks. Unfashionable light-blue jeans with an elastic waist—but I didn't give a fuck. I winced while pulling on a purple baggy golf sweater, feeling my arm protest.

Back in the kitchen, Jack opened two cans of Dinty Moore beef stew, placed them on the table, and stuck dessertspoons in both. Brett sat down and immediately tucked in. I grabbed the other while Jack leaned against the counter and attacked a can of tuna.

The stew tasted great, and I looked around the kitchen while chomping the contents of the can. A bunch of car keys hung on a small hook next to the fridge. I finished the can, grabbed the keys, and rattled them. "Fancy a ride in that Pontiac?"

Brett threw his can to one side. "Sounds good to me."

"No point hanging around," Jack said. "We packed the food while you were getting changed."

Going back into more densely populated areas, I knew we would come across more people, possibly still suffering the effects of GA's technology. So far, Brett didn't have any answers for us in that regard. I decided we should keep our distance from all people until we could establish their motives.

I placed a car key in the Pontiac's door and twisted. All internal locks popped up. Jack threw his pack on the back seat and clambered in, and Brett sat next to me. I adjusted the front seat and started the engine.

Brett took a map out of the glove box. He clicked his tongue against the roof of his mouth while working out a route. "Go along the two toward Cleveland and take the fifty-seven down to Elyria. It's less than twenty miles. We can easily get on Interstate 80 from there."

I placed the car into drive and bumped onto the road.

Getting out of town proved slightly awkward. I had to slowly mount curbs and grassed areas to guide the car around blockages in the road. The way ahead cleared slightly as the urban area disappeared from our sides, allowing an increase in speed to around thirty miles per hour until we reached the highway.

5

State Route 2 didn't differ from our previous experiences of highways. Multiple crashed vehicles spread across the road, mingled with corpses. Some cars had pulled to the shoulder, where drivers took advantage of injured parties in the wrecks. All hallmarks of the carnage the first activation had brought. Brett silently stared out of the window, shaking his head at regular intervals. I wondered just how much he had seen around Monroe. He'd told me he was part of the cleanup operation, but I guessed it had only been in a limited capacity. The burden he carried must have weighed heavily, knowing that he was part of the "solution" that caused the devastation outside the Pontiac.

Rubbish drifted around hotels and fast-food joints that lined Route 57. Things were starting to change. When we'd fled New York, it had felt alive with killers and survivors; the infrastructure was still fresh and intact. The heightened sense of abandonment around here gave the impression that civilized life had drained from the landscape. It wasn't obvious at first, but as I paid closer attention to the buildings, the signs became clearer. Not a single window gleamed, corpses were in advanced states of decomposition due to the warm spring sunshine, and the entire area was deathly still.

I thought back to a trip Jack and I had taken to Machu Picchu three years ago. I remembered him asking, "How come they just stopped living here? Why didn't somebody else move in?"

Back then I had no idea and naïvely accepted it as part of history. I never thought that the same thing would happen to major towns or cities in my own lifetime. To imagine Manchester quietly decaying, covered in weeds and slowly being swallowed by nature, seemed ridiculous, but it was probably happening as we drove toward Elyria.

I wondered if we would still have a human population to walk around and marvel at those city ruins in five hundred years.

"A penny for your thoughts?" Jack said.

"I was just thinking about our trip to Machu Picchu."

He grimaced as we crunched over a stray detached bumper in the road. "That's a bit random. I was thinking what we should do if we come across another person like that bloke on the island."

"We keep our distance and take no chances," I said.

"Exit here," Brett said. "We'll be there in two minutes."

I swung the car right and headed along Broad Street, which ran through the center of Elyria.

"Stop the car!" Brett suddenly cried.

I thrust my right foot against the brake pedal, and the Pontiac came to a screeching halt. Jack aimed his rifle around the windows.

I glanced to either side of the road. "What's the problem?"

"Over there. A pharmacy. Didn't I tell you?"

Jack frowned. "You could do it a little less dramatically next time, and not put the shits up me."

I grabbed my rifle from between the back seat and headed for the pharmacy attached to a general medical building. Jack and Brett covered me as I peered through the glass. An aisle ran along the center, with various hygienic and homeopathic products. Medical kits lined the shelves to the right. Two women in white coats both slumped over the counter at the end.

A two-toned electronic beep and an eye-watering stench greeted me when I pushed open the door. I went straight for the right side and grabbed a green plastic case with a white cross on it. I popped it open and found exactly what I was looking.

I returned outside, sat on the step, rolled up my sleeve, and snapped on a pair of plastic gloves. I rolled off the flimsy crusted bandage, splashed on antiseptic fluid, rubbed sterile cotton across my arm, and clenched my teeth as the stinging sensation intensified. Brett unrolled a fresh, more robust bandage and passed it to me. I wrapped it around my arm, feeling pleased that I had hopefully addressed the problem.

"You wanna quick look around town before we head off?" Jack asked. "See if there're any gun shops?"

"Do they have them around here?" Brett asked.

"No harm in trying," I said.

I put my rifle on my shoulder and carried out a quick visual sweep of the area. A hundred yards ahead, a sheet of newspaper danced across the street. Three hundred yards to our left, a flock of birds circled high in the air. Further into town, cars littered the road at atypical angles, mangled and smashed.

"I can pick out a route through the mess," Jack said. "No point getting split from our supplies or have somebody take the vehicle when our backs are turned."

"Let's not hang around here for too long. A quick search, then straight for the highway." I turned to Brett. "You okay with that?"

"Whatever you say until we get to Hart Island."

We got back into the Pontiac, and Jack twisted and turned a mile along the main street. He halted when we reached an area with a host of shops on either side of the road. Most had broken windows. A woman in a blue flowery dress slumped through a bookshop window, impaled on a shard of glass that rose out of her back.

Brett gasped and pressed his hand against his chest. "What the fuck?"

Five naked corpses were propped against the wall of a gym. All sitting tightly together. All beheaded. Somebody had written "This is the End" above their bodies on the brick wall in white paint.

I opened my door. "We just need to make sure we don't join their line. Be on your toes."

Jack walked over to a bakery. He pushed open the door, and a bell tinkled. "Already looted. Might be some survivors around here."

"Can't blame them for that," I said.

I wandered past a store filled with home decorations and peered through the smashed window at the contents inside. A small ornamental glass clown caught my eye. Similar to one that our grandparents once had above their fireplace. I reached in, picked it up, and dusted it off.

"What have you got there?" Jack asked.

I held it up. "When did you last see one of these?"

Jack shook his head and continued down the street. "Useless piece of junk. Come on."

I thought for a moment about pre-activation life. Most people I knew, now probably dead, occasionally shopped for these small trinkets to decorate their houses. But for what? They would all be gathering dust in our decaying world. I decided to keep the glass clown. It provided me with memories of cutting my grandparents' lawn before relaxing on their couch with a glass of sherry. Their clown always smiled at me, no matter how useless. Besides Jack, memories were all I had.

"This one looks more like it," Brett said.

I joined him at the doorway of a café. Inside, cakes rotted below plastic protective shielding on the counter. Eight tables and their surrounding chairs had been pushed all over the place. White cups and plates lay on the floor, some in pieces, still smeared with food or coffee stains.

"Get yourself inside then," I said to Brett.

He went straight for the counter. Jack and I followed him inside.

Flies buzzed around a body on the brown tiled floor. The man wore an apron and was missing three fingers on his left hand. One stupid fly tried to escape the café and constantly bashed against the window. An ideal candidate for the Monroe Genesis Alliance team.

I leaped over the counter, grabbed two husklike croissants and tossed them over to Brett.

He froze and they bounced off his chest.

Jack glanced outside. "Something's coming. Get down."

I hunched down and aimed my rifle over the top of the counter. Brett knelt behind a fallen circular table.

Jack stood by the edge of the window. "A red pickup truck. Two men inside."

The brakes squeaked as the vehicle came to a halt close to the café.

"Are they wearing black?" Brett asked.

"No, both civvies. One's holding a sack; the other's got a shotgun."

"Might just be looters," I said. "Let's keep our heads down and wait it out."

I felt my pulse quicken and shuffled across a few feet to give myself a clear shot at the entrance. Brett stared at me and clutched his rifle to his chest.

"Stay where you are," I said to him. "You know the drill."

The men, both in jeans and T-shirts, stood ten yards in front of the café in conversation, oblivious to the fact that at least two of us could drop them in a second. The shorter man ran his hands through his greasy black hair. They moved to the left, out of sight. I could hear their muffled voices next door. Judging by their apparent casual attitudes, they were on a familiar excursion and weren't expecting trouble.

"We don't want to end up in a close-quarters situation," Jack said. "It's too easy for somebody to pull the trigger."

It would only take us seconds to sprint back to the Pontiac, parked twenty yards to our right.

"Back to the car for cover," I said. "When they come out, we get them to drop their weapons."

"You want to recruit them?" Jack asked.

"I want to talk to them. Find out what they know."

I vaulted over the counter. Jack checked that the coast was clear, and the three of us edged back to our vehicle while aiming at the shop next to the café.

Brett knelt with me behind the hood. Jack aimed around the rear.

Seconds later, the two men casually walked out of the shop. One had his arms wrapped around a full sack; the other followed with a shotgun lazily held over his shoulder.

"Freeze! Drop your weapons," I shouted.

The man dropped his sack and spun in our direction. A can spilled onto the road and rolled to the curb. The other fumbled with his shotgun and started backing away toward their pickup.

"Who are you? We don't want any trouble," Shotgun said.

The other tentatively bent down to pick up the sack while keeping his focus on me.

"Drop your shotgun. We're not going to shoot," Jack ordered.

"You can have these supplies—take them," Sack Man said. He widened the top of the sack, revealing cans and packages. "I'll leave them on the ground."

"We just want to talk," I said.

The other lowered his shotgun. They both glanced at each other. I needed to do something to put everyone at ease and end this standoff.

"Cover me," I said to Jack and Brett.

I held my rifle above my head and walked toward them.

"We don't want any trouble, mister," Sack Man said. "Let us get on our way, and you won't see us again."

"We're not here to do anything stupid," I said. "I want to talk to someone who isn't either trying to kill us or planning world domination."

It seemed impossible to form any trust in a few minutes. We should have been embracing each other as fellow survivors in a decaying world, happy that we'd found each other.

I stopped a few yards short of them and placed my rifle on the ground. The man placed his shotgun down. I heard Jack and Brett close in from behind. They placed their rifles alongside mine.

"There, we're all friends," Jack said.

"Where did you come from?" Shotgun said.

I didn't immediately reply. My mind replayed events since leaving Manchester, and I shook my head, trying to think where to start. Brett's silence was a little more obvious.

"We landed in New York, and that's where we're heading," Jack said.

"You landed in New York and you're going back there?" Sack Man asked, astonished. "Where else have you been?"

"Long story," I said as I came to the realization that these people probably knew nothing of Genesis Alliance, and it couldn't be explained by a quick chat on the street. "Is it just the two of you?"

"Just the two of us," Shotgun said.

This awkward meeting needed some direction. But we stood making stilted conversation, eyes breaking away for fear of making too much contact and appearing aggressive. The fact that we were facing two people standing together and not trying to throttle each other gave me hope.

"I'm Harry, that's Jack and Brett. We landed last Friday, a few hours after the shit hit the fan. We've been through a nightmare and only want to sit down and talk."

"Sure, why not?" Shotgun said. "Let's grab a pop and talk."

The word "pop" took me back for a moment. I hadn't heard it called that in years. He walked past us to the café. Sack Man, who stood around six feet five inches, towering over all us, followed. He attempted to smile, but I could see the anguish pasted across his face.

Jack looked at me and shrugged. He picked up his rifle and headed to the café. I passed Brett his rifle and followed suit. The larger man dragged his sack inside, opened a dead fridge, retrieved four cans, and passed them around.

Shotgun dragged the corpse to one side and straightened a table, and we dragged chairs around it. My can hissed when I popped it open, and I took three gulps of fizzy lukewarm coke. "We use the word 'pop' back home. I didn't know you used it here."

"You're a long way from home, guys," Sack Man said. "Is it the same in the UK?"

"We're not sure. We've had conflicting information," Jack said. "As far as we know, it's worldwide."

Brett remained quiet and fidgeted with a paper packet of sugar. I could imagine a hundred reasons why these two strangers would beat him to death.

Shotgun sighed. "I thought as much. It's been a nightmare around here. A few of us have managed to hole up in a hangar. You're the first people we've come across outside our group that hasn't been insane."

"There're more of you?" Jack said.

"Eight of us," Sack Man said. "An old guy runs the place. He's a bit weird, but it's better to be in a group, right?"

"I suppose so," I said. "What do you remember from last Friday?"

"I remember a car crashing into the back of mine at high speed and my face smashing into the wheel. I woke, alone on I-80, with a massive headache and death all around me. I found him a day later." He gestured to Shotgun. "I was hiding out in an abandoned house, and he just walked right up the street. I thought he was another psycho. They were everywhere."

Shotgun smiled. "When I saw him come out of a house, I nearly ran. I'd been fighting and running for days. I was working in a lab when the killing started, and didn't know what was happening until later that night." He paused and stared at his can. "When I left the secure environment, I found our security guards dead. Somebody tried to smash down the door and threatened to kill me. I called 911 but got no answer. I eventually left and spent days on the run. I'm one of the lucky ones, and thank God someone found me wandering."

The two stories appeared to make sense. Meeting fellow survivors gave me encouragement that if we could destroy the control unit and stop the second activation, society would eventually come back together.

"You're both lucky to be alive," I said. "We had similar experiences after landing. We've been traveling around and have information that might keep you safe in future."

Sack Man leaned over the table. "Information? You know what's happening?"

"Not exactly, but we know part of the picture," Jack said. "Another activation is coming, but we can stop it."

"Activation? What do you know?" Shotgun asked, eyeing Jack suspiciously.

"We'll tell you when we get somewhere safe," I said. "How about we go back to your hangar?"

I wanted to meet more of the survivors and possibly convince them to join our mission. More numbers wouldn't be a bad thing, especially with Jerry and Anthony on our tail.

"I'm not sure Bob would like it."

Brett split the sugar packet, and brown grains spilled over the table.

"He's quiet," Sack Man said, gesturing toward him.

"He's traumatized," I said. "Only says a few words."

Sack Man nodded in understanding. "There's a woman back at the hangar who's still nuts. Bob keeps her chained up."

"Chained up?" Brett said.

"She would kill you given half a chance. Better to be safe than sorry."

"We need to head back in a few minutes," Shotgun said. "He starts to panic if we're not back on time."

"So that's it?" Jack said. "You don't want to know more about Genesis Alliance and the activations?"

Shotgun finished his can and tossed it over the counter. It landed with a rattle. "I'm sure it's a great story, but we're pushed for time."

Jack stood and his chair legs screeched along the tiles. "It's not a story. It's information that could save your life."

"I think we should hear them out," Sack Man said. He seemed the friendlier of the two. "If they know about what really happened and what's likely to come . . ."

Shotgun grinned, quite smugly in my opinion. "No offense, guys, but you look like trouble. We've heard all kinds of crazy talk and don't need any more."

"If you want to end up as slaves, be my guest," Jack said and stormed out of the café.

"Sorry about that," I said. "He can sometimes fly off the handle. Is the quickest way back to New York along Interstate—"

Jack burst back in with a look of panic on his face. "They're here. Get behind the counter."

"Who's here?" Sack Man asked.

"Genesis Alliance. The people who caused all of this."

I ran to the doorway and peered outside. At the top of the street, three hundred yards away, a black Rover slowly headed in our direction. Men dressed in black, possibly twenty, fanned across the street, walking behind the Rover and pointing their weapons at buildings. The two men, Brett, and Jack scrambled over the counter. I took one last look at the approaching force and joined them.

"What are they looking for? Did you lead them here?" Sack Man asked.

"No," I said. "They're probably searching for survivors on their way to Hart Island. If you cross them, they'll kill you."

Shotgun looked pale. His hands trembled on his weapon. "What do we do?"

"Just keep your head down," Jack said. "If they find us, we won't have a choice."

The engine noise grew louder. Raised voices echoed along the street. We had to hope they didn't enter the shop and poke around. At least we'd have the element of surprise, but the odds were stacked against us.

The larger man tapped me on the shoulder. "Why Hart Island?"

I put my finger to my lips and looked over the counter. I ducked down immediately as the front of a Rover appeared from the right, trundling along at around three miles per hour.

Footsteps crunched on debris outside. Somebody paused by the café window. I tensed and curled my finger around the rifle's trigger.

The footsteps continued away, but another set followed.

"Are we looking in any of these?" A man shouted.

"We haven't got time," another said. "The convoy's on its way, and we need to keep ahead of it. You can answer to the boss if the path isn't cleared."

The main body of men passed outside, loudly talking with one another. I heard one mention something about looking forward to a beer this evening. The larger man tried to suppress a sneeze but let out a short grunt. Jack shook his head.

Voices faded away. I wanted to make sure they were well into the distance before we moved. Shotgun sat with his back against the counter, his eyes tightly closed. A bead of sweat rolled down the side of his face.

We waited another five minutes in silence. Brett crouched at the far end of the counter, away from us. Jack or I weren't about to tell his story, if that's what his problem was.

"I'm taking a look," Jack said. "If they come back this way, I want to be out of here."

He slipped over the counter, and I watched him creep to the door. He looked back. "I think they're gone."

Sack Man let out a deep breath and wiped his brow.

"Take us back to your hangar," I said. "I'll give you the information you need."

He rapidly nodded. "I know a few back roads. We can be there in ten minutes."

"I suggest we move, now." I put a friendly arm around Brett and led him outside. "You're safe with us, mate. Don't stress."

"I don't know what to say. What would you say?"

"Tell people you came over with us. That'll do for now."

I genuinely felt sorry for him. I could tell he was a decent man who had been forced to play a part in a wider evil plan. In our previous lives, I'm sure we would have been good friends had we met.

The other two men clambered over the counter and headed out. Jack stood outside, looking in the direction of GA's travel. I joined him and gazed into the distance. The road curved away as it left the main part of town.

"I only want to be that close again when we're taking the bastards out on Hart Island," Jack said.

"Did you hear what they said about the convoy?" I asked.

"It's probably not far behind if they were an advance party."

"They're moving at a snail's pace," Brett said.

"Doesn't matter," I said. "We need to get you down there as fast as possible."

I turned at the sound of the pickup truck's engine starting. Sack Man leaned out of the passenger window, still looking slightly rattled. "Follow us. It won't take long."

"What're your names?" I said.

"I'm Dave, he's Arun."

We slipped inside the Pontiac and quietly closed the doors.

Jack started the Pontiac and pushed it into drive. "What about these two? They wanted to dump us before GA showed up."

"I think we need to give people a chance," I said. "At least we know a little bit about what's behind it all. They've just seen their world go to shit without explanation. I don't blame them."

"I suppose you're right. I'm keeping my distance, though." He looked over his shoulder at Brett. "You okay, Chief?"

Brett gazed out of the window. "I'll live. I think . . ."

Jack turned in a semicircle and followed the pickup. It steered down a side road, passing through a small new development of three partially constructed houses and headed for what looked like a dead end. The pickup turned right, disappearing behind a yellow-painted bungalow, and as we followed, the road turned into a snaking mud track with a stripe of grass running along the middle and hedges on either side.

The track led to Elyria airport. The pickup crossed the tarmac, in front of two hangars, and came to a halt just before the large sliding door of the first. Both men sprang out and rushed inside. Dave returned a minute later with another man, old with gray hair, stiff and vigorous. He approached the Pontiac and gestured to me to lower my window.

I dropped it and heard the buzz of a generator. Not the smartest idea if they wanted to remain inconspicuous in this location.

"The name's Bob. Park immediately on the right side—go on," he said, beckoning us away.

"Short and sweet," Jack said.

Bob slipped back through the gap. The door wound open a few feet. Jack eased into the hangar and parked to the right of three small single-engine planes. I would normally be excited and curious to examine them, but as the hangar doors closed and the darkness descended, I felt less enthusiastic. We disembarked and stood by the car.

Rapid footsteps echoed to my right. Metal scraped across the concrete floor. A figure charged out of the gloom. I spun and aimed at a greasy-haired woman in a filthy lilac dress. Brett jumped behind me. A trailing chain, bound around her wrists, snapped rigid, halting her forward momentum. She yanked at it, panting vigorously while staring at me with hunger in her eyes.

Lights along the ceiling thumped alive from back to front in sequence. Bob stepped from behind a plane. "Welcome, welcome. Put down your weapons. You're safe here."

"Who the hell is that?" Jack said, thumbing over his shoulder at the woman.

"Don't worry about Amanda. I took her in four days ago, and she acted sweet as apple pie. She attacked Dave with a hex driver on Wednesday, and we couldn't calm her down."

"She was normal for two days, then attacked?" I asked.

"That's right. Turned completely nuts. Must have swallowed another dose of that damned chemical."

"What chemical?"

He smiled and put his hand on my shoulder. "Dave tells me you've got some information. We can compare notes while I get you something to eat."

Our last meal had been in Vermilion just after midday, only two hours ago. But since we'd landed in this mess last week, I never turned down food. "If you've got something, we'd be grateful."

"Follow me, gents."

I glanced back at the woman. She attempted to rip the chain free again and scowled at me.

Bob headed for the far end of the hangar and broke into a half jog before slowing after several awkward strides. I smiled to myself, remembering how my granddad used to do the same thing. I think they did it to prove they still had a level of vitality.

I slowed, allowing him to get thirty yards ahead and walked alongside Brett. "Any idea what he's talking about?"

"I doubt it's anything to do with chemicals. She's been triggered again by something."

"Like what?" Jack said. "Are you saying this could happen to anyone we meet?"

"No idea. Could be a malfunctioning device. She might have had a delayed reaction. It's probably wise if we treat everybody with caution."

"That's just great. Can't you people do anything properly?"

Brett sighed and shook his head.

I searched for potential exit points and areas to use for cover. The appearance of GA had me paranoid, and if they swooped in on the hangar, we needed at least half a plan. The revelation about the woman's behavior also concerned me. The inconsistent nature of the post-activation left us with little option but to trust nobody.

We reached a gray door marked with orange safety flares. Bob led us through to a basketball court–sized room with diagrams of engines and pictures of planes around the walls. Wooden tables with metal legs, like army chefs used in the field, were piled with food supplies. Eight camp beds were set up at the far end, with blue mummy-shaped sleeping bags neatly lying on top of them.

"Sal," the old man shouted, "bring three bowls of your lovely stew."

A thin old lady with white hair pulled back in a ponytail appeared from a side room. She was dressed in a crumpled cream trouser suit, sleeves rolled up to her elbows.

"Three more, Bob?" she asked and rested her wrinkly hands on her hips. "I bet you boys have had an adventure getting here."

"You could say that," Jack said.

Bob gestured to three seats in front of a desk. "Sit down and let's talk. I need to know what happened today."

"You seem to have a nice setup here," Brett remarked.

Bob glanced down, tutted, and swept crumbs off the surface of the table. "We're preparing for the end of the world, young man. Just like we did during the Cold War, but this time it's real. Every day we gather a straggler. Arrange their accommodation and provide a safe place to rest while we wait. At the moment, we number eight, but we expect to build until it finally happens."

"Until what finally happens?" I said.

The old lady carried in three steaming mugs on a tray and placed them in front of us.

Bob smiled at her, then focused back on me. "Rescue, of course. You don't think they'd leave us all here, do you?"

I shifted uncomfortably, trying to think of a reply that wouldn't cause offense. Bob had shown no guile when he spoke. I could only think that he believed, without question, that the National Guard would descend on the hangar at any moment.

The old lady cleared her throat. "What he means is that we'll all help each other until the Army sets things straight."

"I don't want to be the bearer of bad news," Jack said, "but the Army isn't coming."

"Oh, stop teasing us," Bob said and rolled his eyes. "They'll be starting in the cities first. This chemical warfare can't last forever. We'll have nuked them."

"We've come from New York. It's worse than here," Jack said.

"Nuked who? What do you mean?" I asked.

"It stands to reason that this is the action of the Chinese. I noticed them sneaking up the rail, didn't I?" He looked at the woman, who nodded. "They've attacked us. We've struck back. Now it's just a matter of waiting for the effects to subside and standing on our own two feet again."

"Sorry, Bob," I said. "This is altogether different. There's no easy way to say this—"

He jabbed his finger toward my face. "You can't scare me. I'm too old and have seen too much. Tell me about those people in town."

"They're . . . well, there's an organization called Genesis Alliance who did all of this," I said. "What you see around you has happened on a global scale. Small pockets of survivors like you have here are probably all that's left. They used some sort of technology to send out an *activation*. That's what happened last Friday—"

"How do you know?"

"Because we've met them," I said. "They've got a base in Monroe and are heading for a place called Hart Island. There's going to be another activation soon that will pretty much change you into their slaves."

"But there's a way we can help you, and the others here," Jack said.

"What's up with you?" Bob said, looking at Brett. "Cat got your tongue?"

"No, it's just that . . . I . . . ."

Bob narrowed his eyes before referring to a map on his desk. He briefly mumbled to himself about our story and slapped his hand firmly on the table. "Are you saying we've been invaded?"

"Not invaded, as far as we know," I said. "But they're taking over and will be using the remaining survivors to clear up the country by the same technique as previously deployed."

"They're a clean energy company or something like that," Jack added.

Bob cackled. "You've got to be kidding me, right?"

"Does it look like we're joking?" Jack said.

"I doubt they're coming here," I said. "They seem to mostly rely on the technology to do the work for them. We think we can help you all escape the effects. We've been told a way."

"If what you say is true, I need to know how," Bob said.

"This might sound odd," I said. "You have to cattle prod yourself on the head several times, which might work. The other way is by creating a small EMP device—"

Bob frowned. "A what?"

"That's what he said," Jack replied. "You have to use a prod."

"And you've done this to yourself?"

"No, one of the GA tech team used a special tool on us—"

Bob locked his hands behind his head and sat back. "Are you sure about this prod? If I'm to do it to my team, I need to give them a reason."

"It's the only way possible," Brett said. I was glad he'd finally chirped up. His silence made him look suspicious. "It's not one hundred percent guaranteed, but it gives you a chance if the next activation happens."

"It might not even happen," I said. "We're gonna try to stop it at Hart Island."

Bob looked to his left and drummed his fingers on the table. I could understand his questions, and he seemed friendly enough. He surveyed the map again, stroking his silver beard and placing his finger on various points, mumbling about Hart Island.

The old woman arrived with three large bowls of stew and a hunk of freshly baked bread. My stomach growled in appreciation and, despite the heat, we tucked in, blowing wildly to cool the food. The time eating gave me a chance to think of what was happening here. Bob and his group were living on false hope, and our information had probably crushed it. I was curious to see how he reacted.

"Looks like you're enjoying the food, boys?" Bob said.

"First proper cooked meal I've had in a week," Jack said.

"Compliments to the chef," Brett said.

The old woman, Sal, brought three steaming mugs of coffee and a cake to the table. They certainly had a nice setup, as Brett had previously observed, although it could be destroyed in a flash if GA got their way.

Bob kept his twinkling light-blue eyes on me while I finished my cake.

"You don't believe we'll be rescued?" he asked.

"Not a chance," I said. "The best thing we can do is stop the second activation and take the fight to Genesis Alliance."

"There are eight of us here. How can we help?"

"First, we can make you safe," I said. "Then, we can discuss if you're prepared to join us and destroy their infrastructure."

Sal took our plates away. Bob went to slap her on the backside as she walked past him, until she gave him an icy stare.

He leaned forward. "Tell me more about Genesis Alliance."

"We met a member yesterday," I said. "He gave us the info on Hart Island."

"Well, I think I need to know the full story if we're joining the fight."

"He was press-ganged into an organization that did all of this. They carry out activations through devices spread around the world. I've seen two of them in southern New York state and Hermitage. You can also trust us."

"Why are they doing this?" Bob said. "I don't understand the motivation."

"We don't know," Jack said and glanced at Brett. "We've had to fight our way to Monroe and back just to get these snippets."

Bob pointed at Brett. "Does he know something that he isn't saying?"

Brett bowed his head. "I arrived with Jack and Harry last Friday."

Only actors on the Syfy channel outdid Brett for bad acting. I put my arm around him. "He's been through a lot, Bob. Go easy on him."

"How did you know they were in Monroe?"

"We met one of them in southern New York," Jack said. "He told us the location of the main U.S. contingent. There's a bigger force on their way from the UK."

I wondered how suspicious we actually sounded. If I were in Bob's shoes, and a group of survivors turned up with this information, I'd be asking questions and thinking they were part of it.

"You just met one out of the blue?" Bob said. "And more are coming?"

"That's right," Jack said, his mouth still stuffed with cake. "This isn't a small operation."

Bob sighed and pulled a black book from his pocket. "I have something to show you that you might find interesting."

He licked his finger and flicked open a few pages before placing it on the table. "Read it. Transcripts of the radio contact I've had with a man named Anthony Olney."

My heart sank as I reached forward and grabbed the soft leather-bound book. I read the first page, his written journal of events, all dated and with times filled in. The book began with details of every call made by Bob, including some contact with pilots in the air. Then a period of radio silence until the first transcription of his conversation with Anthony.

113

Anthony had told Bob that he was part of the surviving government and was rallying the country to gather up all survivors and organize their sanctuary. Bob replied, saying a group of survivors were in a hangar close to Elyria. Anthony instructed him to wait for rescue.

The book recorded radio silence again for a few days until early this morning. Anthony transmitted again, telling him to keep an eye out for two British men named Jack and Harry and a New Zealander named Brett.

With Anthony and Jerry on our trail, and in the local area, it was only a matter of time before they showed up here. I closed the book and looked up at him.

"The guys told me your names," Bob said. "I could have radioed Anthony, but it didn't feel right. I wanted your side of the story, and you saved my men in town."

"You're on very dangerous ground here—" Jack said.

"What do you mean?"

"Anthony is their hatchet man," I said. "He slit a woman's throat and blamed it on us. Beat a man's brains out with a bat. If he knows your location, I suggest you find another one, and quickly."

"We were going to move to my farm, but as things were going well here . . ."

"If Genesis Alliance comes here," Jack said, "they will be well armed and will show you little mercy."

"Why do they want you?"

"They want us because we've taken a few of them out," Jack said. "We burned down the local leader's house. That's why they're going to Hart Island."

"You've led them here," Bob said.

I slid his notebook back across the desk. "We're not special cases. You've seen the world outside. The threat is real, and you need to move."

"They already know about you, and that fact should give you enough motivation to find another place," Jack said.

"Bring Dave here," I said. "Ask if those goons in town looked like a friendly force."

"He already told me they looked like a mean bunch. We'll head over to the farm and work it out from there. Do you mind helping? It shouldn't take long." Bob looked at Brett. "You sure you're okay, son?"

"I'm fine. Just a bit under the weather."

"You're certain using a cattle prod on crazies will work?" Bob said and rubbed his beard. "I guess we could always give it a go on Amanda."

Brett gave a single firm nod. "It's the best solution available."

Our story would sound silly to any rational human, but we were living in irrational times. At least Bob considered our words and acted.

He called the other seven into a group in the center of the hangar. Besides the old lady and the two men we'd met in town, the other three men and two women looked bedraggled and worn out.

Bob stood on a small wooden box, like a second-rate politician. "Ladies and gentlemen, it's come to my attention that we have a potentially immediate threat. Unfortunately, it means we have to leave our location and find a new home."

The group whispered among themselves; two shook their heads. He continued, "It's not a bad thing. We can use my farm. You know I have a limited amount of supplies, but we can take what we have built up here and carry on expanding our community."

"What threat? We were okay until those two turned up," said a man in a dirty yellow shirt and brown trousers.

"They've come here to warn us," Bob said. "Apparently, another disaster wave is coming. I've been provided with a solution by which we can stay safe. The first priority is moving from here. I'll provide more details once we get to the farm."

The group looked at each other and continued whispering.

He clapped his hands. "Get to it, guys. We've been compromised and need to relocate." He turned to us. "Bring your car to the back, and help me load the stores. You're helping me explain what's going on once we arrive."

"No worries. You're doing the right thing," I said.

Jack nodded toward Amanda. "Are you going to test the prod on her?"

"After we clear ourselves, I'll come back and cure her."

"Why not do her first, and show your group that it works?" Brett said.

"Prod's at my farm. Do you want her in your car?"

None of us needed to answer his rhetorical question.

For the next twenty minutes, we loaded food and equipment into the back of our vehicle. Bob busily ran among his group members, helping carry boxes and giving words of encouragement. Amanda struggled against her restraint and shouted insults at anyone who passed.

I got the impression Bob was well liked among the group. Survivors in this world had little choice of companionship if they wanted to form a group. I could think of worse choices than for him to be in command.

After finishing packing, we formed a convoy with the vehicles outside the hangar. Bob led from the front, weaving along back roads through the countryside.

"They seem to be doing all right," Brett said.

"If you keep acting like you were back there," I said, "people are gonna smell rat."

"Fair point. The problem is knowing what to say."

I had to keep reminding myself he was a tech geek and in a difficult situation, but we had to be tight and convincing when coming across survivor groups. People would be paranoid, scared, and suspicious.

I peered through the window for any signs of GA. My thoughts drifted back to Bernie, for some reason; the thought of him waddling out of his bedroom in pants and vest made me smile. The activation had made me evaluate friendships in my previous life, and I realized that I hadn't spent enough time with the people who mattered. We all had busy lives, and I'd used it as an excuse. If we managed to get through this, I wouldn't make the same mistake again.

The convoy snaked through narrow country roads with fields on either side. The sparsely populated area probably provided ideal survival ground—the opposite of our intended destination, although I had no intention of hanging around Bob's farm, especially now that we knew about the convoy.

We rattled over a cattle guard and entered a rural property with a smart Victorian farmhouse at the end of the road; a darkly stained, rickety wooden barn stood opposite, surrounded by lush green grazing fields.

The vehicles stopped in a disorganized formation at the front of a house on a cobbled yard. I got out of the car and stood behind the group already surrounding Bob.

"Unload into the barn, and we'll discuss arrangements," Bob said and disappeared inside the house.

He quickly returned with a wooden cattle prod and a shotgun. Dave stared across a field at a distant plume of smoke. Bob clicked his fingers. "Come on now—this isn't the time for daydreaming."

Someone has to play leader in these types of situations. Bob seemed officious but friendly. I respected him for taking control and trying to organize things. An every-man-for-himself attitude would only further fragment the decimated population. It certainly wasn't for Jack, Brett, or me to start dishing out advice to local people in Ohio, telling them how to run their wrecked lives.

We unloaded the contents of the Pontiac into the corner of the barn and relaxed against its timber wall. Jack pulled out a packet of cigarettes he'd taken from the café in Elyria and lit one up. Brett tugged at weeds that sprouted between cobblestones. I sat back and closed my eyes, enjoying a peaceful moment as the sun beat against my face.

Footsteps approached. I opened my eyes to see Bob jogging over. "I'm going to call the team meeting in five minutes. You need to tell your story, and I'll be the first to take the cattle prod."

"No problem. I'll do it," Brett said.

"You seem in a hurry, Bob," Jack said. "Why not chain Amanda up and bring her over for a demonstration?"

"I lead by example. My priority is to keep everyone safe and show them we're all equal."

"Whatever you want," I said. "We'll do our bit and leave. We're up against the clock."

Bob crouched in front of me. "I'm going to put Hart Island to a vote. We can come with you and stop this thing."

"Speed is the key. You also have to understand that the risk is significant."

"Doing nothing is a bigger risk," he said. "Convince the guys, and we'll follow you."

I considered whether a larger group would slow us down. Numbers would help to combat any threat we encountered on our way, but a smaller group would be more nimble. Brett might also be compromised when we arrived at Hart Island, when he did his thing. I doubted all would be as accommodating as Jack and me.

Bob stood in the middle of the courtyard. "Meeting in the barn in two minutes."

The group trudged in through the two main doors, one after the other, and stood in a semicircle in the center. The barn had a straw-covered floor and an assortment of farming tools neatly placed along one side. Hay bales were stacked at the back. Behind them, I could see cracks of light shining through the thin gaps of a doorframe.

We stood to Bob's right, in front of the group.

"These three have a story for you. The devil is coming and we need to be ready. They have a procedure to help you avoid the consequences of another radiation wave from the enemy. They'll explain it from here."

Jack stared at him. "We never mentioned a radiation wave."

I elbowed Jack. "I'll take it from here."

It seemed pointless trying to undermine Bob's understanding. The theory mattered little. The remedy was the most important thing, along with a warning of what people were facing. I decided not to pull any punches when taking the group through events. They had to know the reality of the situation and the consequences of not acting.

Looking around the barn at the various faces, I viewed a mix of emotions as I took the group through our own experiences since landing in New York. At first they listened intently. When I explained about Genesis Alliance and the information we'd gathered from Brett, the mood seemed to change. A couple of people stood open-mouthed; one lady put her hands over her face and muttered. A man put his hand on his forehead and tried to speak. No words came out.

Bob stepped toward the group and raised his cattle prod. "If you want to avoid being turned into a fruitcake, I need to buzz you."

"Are you serious?" a woman said.

"I'm afraid it's all true," Jack said. "We will stop it if we can, but . . ."

"How long have we got till the shit hits the fan again?" Arun asked.

"Four days," I said.

He looked at Bob. "If you believe it, you go first."

Arun had displayed cynicism back in town. I didn't expect everyone to believe us, and it came as no surprise that he'd piped up.

"I will lead by example," Bob said. "After that, I want you all to form an orderly queue."

He dropped to his knees, facing Jack, and passed him the prod. "It's primed and ready to go. Just hit the button on the handle."

Jack walked to Bob's rear. "You know we've never done this before?"

"Yes, yes—get on with it," he said impatiently, shaking his head.

Jack held the prod out, looking like the Queen knighting a subject, and pressed it against the back of Bob's head. Bob gasped after the electric snap, leaned forward, and screwed up his face.

"Hit me again."

Jack repeated the procedure. There was a sharp intake of breath. Bob's eyes widened and rolled up in his head, and a string of saliva hung from his mouth.

"Are you okay?" I asked.

Bob's head dropped and he groaned. He slumped to the ground and made a strange croaking noise. Brett gasped and took a step back. Sal screamed.

"Shit," Jack said.

He rolled Bob onto his back and slapped his face a couple of times but received no response. Jack leaned over his nose and mouth before grabbing Bob's wrist and checking his pulse.

The group converged on their stricken leader.

"Oh my God," a woman gasped. "Is he breathing?"

"You've killed him!" a man said.

Jack clasped his hands together and pumped Bob's chest. I knelt next to his body and noticed a wet patch forming around the crotch area of his cream chinos.

I'd seen this before in my local village pub. The heart of one of the old regulars had packed up as he sat in his favorite chair, drinking whiskey. We'd tried to use our medical training from the Army, pumping his chest to get oxygen to his brain in order to preserve function until the ambulance arrived. It didn't work; besides that, an ambulance wasn't about to show up at the farm any time soon.

Jack stopped pumping, reached up, and closed Bob's eyelids. Sal cradled his head and sobbed. A pistol slide sprang forward.

Arun aimed at Jack. "Give me one good reason why I shouldn't shoot you."

Jack reached for his rifle. "Jesus Christ, it was an accident!"

"Accident or not, a man's lying dead and you're responsible."

"Who makes you judge and jury?" I asked and raised my rifle.

Dave grabbed Arun's shoulder. "He didn't mean it. We don't need any more killing today."

Arun stared into my eyes. "I don't care about the old man. He's been jacking me around for days. I'm more interested in you three. You show up with a crazy story and ask us to line up to be electrocuted."

"Everybody calm down," Brett said and stood between Arun and me. "We can talk this through."

Arun broke eye contact and looked over my shoulder toward the barn door. A vehicle approached outside. Its engine cut and two doors slammed shut.

"I haven't finished with you three yet," Arun said. He gestured the others toward the entrance with his gun. "Let's find out who our visitors are and deal with these three after."

Sal wiped tears from her cheeks. "I'm staying with Bob."

"You're coming out with us. Bob was your husband. You need to be part of the decision."

Dave eased Sal up by her arm. The group stepped around us and left the barn. Warmth had turned to cold stares. Arun closed the large double doors, and a bolt squeaked along its rail.

I peered through a small gap between two decaying pieces of timber. Three men, dressed in black, stood in front of a Rover at the property's entrance, around forty yards from the group. Arun led the other five members of the group toward them.

"Let's get the hell out of here," I said.

"You read my mind," Jack said.

I took one last look out front. The group reached within thirty yards of the GA goons. Anthony stepped from behind the Rover, holding an M60 at his hip and opened fire.

Rounds ripped through the survivors and peppered the barn. Jack and I dove to the ground. Brett froze.

"Get down!" Jack shouted.

Brett pressed his hand against the left side of his chest, pulled it away and looked at his blood-soaked hand. He dropped to his knees, his eyes glazing over, and he fell face first and joined Bob on the dirt.

I crawled over to him and twisted his head toward me. His eyes stared back vacantly. There was nothing I could do. Our plan had died with Brett, and we would follow if we didn't act quickly.

Somebody barked orders outside. Another burst of automatic fire hit the barn. Wood chips sprayed from the decaying doors. A round ricocheted off the farming tools to our right and whizzed in an unknown direction.

"Back door, now," I said.

"We can take them out," Jack said.

"Fuck that. Four against two, and they've got a machine gun."

I wriggled to the hay bales, crawled over them, and dropped to the far side of the barn. The rusty bolt on the back door required a few twists of encouragement before it opened. Jack landed beside me, and I pushed the door open.

We sprinted for the trees on our left, keeping our flight obscured from anyone at the front of the property, and threw ourselves down behind them. I shouldered my rifle and checked for any signs of pursuit. Nobody followed, indicating that perhaps the survivors didn't have time to tell the goons about us before being cut down.

Using the cover of woodland, we carried on, putting distance between the farm and us, eventually meeting up with a country road that led to Interstate 80.

Brett's death had increased my determination to succeed against Genesis Alliance. He was a likeable guy who had been put through hell by these people. I appreciated his brave decision to join our fight, putting him miles out of his competence zone and perhaps placing his family at an even greater risk.

"That's our plan for Hart Island—screwed," Jack said. "With Brett gone, how are we supposed to destroy that thing?"

"Maybe find Morgan and his group. They might have some ordnance or could help us find some. If GA is right up our asses, I think we need a stronger force."

Brett's reward for having the courage to stand up to GA was a bullet. I vowed to honor his memory and complete the mission we'd started together—and return the compliment to Anthony.

6

We struggled to find a usable vehicle in the near vicinity. A group of badly damaged and charred cars cluttered around the intersection. Two were mangled together at the front end after meeting in a head-on collision.

I jogged along the inside lane and spotted an electric-blue Honda Goldwing motorbike on its side, its rider pinned underneath. I grabbed the handlebars and strained to right the bike. Jack pulled the corpse away by the helmet.

"So we're sticking to the highway?" he said.

"Best way to build up a lead. Straight to New York."

He straddled the bike and started the engine. It sounded too loud on the silent highway. Jack had been a weekend biker in England. I'd always thought of motorcycles as death machines, but in our current circumstances, a bike appeared the perfect way of eating distance. With a convoy heading the same way, not to mention the imminent arrival of a larger, more powerful force, we couldn't hang around.

I took the pillion, and neither of us bothered with a helmet. *What did it matter?* I thought; health and safety had died in the activation too.

"Next stop, Hermitage?" Jack shouted above the whining engine.

"That's not even funny."

"I think we should go back to Jerry's barn and burn it down. If we can take out that device, it might leave GA with another hole in their communications."

"It's on the way, so why not?" I said, remembering Bob indicate the location of Hart Island on his map. "If we head into the city from the north, it'll give us a view of the island."

Wind rushed against my face in the brilliant sunshine. I purposefully avoided mentioning Bernie and so did Jack. Riding on a motorbike made any reasonable conversation difficult, but I thought we could both benefit from paying respects to someone who had been an integral part of our initial survival.

With the time approaching four in the afternoon, we zipped between obstacles at a decent pace. The Newburgh-Beacon Bridge lay just over four hundred miles away in southern New York State. At our current speed, and allowing a short stop in Orange County, we could make it by the early hours of Saturday morning. I earmarked the bridge as a place to stop and get a couple of hours' sleep before entering the city.

———

The bike's fuel light blinked on just before Bellefonte. At half past nine in the evening, darkness had already descended. I thought it a blessing in disguise because I would feel far safer in a car at night.

Jack stopped next to a lone Jeep. Two people lay next to the passenger door. Moonlight reflected off their pale green skin, and I cupped my hand over my nose. More importantly, the inside of the vehicle appeared clean. I jumped into the driver's seat. The keys were still in the ignition, and I gave them a hopeful twist.

The engine roared into life, and the fuel gauge flipped to three-quarters full. I placed my rifle between the front seats while Jack buckled up. Moonlight allowed us to drive with dipped headlights, and I felt a sense of purpose as the Jeep cruised at fifty miles per hour, curving between lanes.

We occasionally bumped over stray objects in the road, but I threw my previous caution to the wind. Brett's death had dealt a severe blow to our plans, but we had to continue. The more I thought about meeting with Morgan's group, the more it made sense. Without a tech geek in our midst, we probably needed a stronger force to end the local threat. We would certainly need a small organized army to defeat the larger incoming threat.

Jack seemed to be getting more used to his environment. I thought our new objectives channeled his emotions and helped him come to terms with our situation. Being in a position to do something returned him to his former self, focused and single-minded. When we were simply surviving, he acted irrationally and came close to having meltdowns.

We stopped for a short break at Bloomsberg, leaned against the hood, and shared a bottle of Gatorade I'd found under the front seat. Something buzzed in the air, and I peered into the clear night sky.

"Sounds like a chopper," Jack said.

I looked back in our direction of travel. A white beam shone on a distant section of highway. "Kill the lights. Into the trees."

I crouched behind the trunk and peered between branches. The buzz grew quickly louder.

"Who do you think it is?" Jack asked.

"I'd put money on it being GA."

Twenty seconds later, a helicopter thumped overhead, perhaps only two hundred feet above the highway. A searchlight shone along the lanes, and I felt a light breeze against my face as the chopper passed. I leaned out and watched it blast along the length of the highway and disappear into the distance.

"Looks like they've found a quicker way to Hart Island," I said.

"Some of them, not all. Doesn't change our plan, though, does it?"

"No. We can still beat the convoy and take on small numbers with Morgan's help."

He took over the wheel and picked up Interstate 84 at one in the morning. This section of road had been relatively clear on our way to Monroe, and it was doubtful that the density of wrecks had increased in the last few days. My eyelids felt heavy, but I had to remain vigilant for any movement in the shadows around us.

Jack slowed to navigate around a large truck lying on its side, then suddenly slammed on the brakes.

I jerked forward and thudded against my seatbelt. "What is it?"

He grabbed his rifle from the back seat and aimed forward. "There's a bloody spike strip on the road."

I quickly looked around in all directions. Something moved through the trees to our left. "Smells like an ambush. Get the fuck out of here."

Jack slammed the Jeep into reverse. The engine whined as he weaved backward. I kept my eyes fixed on the thin woodland next to the highway. A figure ran to the opposite shoulder and kept pace.

I wound my window down and tracked the figure's movement with my rifle.

"What the hell are they doing?" Jack asked.

After meeting Amanda in Bob's hangar, I wasn't taking any chances. A rational person surely wouldn't run after a car on a dark highway. "Stop, so I can take a shot."

Jack hit the brakes, and our Jeep came to skidding halt. A bearded man, wearing only a pair of jockey shorts, crouched next to an ice truck fifteen yards away from us.

I lowered my window and aimed. "Back off or I shoot."

He screamed like a banshee, stood, and headed directly toward me, holding something concealed behind his back.

"Shoot him," Jack said.

"Stay right where you are," I shouted.

He paused, titled his head, and hissed through clenched teeth. I couldn't be certain in this light, but it looked like he had several human fingers dangling from a necklace on his bare chest.

I gently squeezed the trigger. If he took a step closer, I would drill a round through his forehead. He changed direction and headed to the front of the Jeep, trudging like a Neanderthal man. A large fire axe dropped by his side and its blade scraped against the road surface.

"What the fuck is wrong with him?" Jack asked. "He's another Amanda."

He stood two yards in front of our hood, raised the axe above his head with his right hand, and glared through the windshield with rage in his eyes. He spat at it, and a thick trail of saliva dribbled down the glass in front me.

"Fuck this," Jack said.

He put the Jeep into drive, and as the man managed to free the axe and drew it back again, pressed the accelerator. We smashed directly into him, and he disappeared with a scream. I felt his body scrape against the underside of the Jeep, and the left rear tire bounced over him. Momentum took us straight over the spikes, and we advanced unsteadily through the debris.

I looked back between the two front seats at the road behind us. The man lay motionless, arms by his side. Our tires quickly deflated, and Jack struggled to control the Jeep. We came to a juddering halt fifty yards away from the trap.

"He's not getting up anytime soon," I said.

"What the hell was that about?"

I jumped out and swept the area with my rifle. "Just another poor victim of GA. Every one of these meetings emphasizes why we need to destroy those buggers."

"Agreed. Let's get another car, and quick."

We shouldered our rifles and advanced along the highway in search of another vehicle. After quickly identifying a Chrysler whose only occupant was a corpse hanging out of the driver's door, I pulled it out and we were on our way again.

———

Just after three in the morning, we reached the outskirts of Montgomery and merged onto the road toward the house and farm, both of which held strong recent memories for me. Bernie and Jerry. Complete opposites and the wrong one had remained alive.

Jack slowed the car to a crawl as we approached the farm's entrance. "Which one first?"

"The house. We should set fire to the barn when we're ready to leave. Don't want to advertise our location. If Jerry's around and sees the smoke coming from the direction of his place . . ."

Jack nodded and accelerated toward the house.

We rumbled along the lane, past the burnt-out silhouettes of two properties. I peered back to Jerry's farm on our right. No vehicles were parked around the farmhouse, and one of the barn doors hung open.

"So far, so good," I said.

Jack swung the vehicle onto the crunchy gravel drive of the large white house and flicked on the Chrysler's main beam. Neither of us said a word at what initially greeted us.

Bernie's rotting body gently rocked in the breeze, suspended from the porch's roof by a rope around his neck. His clothes were filthy from his burial. I felt an intense rage bubble inside and clenched my fists.

Jack growled and punched the steering wheel. "Those bastards. Are there any depths they won't sink to?"

"Jerry's been here. Who else knew about Bernie and would do this?"

I jumped out of the car and scanned the dark swaying trees that lined the edge of the property. Jerry could be close, and if he was, I wanted him hanging in Bernie's place.

"He might be at his farm," Jack said.

"God, I hope so."

We backed over to the ornate colonial porch. Jack glanced up at Bernie, swallowed hard, and bowed his head. He briefly closed his eyes, and his jaw twitched—something he often did when trying to maintain his composure. If it happened in a bar, that was my cue to get him out of the place, but this was altogether different.

A piece of A4 paper hung from Bernie's chest, held in place by a hunting knife that had been pushed in right up to the hilt. I leaned forward and ripped the paper down.

"What does it say?" Jack asked, looking over my shoulder.

I crumpled it up in my hands and gritted my teeth. "'You're both dead men. Jerry.'"

Jack crouched and took a deep breath. "Let's get to his farm. I'm going to gut him like a fish."

"Seems like a lot of effort just to send a message," I said and glanced back at the road, conscious that this must have happened in the last few hours.

"He's ensured that he's going to be the focus of my effort. When I get my hands on him . . ."

I wondered if there was a lot more to Ron's inner circle than just being deluded losers. You've got to be one sick bastard to pull a stunt like this.

Jack reached up and grabbed the knife from Bernie's chest. He slid it out, and I heard a metallic click. I grabbed his shoulder and ripped him back. "Get down."

I covered my head with my arms, and Jack followed suit. An explosion ripped through the air. Warm parts of Bernie splattered over my legs, back, and arms. My heart raced as I patted myself down for damp patches. I had learned this technique in the Army. With adrenaline pumping, an injury requiring immediate attention might not always be felt.

"Are you okay?" I asked.

Jack grimaced and rose to his feet. He peeled a large flap of skin off the side of his jeans and wiped himself down.

The bottom half of Bernie's body lay on the porch floor in a mangled mess. His neck still hung in the noose above, but only his chest and one arm were still attached. The house and porch were covered in a mix of shrapnel damage and our former friend.

"Bastards!" Jack shouted at the top of his voice. "I'm coming for you, do you hear me?"

"Jack," I said, "we need to make sure it's on our terms. If they're around, they'll have heard the explosion. We've got to move."

"I'm not leaving him like that, no way." He grabbed the rope and cut it above the noose, and we carried Bernie's remains to the back of the house.

A spade was wedged into the turf next to the site of his exhumation. Jack dropped the parts into the grave. I placed the upper half on top and quickly scraped a thick layer of dirt over the hole.

I looked at my clothes and shuddered. "Quick wash before we go. Then, straight to Jerry's."

Jack nodded and followed me toward the back door.

I pushed it open and made my way to the kitchen sink. The tap ran, but I resisted the temptation to have a drink, instead washing my face, hair, and arms clean. Jack took my place while I carried out a quick search of the ground floor. I sighed when looking in the dining room. Four dirty plates were still in position around the table—the place where we had eaten breakfast before

131

heading out to Maybrook; it had turned out to be Bernie's last meal. So much had happened since, that it seemed months rather than days ago.

It also made me think of Lea. If Jerry and GA were prepared to do this to Bernie, I dreaded to think what they would do to her. My hopes lay with Martina saving her bacon, or the technology team, who at least seemed to have a shred of human decency.

I returned to the kitchen, still concerned about the sound of the grenade alerting any nearby patrols. "Ready for Jerry's? Then we'll head to the city."

Jack wiped his face with a blue hand towel, threw it on the kitchen floor, and picked up his rifle. "Wild horses wouldn't stop me."

I drove the Chrysler to within two hundred yards of the farm. We hopped over a fence into a neighboring field and cautiously advanced to the back of Jerry's barn—the same direction as our initial assault after his escape following Bernie's murder.

Jack edged around to the open door while I provided cover. He slipped into the barn, and quickly returned. "It's gone."

"What? The device?"

I brushed him to one side and peered into the gloom. Only a large square imprint in the dirt betrayed the device's former location. Most of the supplies had been taken; a few empty cans dotted the ground. A high-frequency radio lay smashed to pieces in the center.

"Reckon they've taken it to Hart Island?" Jack asked.

"Maybe. I'm starting to think Jerry was in that chopper. How else could he have made it to Orange County before us?"

"Wouldn't mind searching a camp. Get my hands on a couple of rocket launchers."

"We might need something like that. Who knows what HQ is turning up with?"

Jack rummaged around the clutter lining the far wall and held up two prods. "Thought they might have taken these."

"Probably don't need them if they've got a tool like Brett's."

Jack pressed a button on the handle. A blue light snapped between the two prongs, momentarily lighting up the barn.

"At least we've got something to take to Morgan," I said. "Let's get out of here."

"Not yet. I want to leave him a message."

He crossed the farmyard to the house, and I tried the door.

"It's locked, Jack. Do you really want to bother?"

He returned to the barn, came back with a mallet, and passed me his flashlight.

Jack smashed the living-room window and carefully knocked around the edges to remove sharp pieces of glass. I realized trying to stop him would be futile; he was intent on destroying Jerry's property.

He climbed through the window and glanced back. "You joining the party?"

I shook my head and tossed his flashlight through the window. "I'll watch from outside. Just get on with it."

He shined it around the room and headed for a display cabinet. Jack took out framed pictures and threw them all against the wall and smashed Jerry's small fantasy ornaments with the butt of his rifle. He tipped over the bookshelf, kicked over the couch, picked up a DVD player and threw it at a retro record player. I felt a small amount of satisfaction at seeing Jerry's property being destroyed. He deserved it, and I hoped it had a therapeutic effect on Jack.

Jack tipped over an armchair, took a lighter out of his pocket, and set fire to it. He encouraged the small licks of fire with paper that he ripped from a large atlas. Once the flames took hold and the fire started to crackle with a healthy rage, he jumped back out of the window.

Jack rubbed his hands together and slung his small pack.

"How did that feel?" I asked.

"Like we've given him a virtual punch in the face. That will have to do, for now."

———

Picking back along Interstate 84 in the dark used up a lot of energy-sapping concentration; the car took a bit of a battering off the side of other vehicles and loudly banged over debris on the road. Thankfully, it only took an hour to reach the Newburgh-Beacon Bridge, a nice sign of progress. I suggested to Jack that we not enter the more heavily populated areas of New York until daylight. He agreed and I stopped on the bridge at half past four in the morning.

I gazed along the moonlit river in both directions. Looking south, faint orange glows burned against the dark skyline, perhaps the route of a Genesis Alliance advance party. I couldn't imagine they'd be collecting any prisoners or messing around with siege tactics. I sat down next to Jack against the concrete sidewall.

"I'm getting pig sick of this traveling about with threats around every corner," Jack said. "I can't wait to get out onto the open water."

"You want to sail to England?"

He sighed and rubbed his face. "Wouldn't be the worst idea in the world. We've spent half of our time here, struggling up and down roads, and all we've achieved is a black eye each, weight loss, and a couple of dead and missing friends."

"Keep your chin up. We've discovered a lot too and have an opportunity to strike."

Jack picked up a stone and hurled it across the road. It clanked against a metal railing on the opposite side.

I wondered if Bernie dominated Jack's thoughts. If we'd stayed in his apartment, the chances were that we might have ended up with a group of survivors in New York. Then again, in a densely populated city area, more killers lurked. Choosing the right answer had proven impossible, but so far I thought we'd made reasonable decisions. We were still alive and could help people in the city.

We sat in contemplative silence for ten minutes, and I closed my eyes. A sound like crashing thunder rumbled in the distance. The clear night sky showed no signs of an imminent storm, so I strained to listen as the sound grew steadily louder.

Jack sat up and peered west. "Whatever that is, it's coming toward us."

"Into the car," I said.

I lay across the front seats, Jack dived in the back. The rumbling sound changed into a bashing of metal. I leaned over the back seat.

Two bright headlights stabbed through the dark. Others followed. The lead vehicle closed in, and the noise intensified. The GA convoy—it had to be.

Jack glanced at me. "Think it's them?"

"We'll find out in a minute. Hold your fire unless they see us."

A large snowplow powered past and smashed a Mustang to the side of the road. It barged aside anything in its path, creating a clear route for the following vehicles.

I raised my rifle to just below the window, ready to thrust it up and fire if required.

Two noisy five-ton trucks came next, common logistical vehicles for armies across the world. I couldn't see the drivers in the dim light and tried to keep my night vision by focusing away from the dazzling lights. A flatbed followed, with two activation devices strapped to its back, similar in size to the one in Jerry's barn. Six black Range Rovers brought up the rear.

"How did they get here so quickly?" Jack said.

"Drove nonstop, like us."

I thought about the implications of what we were seeing. GA was executing its plans for the second activation, and crucially, its members were now ahead of us. Brett had mentioned the technology team needing time to set things up, so the timeline matched the notebook. The countdown had begun.

We watched the convoy as it crossed the bridge and continued down the highway. The engine noises died down as the red taillights disappeared from the horizon. A solitary black Rover crawled into view, possibly acting as some kind of backmarker. I resisted the tempting urge to pump it full of lead.

After waiting another fifteen minutes without seeing anything else, we crawled out of the car and sat by the road.

"We need Morgan and his group," I said.

"Yep. Can't take on that with two rifles."

"And whatever else is coming."

Occasional distant noises punctuated the last two hours of darkness, mostly sporadic gunfire. A long, loud crashing noise echoed as dawn began to break. Perhaps a building collapsing after a fire or something more sinister, related to GA's advance.

Conscious that I should at least get an hour's sleep before we headed into the city, I stretched across the back seat. We didn't have to worry about what was behind us anymore. All the danger lay ahead.

———

Jack shook my shoulder. "Harry."

My mouth felt like the Sahara. I swallowed and rolled over. "How long have I been asleep."

He had a look of urgency on his face that made me bolt up and reach for my rifle. "Ten minutes. Someone's coming."

I sprang to the back window. Through the murky dawn light, a pair of dipped headlights headed through the cleared path. "Just one set of lights?"

Jack nodded. "Let it roll by. Ambush if needed."

I lowered the rear window in case I needed a quick, accurate shot. A risk I wasn't prepared to take with a convoy, but a single car away from the pack would be easier pickings.

The car approached at a steady pace and slowed when it reached the bridge.

I raised my head just before it pulled level, hoping to catch a glimpse of the driver. A blonde-haired man, dressed in a red fleece, stared straight back at me.

His head jerked back against the rest and the engine roared. Car tires screeched against the road surface. His car bucked forward and veered to the right. It slammed into the side of a caravan, twenty yards head, with a metallic crunch.

I kicked open my door. "Go, go, *go!*"

Jack ran to the driver's side and pointed his rifle through the window. I covered him and swept around to the passenger side. Only one man in the car. Back seat empty.

"Don't move an inch," Jack said.

I opened the passenger door, keeping my rifle trained at the man's face. Blood trickled from his nose. He groggily looked in both directions and held up his hands.

"Don't shoot—don't shoot, please."

"What are you doing on the road?" I asked. "Who are you with?"

"I could ask you the same thing. Lower your guns . . . please."

"What's your name?" Jack said.

"Rick. Stop pointing that thing at me, please."

"Where are you heading?" I asked.

"Eastchester, to see my bro."

I needed to press for more information. Bring out the possible maniac inside of him. "Why now? What have you been doing for the last couple of weeks?"

"I've been keeping a low profile since it all went crazy last Friday. What's with all the questions? Who are you guys?"

"Just a couple of survivors," Jack said.

"What's your story?" I asked.

He frowned at me. "My story?"

"You heard me. Run us through your events since last Friday."

I thought it would be the best way to judge whether, like us, he'd managed to evade being activated. Or if he had a few days of memory loss, like other killers we'd met along the way. If so, he posed a risk of flipping again like Amanda. Whatever he had to say, it needed to be convincing.

"I was alone in the lab when I felt funny vibrations, like little shock waves. The next thing I knew, people were shouting, screaming, guys attacking each other, killing themselves—all kinds of weird shit."

"Where do you work?" Jack asked.

"A pressurized environment, dealing with chemicals. I hid in the roof after the shit hit the fan." His head sank. "My colleagues . . . they were killing each other."

He probably avoided the effects the same way we did, but on ground level, which was a whole lot worse. I remembered the carnage at the airport and shivered.

"How long did you stay up there?" I said.

"A day. I had lunch in my pack. To be honest I felt sick, wasn't hungry. What happened to you when shit started going down?"

"We were on a plane," Jack said. "Some might say we were lucky, but it doesn't feel like it to me."

"Where did you go after that?" I asked and lowered my rifle. Jack followed suit. Rick seemed to be conscious of his surroundings and didn't appear to be a threat.

His shoulders relaxed and he let out a deep breath. "Thank you. Most of the people around the complex were dead, but I met a couple of psychos on my way back home. One chased my car. Another stood in front of it. He threw a rock at the windshield. I swerved around him. In my mirror I saw them attacking each other."

"That figures. So you've just been hiding at home?" Jack said.

"I stayed in the house, drew the blinds, and locked the doors. Things seemed to calm down after a few days, until yesterday. A naked man smashed through the front window with a hockey stick."

"He came for you specifically?" I said.

"I don't think so. I'd heard clattering all morning, coming down the street. He broke into other houses before mine."

"What did you do?" Jack said.

"I didn't have a choice. He screamed, 'Kill, kill, kill' but was all tangled up in the blind. I stabbed him in the throat."

Jack grunted in appreciation. "We've seen a lot of that kind of stuff from New York to Monroe. You can't reason with them."

"We've an old saying here: 'It's better to be tried by twelve than carried by six.' I wasn't going to stand there and let him kill me. Do you know how far this thing has spread?"

I shook my head. "It's all over the place."

"Seriously?"

"Globally," Jack said. "The whole place is goosed. Where did you say you were heading?"

"My brother's place in Eastchester. He's ex-Army, has guns and rifles. I figured if I'm going to survive through this, I'm going to need his help. What about you guys?"

"New York City and Hart Island," I said. "We know of a group of survivors from the plane."

"And we might be able to help them," Jack said.

"Eastchester's on the way. Mind if I join you?"

I looked at Jack, who shrugged. At some point we had to believe in people, and Rick seemed genuine.

"We could always do with some local knowledge," I said. "Hop in the Chrysler."

The sun continued to rise as we headed over the bridge. Nature's wonders had stopped being things of beauty to me. Dark and light were considerations in our strategy for survival and attack. We had three days until the second activation, and possibly two until Headquarters showed up in whatever guise.

Rick sat in the front with Jack. Although I felt sure he had good intentions, I took no chances and kept my rifle pointed at the back of his seat. He nervously babbled about his life story. We told him the short version of events since landing at JFK. As conversation continued, he relaxed a little.

"My bro will know what to do," Rick said. "Wait till we get there; you'll see, he'll have a plan."

Jack sighed. "Don't count your chickens, Chief. We came from that direction last Sunday. Total bloody mess. He'll be lucky—"

"You don't know my brother. He doesn't need luck."

"What makes you think he's alive? I'd prepare myself for the worst," Jack said.

"Well, I'm alive. It could be genetic, right? You two are both okay."

Jack and I both sat in silence. I certainly didn't have the heart to tell him that his environment probably saved his bacon.

We proceeded quickly along the GA-cleared route. Rick instructed Jack to take the next exit. For some reason, probably habit, he flicked the indicator on. Ahead, a tangle of cars blocked the exit road.

Rick pointed to the shoulder. "Pull over here; we can go through the trees."

Jack brought our car to a gentle halt and turned to Rick. "We take things nice and easy. Only fools rush in."

I visually scanned the surrounding area through my sights. Rick quickly moved past me and headed for the trees.

"How far is it from here?" I asked.

"Two minutes. This way."

He strode with purpose along a beaten path through the woodland. Jack and I followed, flanking him on either side, rifles at the ready. The path led to a cul-de-sac cramped with Gothic Revival–style houses. Rick froze and glared at the nearest. A body lay at the end of the driveway. He broke into a jog.

I reached forward to grab his arm but clutched thin air. "Slow down. Be careful."

He ignored me and ran for a DHL van parked at the front of the property. As I closed in, I realized the body was a deliveryman's. His bright red and yellow jacket hood flapped in the breeze. Rick stood over him and bit his right fist. Dried streaks of blood led a couple of feet to a street drain.

He raced to the open front door and knocked on it. "Hey, it's Rick—are you here?"

Jack cut across the grass and covered him. "You don't know what you might find in there. Let us clear the house. We're armed."

"He'll be in the basement. That's where he keeps his stash."

We followed him into the house. He rushed through a living area containing a blue couch, a recliner, and a flat screen TV. The place stank of stale cigarette smoke and death. I noticed a trail of purple splashes on the green carpet.

Rick paused above a flight of stairs. "Are you down there?"

Jack looked at me, raised his eyebrows, and motioned toward the carpet. Rick thumped down the stairs. Moments later I heard a cry from the basement.

"Oh God, no . . . no!"

I clambered down and bumped into Rick after rounding a corner at the bottom of the stairs. Small windows, just below the ceiling, provided enough light to see his brother. He slumped against a chest of drawers and had a deep diagonal slice across his right wrist. A bloodstained bayonet lay by his left hand.

Rick approached, knelt, and held his brother in his arms. The corpse made a strange burping noise. He jumped back and turned to me with tears in his eyes. "I thought he'd be okay. He was one tough son of a . . ."

I decided to give Rick some space and check out the basement. None of my words would bring him any comfort. What could I say?

Nothing looked immediately useful. To my right, an old computer sat on a desk, and a dusty exercise bike was propped against the wall.

Jack appeared around the corner, took one look at Rick and his brother, and turned away. I imagined finding him in similar circumstances and shuddered.

I sat on the swivel chair in front of the computer and flicked through a newspaper, dated the day before the first activation. Some of the readers' letters looked strange when viewed in current context. One complained about cyclists in the city; another, about garbage collection. A lady seemed to have a deep grudge against the mayor.

I turned to the sports pages, perhaps for a final touch of the old world, and wondered if I'd seen my last game of football or swung my last club.

A floorboard creaked overhead. Rick glanced up. I put my finger to my lips.

Two seconds later another creak, then another. Somebody was crossing the living area in the direction of the stairs. My heart thumped against my chest, and I shouldered my rifle.

Rick crept over to me. "What are we going to do?"

"Looks like we've been followed," I said. "Presume guilty until proven innocent."

"Too much of a coincidence," Jack said. "One rule, Rick. We don't let anyone get close."

I looked up as the noises above continued. The door at the top of the stairs groaned open.

"I know you're down there," a female shouted. "Come out with your hands up."

Jack placed his back against the internal wall and leaned around the corner. "How about you come down here with your hands up?"

After a lingering moment, probably shorter than what it seemed, she replied, "There's three of you; why would I do that?"

"You've just explained why you should. Three against one," I said. We had to establish her faculties. "Why did you follow us?"

"Just one of you come up. I only want to borrow a lawnmower," she said.

My heart sank. To escape the basement we would probably have to kill her.

"Bollocks," Jack said. "She's activated."

Rick shook his head. "She wants a fucking lawnmower?"

"Activated people don't have a recognition about the events around them. They act normally until they have a chance to strike."

"What do you mean 'activated'?"

"Crazy. You've seen them yourself," I said.

"It's all so damn weird," Rick said, and he looked back at his brother. "Do you think he killed the guy upstairs?"

Cupboards and drawers slammed overhead.

143

"We've come across some pretty unpredictable behavior," Jack said. "We can talk about what they did to the planet after we've sorted this situation out."

"Who are *they*? Do you know who did this? You can't—"

"It can wait for now. Trust me," I said.

His eyes narrowed and he pointed to the corpse. "No it can't, not if you have something to do with my brother's death."

"Yes, it bloody well can," I said. "We deal with this, and then we talk."

A glass object smashed at the bottom of the stairs, followed by a whoosh of flames.

Smoke drifted across the basement ceiling. I grabbed a folded blanket from under the desk, edged to the stairs, and tried to beat the fire, keeping my body out of view. A round smacked into the wall above my arm.

She must have made and tossed down a homemade type of petrol bomb to smoke us out.

"Give me a bunk-up to the window," Jack said.

"A what?" Rick said.

"Don't worry about it, Rick," I said and passed him my rifle. "Keep an eye on the entrance. If she comes down, turn her head into a block of Swiss cheese."

I immediately knew what Jack had in mind. He made his way to the window, stretched up, twisted the lock, and pushed it open. I clasped my hands together and rested them on my right thigh. Jack hoisted himself on my improvised support and wriggled through the window onto a lawn outside.

I passed him his rifle. "Good luck."

"If I'm not back in two minutes . . ."

Crackling flames licked the roof above the stairs. We weren't engulfed in smoke, but very soon it would be a serious issue. I took my rifle from Rick and stooped by the wall.

Faint footsteps creaked overhead. Jack on his way. I shouted to draw the woman's attention. "One of us is coming up. Do you promise not to shoot?"

"Come up—" she said.

I heard one more creak before a shot rang out. Something heavy tumbled down the stairs.

I prayed it wasn't Jack and aimed around the corner.

A woman lay in a strange upside-down position, arms covering her face. Her hair singed in the flames and her jacket caught fire.

Jack shielded his eyes and peered through the thickening smoke. He coughed twice. "She set fire to the couch too. It's not pretty up here. I'll come back to the window."

Rick looked down at my rifle. "How many people have you killed?"

"Only ones that want to kill me," I said.

"Do you know when it might all end?"

"A techy guy gave us some info that might just—"

Jack ducked by window. "Hurry up. We're gonna be seen from miles around."

"Where are the weapons, Rick?" I said.

"This way." He led me to a large wooden chest next to the fridge. "He keeps his guns in here."

I slid the chest to the center of the basement. Smoke thickened around me, and I squatted to breathe fresher air.

Rick knelt by his brother and fumbled with his belt.

"Got any tools down here? We need a bar, a hammer," I said and pulled my sweater over my mouth and nose. The back of my throat stung, and my eyes streamed. I suppressed a cough and rattled the chunky brass padlock.

He threw me a bunch of keys. "It's the small one."

I clicked open the lock and swung open the chest, revealing a small host of weapons and boxes of ammunition. I reached for a hunting rifle. Rick threw out an arm and held me back.

"What's wrong? We'll choke down here," I said.

"It's like we're looting my dead brother's house . . ."

"Not being funny, Rick, but—" I coughed five times in quick succession. "You need to make a decision. Now."

He lowered his arm. "Get what you need."

I thought about giving him a sympathetic pat on the shoulder but didn't want to waste any time. I grabbed a Remington hunting rifle complete with telescopic sight.

"Hurry the fuck up," Jack said.

Rick squinted and blinked. We probably had a minute before being overcome. He slid a magazine into the grip of a Glock.

"We'll sort the weapons outside," I said. "Just grab it for now."

He passed me seven boxes of rounds, which I threw through the window. He tossed out a Colt revolver and a Glock.

It felt like my lungs were about to burst. "Let's get out of here."

He scrambled over and crouched by his brother for a few moments. I pulled the chair over to the window, grabbed the frame, and hauled myself out. I rolled on grass away from the billowing smoke pouring out of the window and gratefully gulped clean air.

"Rick, come on, you'll die down there," Jack said.

Rick threw a black bag and two hunting knives out. Jack grabbed his arm, assisting him to safety. He flopped on the grass next to me and leaned back on his elbows. None of this could have been easy for him.

Jack stuffed guns and ammo into the bag and slung it over his shoulder. I grabbed the Remington in my left hand and peered up at black smoke, pumping into the clear blue sky.

"Back to the car before any others show up," I said.

We jogged to the highway, although my tight chest hindered my pace. I jumped into the back, letting the others take the front.

Jack punched the accelerator and headed in the direction of New York City.

———

"That rifle's a decent score," Jack said. "Could have done with it in Ohio."

Rick stabbed his finger at Jack. "Hey, that's my bro's stuff— have some respect."

I acknowledged him with a raised hand but kept my eyes firmly on the road ahead. We would soon be in an urban jungle with threats everywhere; sentimentality would only lead to mistakes. I realized my thoughts had a hint of callousness, but our time for remembrance would come if we remained focused on our immediate objectives.

"Do you know the way to the Long Island Expressway in Queens?" I asked.

"Is that where the other guys are?" Rick said. "If the highway stays like this, maybe twenty minutes."

"It's where they were. We need to stop, check weapons, and get ourselves ready."

"Take the next exit. I know a good spot."

Under Rick's direction, Jack took us through a small housing development, under the highway, and toward the edge of a tree-lined reservoir. He parked on the grass on the side of the road.

We sat silently for a few moments, surveying all around. I lowered my window and listened for any suspicious sounds in close proximity. A large white bird flapped over the reservoir.

"Let's do it here. Stay alert," I said.

I popped open the trunk and pulled out the black bag. Jack checked the hunting rifle over with an air of efficiency. Rick had kept hold of the Glock after leaving the house, and gave it a once-over.

I placed rounds into the Colt's cylinder and threw it back in the trunk before topping up my rifle mag.

"I get a feeling there's something you're not telling me," Rick said. "What was it you said back at my bro's? Something about a techy guy?"

"Do you know where Hart Island is from here?" I asked.

"Sure, it's close. What's that got to do with anything?"

"Some of the people who caused this mess are probably there," Jack said.

Rick's eyes widened. "Seriously? Let's go. I'm in the mood to kick some ass."

I shook my head. "We can't just rock up, all guns blazing. There're too many of them."

"We get the others from New York to help us, right?"

"We'll see," Jack said. "First, they need to be alive; second, they have to believe us."

"Who are these fuckers in Hart Island?" Rick said.

"They're a group called Genesis Alliance," I said. "They used a network of devices to send something called an activation. There's another one coming on Tuesday."

"Will it turn us into psychos?"

"No," Jack said. "We've been neutralized and can help you too."

Rick folded his arms and glowered at Jack. "How do you know all of this?"

"We met a member of their techy team. They killed him yesterday afternoon after he decided to help us. All we've got to do is zap you several times on the head with a cattle prod."

"For the sake of full disclosure," I said, "we tried it on an old guy in Ohio, and he dropped dead."

"A cattle prod shouldn't kill you, man. We used to play around with them as kids."

"Just warning you. If you do it, it's at your own risk."

"What choice have I got? I don't want to end up like my . . ." he looked away.

"Are you one hundred percent sure?" I asked.

Rick placed his Glock on the grass and turned back to me with a steely resolve in his eyes. "I'm ready—go for it."

I retrieved a prod from the trunk and passed it to Jack. Rick seemed very trusting, although if I were in his shoes, I'd also take the gamble if it meant avoiding a second activation. Any survivor wanting to make it in this world had to adapt to strange choices. If I thought deeply enough about killers, I might come to the conclusion that we were murdering innocent people. Getting wrapped around the axle about the morals of our predicament would only damage our chances of seeing this thing through.

Jack circled Rick and held the prod toward the back of his head. "Ready?"

He took a deep breath. "They told you it would work, right?"

"We'd have to be some kind of weird perverts if we were lying," I said.

"Do it."

Jack pressed the button. The prod let out an electric snap.

Rick lurched forward and grabbed the back of his head. "Argh, you mother—"

"Can you handle a few more?" Jack asked.

"Do I need to?"

"Apparently," I said.

He stood upright and tensed his arms by his side in anticipation. Jack zapped five more times. Rick took it like a man. I was glad Brett had been able to use his strange device on me.

"What happens if it doesn't work?" he said.

"It'll work, don't worry," I said, completely unsure of my words. "Even if it doesn't, you won't die; you'll end up heading to Genesis Alliance to be turned into a laborer."

"Laborer? What else are you not telling me?"

Jack threw the prod in the trunk and slammed it shut. "GA is going to mount a cleanup operation using survivors to do the grunt work."

"There's nothing more to it," I said. "All you need to know is they're dangerous, probably on Hart Island, and we need to hit them within three days."

"Can we see Hart Island on our way to the Long Island Expressway?" Jack asked.

"I don't think so, unless we took a detour. We should get going and find your friends. I want a piece of Genesis Alliance."

"Food first, guys," Jack said. "Let's try a house on the other side of the highway."

Our growing experience in searching houses, avoiding the corpses, and finding supplies had led to increased operational efficiency. We returned to the car with canned Vienna sausages, cheese-flavored Doritos, bottled water, and Coke. I split the food, and we shared our views on the possibilities of an unaffected enclave in northern England. The general conclusion was, if it existed, we all wanted in, away from the nightmare Genesis Alliance had created elsewhere.

"I saw something yesterday evening that might be connected to all this," Rick said. "Two jumbo jets flew over my house."

"What time? Heading to New York?" I said.

I feared that this could be the first tangible piece of evidence that HQ had arrived.

"Around six. I think they were going to Albany. Not sure where else a plane that size could land in the area."

"Where's Albany?" Jack asked.

"A hundred and fifty miles north. Do you think it's Genesis Alliance?"

"They're sending a force over from the UK. We thought by boat," I said. "Doesn't change our plan, but it injects more urgency, not that we needed it."

"Just how big is Genesis Alliance?" Rick asked.

"Big enough," Jack said. "Are you with us?"

"Sure, a chance to avenge my brother, family, friend, and all those other folks. I'd be pissed if you didn't want me to come for the ride."

He aggressively threw half a hotdog at a nearby car—a pointless gesture, I thought. His mind was probably all over the place. Whose wouldn't be after finding their brother dead and learning about Genesis Alliance?

Jack eased the car from the grass and back onto the Hutchinson River Parkway. A straight path cut through the middle lane. Cleared for us, courtesy of GA.

The closer we got to the city, the more buildings lined the edge of the highway. Perfect vantage points for concealed shooters or hidden crazies. I pushed the thoughts to the back of my mind. So far we'd come across very few people. I suspected most of those alive, with their senses intact, would be hiding.

There were intermittent signs of recent activity; a chilling warning, spray-painted on a Dell advertising board, advising drivers against entering New York due to toxic spills. Another board had the word 'Help' sprayed in red over a Big Mac, and an arrow pointing left.

We didn't stop for anything. I spotted a person walking across a golf course a few minutes before we reached the Bronx-Whitestone Bridge. He turned and ran in the opposite direction when he noticed our vehicle.

Jack pulled the car to the side of the highway when the bridge came into view, and swore under his breath. An alternative route would be required. I disembarked and advanced up the rise of the bridge to get a better view of the scene.

Something moved ahead. I dropped to one knee and aimed.

A fox ran from an open SUV door, straight past me, and vanished in the wasteland on my left. I peered into the SUV and realized this might be the fox's regular feeding spot. Most of the left arm and parts of the driver's face had bone exposed. A green-faced passenger, heavily bloated and missing a nose, sat next to him. His body strained against the seat belt, on the brink of a disgusting explosion.

Near the top of the rise, I saw the true extent of damage only glimpsed from farther away. The bridge's midsection looked as though it had snapped. Two previously adjoining road sections slumped into the river. A dramatic and unwelcome view.

Rick shielded his eyes from the sun and gasped. "Jesus, GA must have some serious firepower."

"I don't get why they did it," Jack said. "What's the point?"

"Who knows what goes through their twisted heads?" I said.

I looked east, across the wasteland. A distant bridge also appeared heavily damaged. Closer to us, along the coast, pontoons jutted out from the land around half a mile away, a potential option if we wanted to avoid the claustrophobic confines of Manhattan.

7

"We could cut through Manhattan, take the tunnel," Rick said.

"I don't fancy having a flat tire in a tunnel—seen that kind of thing before," Jack said.

"It's got to be a boat; we'll see anyone coming," I said.

Rick and Jack loaded our food supplies and cattle prods into the large bag. We hopped over a small wall and hiked across the weed-infested wasteland.

Boats dotted the glinting East River, some at anchor, a few purposelessly drifting, most aground at random points along the shore. Rick led us behind a copse of trees that blanketed the faint eerie sounds of the city. He staggered down to a dark sandy beach and headed for a row of jetties.

He broke into a jog for the closest boat. I'd already pinned him as an excitable chap and planned to brief him about our generally slower and more cautious mode of operation.

Jack and I shouldered our rifles and surveyed the area.

Rick stamped along the first jetty to a secured white cruiser. He spun and raised his arm in a salute. I waved back.

The name *Candy Cane* stretched along the side of the boat in flamboyant red lettering. Even in my ignorance of boats, I couldn't help feeling impressed with its sleek contours. Rick climbed to the cockpit and checked the controls.

Jack kicked the cabin doors open and immediately ducked through the door. I followed, gazing around at the luxurious interior. A white-cushioned seating area curved around a solid timber table. On the opposite side, a row of kitchen units ended with a bar in the corner. Through the rear door, a very comfortable-looking double bed with an en-suite shower room. Expensive branded clothes and shoes filled the closets.

The boat made a rumbling noise and vibrated slightly after Rick started the engine. I rushed back out to the sun deck.

Rick stood behind the wheel, elevated a few feet above me. "Where to, boys?"

"Flushing Bay seems about right," I said. "That's probably the closest place to reach the Expressway."

He eased the boat toward the center of the river while Jack and I settled on a comfortable blue leather bench. The boat picked up speed, and we bounced along with a stiff breeze in our faces. A slight smell of burning fuel provided a welcome relief from decomposition and rot. Rick slowed the boat as we cruised past Rikers Island and veered toward Flushing Bay.

I gazed at La Guardia Airport. Deserted and reminiscent of JFK. A few planes were spread around the runway, parked at strange angles. After we chugged deeper into the bay, Jack and I joined Rick in the cockpit. He aimed for a marina with the imposing Citi Field Stadium directly behind it.

"You're good with boats, Rick—did you have one before the end?" Jack said.

"I worked on a cruiser in a former life, serving drinks to big shots." He spat the last five words. "It wasn't all bad; my boss paid for skipper training."

"How did you end up in a lab? Sounds like you got screwed," I said.

"It's a long story. I'll tell you another day . . ."

Although it hadn't been long since our last meal, entering a dangerous city left the timing of our next unknown. Numerous things could happen that would deprive us of food. Better to get more energy into our systems while we had chance, I thought.

"Take us in nice and slow, Rick," I said. "I'm going to prepare us a snack before leaving."

I returned to the cabin and heated water on the gas stove to make some chicken-flavored instant noodles. My watch matched the time on the wall clock. Quarter past eleven on Saturday morning. We'd made excellent progress since our escape from Monroe, but I was aware that we'd dropped our guard to make up the ground. Back in Queens, we couldn't make the same concessions.

I took a large bowl and three forks back to the cockpit, along with a bottle of sparkling water.

Rick smiled, the first genuine one since I'd met him. "We docked here when taking clients to see the Mets."

"Go for it," I said.

I picked up a folded map from a shelf and oriented our docking position in relation to the expressway where we'd last seen Morgan. After that, I ran my finger across to Hart Island.

Rick expertly guided the cruiser while swooping his fork into the bowl I placed on the dash. He tossed it overboard after finishing and focused on the controls as we crawled to within twenty feet of dry land.

Jack and I aimed at the surrounding boats in case there were any nasty surprises. Our cruiser gently brushed alongside a vacant jetty. From here, we could spend no more than two days trying to build our army. Any more, and we'd risk facing HQ and a second activation.

———

I jumped onto the jetty's wooden planks and secured our rope to a post.

"Weapons check before we head off," Jack said.

We individually tested our firearms on the sundeck. I glanced across to Rick who showed no signs of nerves. This morning gave him all the motivation he needed to act. Wellins Calcott once wrote, "He that has revenge in his power, and does not use it, is the greater man." On this occasion, I disagreed.

I gathered the other two in a huddle and spread the map across the deck "Here's the plan. We gather everyone we can in the next forty-eight hours, starting with a search of Aldi. After that, we hit Hart Island with everything we've got. It might be three days to the activation, but we don't know what time it's going off."

"And if there's only three of us?" Rick asked.

"We come up with a strategy to beat them," Jack said. "We should scout out Hart Island tonight or tomorrow. Find out their positions."

"Tonight," I said. "Gives us more time to work on it and think about what we need."

I shouldered a pack filled with the Coke, water, cookies, and dried fruit.

Feeling organized for the first time in a week, we headed into Flushing, fed and armed. This time we also had the experience of the past nine days: ignoring the dead, identifying friend or foe, staying away from any black Range Rovers.

We headed for Citi Field, home of the New York Mets. Jack and I had planned to catch a game last week. It stood solemnly, empty and quiet as garbage drifted around its base. I ignored the temptation to look inside.

Stadiums had always fascinated me. I'll never forget walking into my first big game as a child, hearing the roar of the crowd, smelling the enticing waft of junk food, and marveling at thousands of people, tightly packed together, focusing on the same thing.

"I know what you're thinking," Jack said.

"Doubt I'll ever feel it again."

"Van Wyk's on the other side; it's straightforward from here," Rick said.

I checked the map and confirmed our route from Citi Field, along the road, to the junction of the Long Island Expressway. It seemed sensible to use vehicles for cover and to avoid suburbia.

We continued past the stadium along Roosevelt Avenue. After crossing a rail track, we dropped onto the expressway, heading south.

It took thirty minutes of brisk movement to get to the store, weaving between battered vehicles and stepping over bodies and pieces of wreckage. We encountered no immediate signs of life, although a single distant scream momentarily halted our progress.

The mound of bodies in the Aldi parking lot had increased in size, although not significantly. Around forty fully clothed corpses were piled next to a row of shopping carts, rotting in the midday sun. I ran my hand over the splintered door, remembering the woman slamming her axe against it, in pursuit of Morgan and Harris.

Jack shoved the door open and entered. I followed into the dimly lit supermarket and lowered my rifle. Most aisles had been cleared, apart from a section of electrical goods. Empty cardboard boxes littered the floor. Although the group wasn't here, the signs were positive.

"Must have found a safe place," Jack said. "Transported the useful stock."

"A defendable building with living quarters," I thought aloud and turned to Rick. "Do you know what might fit the bill?"

"Could be any number of places. Your guess is as good as mine."

I pulled the map out of my back pocket. "We can cover the area between here and the boat. Reassess after we've swept Flushing. Let's get out of here and organize a plan of attack."

We filed out into the parking lot. I led us below the expressway and stood next to one of its large concrete supports.

Something moved to our left. Tapping against the concrete.

Jack crouched and aimed. A cat scampered across the road. He lowered his rifle and puffed out his cheeks.

Since I can remember, Jack has loved animals. It would devastate him if he shot one by accident.

I spread the map against the concrete support and studied it. "Through the park, past the golf center, across to Citi Field. Looks like some big buildings around there."

I stuffed the map back in my pocket and headed for the park. An engine rattled in the distance. Not like a car or truck—more like a tractor. The grass below my feet had been recently cut, post-activation, a strange sight in our current environment. Rick ducked behind a tree. Jack and I both followed suit. Surely, it couldn't be?

"Hold steady lads," I said. "I'll be back in a minute."

I ducked through a wooded area, maple to ash, until I caught sight of a man navigating a dark-green riding mower on the other side. He trundled along a golf fairway, cigarette in mouth, throwing up shreds of grass behind him. I had to do a double take before sprinting back to Jack and Rick.

"What the hell is it?" Jack said.

I leaned against a tree and took a few breaths. "You're not going to believe this. A bloke's mowing a golf course."

Jack frowned and peered through the trees.

"Maybe he's just crazy?" Rick said. "Sticking to what he knew before the world crumbled around him?"

"No way," Jack said. "We haven't seen anyone else do shit like that."

"I'll hold him at gunpoint and ask," I said. "We haven't got time to hang around anymore."

"What? Are you crazy?" Rick said.

I ignored Rick and put a round in the chamber. "Jack, cover me in the woods. Rick, move to the end of the tree line and cover the right flank."

"If you sense trouble, get down. You drop, I fire," Jack said.

"Into positions; I'll give you two minutes," I said.

Jack and Rick weaved between the trees in opposite directions. I waited for the second hand on my watch to complete two revolutions.

I moved back to the golf course. The mower swept around the far end of the fairway. I knew Jack would choose a good position and hoped Rick had the sense to do the same.

I broke cover after the mower turned away. The man continued on his line for fifty yards, before swinging back toward me. I immediately caught his attention. The mower abruptly stopped. He stood over the wheel and took off his earmuffs.

He seemed to be trying to recognize me and leaned forward, holding his palm over his eyes. I waved my left hand. He plucked a handheld radio from his belt and pressed it against his mouth.

I jogged over to him with my rifle held by my side, finger on the trigger. He looked around fifty years old, bald, slightly overweight, and he squinted at me.

"I don't want any trouble," he said in a New York accent.

"Who did you just call?" I said.

He pointed to a stadium on our left hand side. "Security. You're not with the company."

"Are you Genesis Alliance?"

"Gene— . . . Who?"

159

I prepared to spring the rifle up. "Don't mess with me. Genesis Alliance. Are you with them?"

He took off a gardening glove and wiped his brow. "Buddy, I've got no idea what you're talking about. I'm with the company."

"What company?"

"The guy who runs it, Morgan, he calls it 'the company.'"

"Bad-tempered twat in a cream blazer?"

"Doesn't wear one of those, but sounds like you know him. He's organizing a new society."

"Where's it based?"

"The stadium. We're building outward once we get more numbers. For now, it's cleaning up the immediate area."

I looked at the mower and surrounding area, most of it neatly manicured. "He's got you cutting grass? Strange priority."

"Hey, I don't make up the rules. I'm just happy to be here."

He glanced over my shoulder. I spun around. A police cruiser rolled across the grass, suspension rocking against the undulating ground. I gestured a "stay down" signal toward the trees.

The cruiser eased its way down the fairway and stopped twenty yards from me. Two men exited, both wearing filthy uniforms. One aimed a gun from behind the open passenger door, and the other stepped slowly forward, holding his gun in one arm and a pair of cuffs in the other. Judging by their drill and dress, they were possibly former police officers.

"What's your business here, sir?" the closest asked.

"I've come to find Morgan," I said and moved my hand away from my rifle. "I need to speak with him, urgently."

He raised an eyebrow and aimed at my chest. "Oh, really?"

"Yes, really. Put your gun down. I'll explain on the way."

"You don't call the shots around here, smart ass. We're taking you in."

"Didn't I just ask you to do that?"

160

His face fell. "Drop your weapon, cross your hands on your head, and step away from the mower."

This felt ridiculous. I considered dropping to the floor and letting Jack and Rick take them out. But that was no way to introduce ourselves to Morgan and his *company*.

I rolled my eyes, placed my rifle on the ground, and raised my hands. The closest man collected it and shoved me toward the cruiser.

"Get in the front," he said. "One move and I'll blow your brains out."

"What's your problem, mate?" I said.

"I'm not your mate. Shut the fuck up."

He needlessly pressed my head down when I stooped to get into the cruiser. I resisted the urge to break his nose and flopped into the seat. They had radios and some sort of mini laptop between the two front seats; I doubted any were in service until the radio beeped and squelched.

"Confirm hostile apprehended," a voice with an English accent said.

The driver picked up the mic and depressed a button on the side. "Confirmed. We're coming in."

The cruiser bumped over the grass and onto a road. It continued along a pleasant tree-lined street and headed for the Flushing Meadows tennis center. Neither of the two aggressive lawmen spoke to me; one drove, and the other kept poking his gun into the back of my head.

I mentally thanked Jack for restraint and hoped he and Rick would stay hidden until I could get back to them after negotiating and making this group aware of the upcoming danger.

The cruiser stopped in front of a large stadium. Its huge angular bowl rose into the sky. Two smaller arenas sat to either side of it, with a number of walled-off areas between, presumably other tennis courts. Two armed guards stood by the main entrance area. They took up alert positions on our arrival. One followed the cruiser with his shotgun barrel. The police officer who had taken my rifle opened the passenger door and reached in to drag me out.

I pushed his arm out of the way. "Thank you, Officer, but I don't need your assistance."

He grabbed a chunk of my sweater. "Whatever."

I shrugged off his grip and got out of the cruiser. He hustled me to the main entrance of Arthur Ashe Stadium and pushed me in the back when we neared the guards. I staggered a couple of paces forward and glared over my shoulder. I could understand how they would have encountered some unsavory characters in the last few days, but I found his behavior a bit trying. We were fellow survivors, and I showed no signs of being a danger.

"Found this one wandering the golf course," he said. "He's a bird; take him down for orientation."

One of the guards, a tall thin man with circular spectacles, seemed to relax and opened up a gold-framed glass door.

"I'm a *what*?" I asked.

"I guess you were in the air when the shit hit the fan? That makes you a bird."

"And the people on the ground?"

"Dogs. We get more trouble from them. Unpredictable bunch, need to be quarantined."

"Which are you?"

"None of your business."

The police officer passed him my rifle.

"Thanks, Charlie, we'll take it from here."

He grunted in reply and turned back toward his cruiser.

"Hey, Charlie," I said, "be careful. It's a dangerous world out there."

He waved dismissively and climbed back into his cruiser. Seconds later, it pulled away.

The other guard, a young brown-haired woman in a blue jumpsuit, raised a small yellow walkie-talkie. "We need a mentor down here for orientation."

"Roger that" crackled back.

"This way. You can wait inside," she said.

I followed her into the gleaming foyer and gazed at the metal-rimmed, semicircular walnut reception desk. A large emblem of a silver tennis ball with a trailing flame decorated the wall behind it. Pictures of former champions lined the upper wall. Morgan probably had his minions polishing the trophies.

The woman stood by my side and stared at the pictures. "Are you a tennis fan?"

"Sports fan. It just feels . . ."

"Strange? I know. I never imagined living here, but we're creating something."

I'd built up a defensive barrier over the last two weeks, so couldn't immediately return with a positive comment. Instead, I bowed my head and fidgeted with my sleeve.

"It's okay," she said in a reassuring way. "We're not the enemy. We need to stick together."

"Is Morgan here?"

"You know him?"

"We arrived on the same plane and met outside Aldi. He acted like a bit of a jerk."

She smiled and stifled a laugh. "We moved from Aldi five days ago. The crazies still eat, and a supermarket is like a big flashing light. Sleeping on a cold vinyl floor was also a pain in the ass. Morgan and the board have been working hard to gather survivors and create a new community here. It's still early, but . . ."

"The board?" I said. "We're all in grave danger. Your community needs to face it down."

"We haven't seen any infected for two days. There are still crazies out there, but their numbers are shrinking. We're sure of it."

"It's far from over. Something big's coming this way."

"You know what's gone down?"

"To a small extent."

She looked over my shoulder. I turned to see a familiar face. A short man with greasy brown hair, wearing a black Rolling Stones T-shirt with a large pair of red lips on the front.

"Harris, right?" I asked.

"Good memory. See if I can remember yours . . . Bernie?"

I felt a mix of anger and sadness at the mention of his name. Every time I'd forged a bond since landing, GA had taken it away. Linda and Bernie. Brett, with his family probably still in captivity. And Lea could be lying in a GA pit for all I knew. They made it personal. I had to convince this group to help.

"The name's Harry, and I need to speak with Morgan, urgently."

He extended his hand. "Morgan isn't going to be pleased to see you. He blamed you guys for that woman showing up."

"I've seen the pile of bodies outside Aldi. Is he really that one-eyed and stupid?"

Harris smiled. "You sound just like him. Come on; I'll take you up to orientation."

I followed him through a series of disorienting blue-carpeted corridors and up a flight of stairs, past framed photographs of past glories. The place was spotless but couldn't escape the odor from the rest of the city. He led me into a small office, sat behind a sturdy oak desk, and shuffled a pile of papers.

He nodded at the bench on the other side. "Take a seat."

I flopped onto the bench and looked at two folders, one with "Dogs" and one with "Birds" written on the spine in white correction fluid. He put on a pair of half-moon spectacles, picked up a pen, and cleared his throat. "I need to take down some information. It's part of the process."

Irritation rose inside of me. I didn't want to lose precious time with corporate bullshit. "Harris, when you realize what the hell's going—"

He sat back in his chair and sighed. "You haven't got a choice— *I* don't have a choice. If you want to speak with Morgan . . ."

"How long's this going to take?" I asked.

"Not long—just need your details. It goes up to his secretary. I'll attach an urgent meeting request."

I couldn't believe what Harris was saying. After the collapse of civilization and the imminent threat of the second activation and a larger, more deadly force arriving, they had me completing a personnel profile and meeting request. I took a deep breath and nodded.

Harris began with asking my name, age, address, occupation, and skills. He continued with questions about my whereabouts when the event first happened and what I'd done since. As I explained my story, he wrote feverishly and didn't interrupt. When I finished, he asked for the location of Jack and Rick. I hesitated, thought for a couple of seconds, and gave Bernie's old address in Elmhurst.

He stood and folded my profile document. "Stay here, please. I think the management team needs to know right away."

Alone in the office, I stretched my legs and noticed a stadium layout pinned to the wall, covered in scruffy handwriting.

I pulled down a section of the blind to get a view of the land outside. I hoped to spot Jack but didn't really expect to see him. I guessed he'd wait for a couple of hours and observe the stadium. If I didn't reappear, his approach might be aggressive. With emotions running high on both sides, it would only take a misinterpreted gesture to start a fight.

Harris poked his head around the door. "They've called an urgent board meeting to discuss your story. You need to come with me."

He strode along the corridor, banged through three sets of swinging metal doors, and climbed another flight of stairs. He pressed his right knuckle against a sturdy set of brown double doors with "Boardroom" stenciled across the top of them.

"You ready for this?" he said. "Just let him think he's boss, and you'll be fine."

I shrugged. "Go for it."

Harris knocked twice.

"Enter," a muffled voice called.

He slipped in, closing the door immediately behind him.

Seconds later, the door opened wide. I stepped into a large meeting room, bathed in natural light from the full-length windows at the far end. Four people sat at a long, oval glass table in the center. I recognized Morgan immediately at the head of the table, wearing a pink business shirt. His neatly combed brown hair didn't look like it had moved a millimeter since I'd first seen him on the plane.

A woman in a cream blouse sat to his right; two men to his left were both dressed in light-blue shirts. They all had a notebook, pen, and glass of water in front of them. Another lady in a purple suit sat at a small desk to the side. She glanced at me and scribbled on a jumbo pad.

Harris took a seat next to her, leaving me facing the group of four. I had to keep my composure in order to rationally explain events.

Morgan steepled his fingers and leaned forward. A clock on the wall ticked around to half past one. I decided to dispense with formalities.

"We're all in immediate danger," I said. "I've come to—"

"I should kick you out of here right now," Morgan said in pristine Queen's English, "but your fantasy story has grabbed my attention. Sit. I'll introduce you to the management team."

"Forget the introductions and fantasy. I'm here to discuss reality and survival."

"I say this to all new arrivals; don't think you're anything special."

"Get on with it, Morgan," I said, not quite believing how quickly he'd set up his own little corporate empire. "We've got important things to talk about."

"I told you he's a loose cannon," he mumbled to his cohorts. "I'm managing director of the company. To my left are our directors of logistics and our head of security."

Both men nodded at me. The security guy had a look of menace about him. Stockily built, with a shaven head, thin lips, and beady eyes. Uneven stitches crossed a recent slash wound on his stubbled right cheek.

"To my right is our director of human resources." A Mediterranean-looking lady, beautiful with long brown hair, smiled. Morgan gestured to the side of the room. "You've met Harris. That's my secretary, taking notes."

Lofty, deluded arrogance, I thought. They were already dishing out fancy titles while the world outside lay in tatters. I wondered if they had already penciled in a team-building event.

"Nice to meet you," I said, scanning the faces. "Now, can we get on with it?"

"Ladies and gentlemen," Morgan said. "You've read his form, so I'll open up the floor to questions."

"That's an amazing story," Security said in a smooth American accent. "You'll forgive me for being a little cynical in our current surroundings?"

"I don't blame you. I've been here less than an hour and already feel the same."

"You know what I mean. Monroe, activations, a force on its way. It's almost as crazy—"

"Why is it so difficult to believe against the context of events?" I interrupted. "It's a bizarre thing to lie about."

"This . . ."—Morgan looked down at his notes—"Genesis Alliance group, where are they now?"

"A team is already here in New York. Expect more to show up. Bigger and uglier."

"You say another *activation* is coming. Will it be like the first event?"

"No—possibly—I don't really know. I think they want to process the remaining survivors to rebuild civilization. You've seen the notes."

"How do you know they weren't just another survivor group?" the HR lady inquired.

"The devices. They used a global network to bring us down. Their techy guy, Brett, told me he was recruited well before the activation, to work on comms. They carried out this shit and have a master plan. Their local team screwed up, and HQ is not happy. I think some arrived yesterday at Albany."

"Do you know how many are coming?" the security guy asked.

I shook my head. "Your guess is as good as mine. But we need a plan to deal with Hart Island as soon a possible."

"I don't believe it, Chip," Morgan said. "How can any organization be that big without coming to the attention of the government? Unless they're a part of it."

"They kidnapped family members and killed any who went off-script," I said. "What have you got to lose by believing me and defeating them? Ignoring the threat would be suicidal."

"I believe him. I mean—" the director of logistics began.

"Let's just assume for a moment he's speaking the truth," Morgan said. "What we have here is an established player in the new world. We can negotiate. Show them what we've achieved."

"You're living in cloud cuckoo land if you think they'll listen," I said. "The clock's ticking and we have to act. I'm not sure we can defeat them on our own."

He glared back and slammed his pen on the table. "How do you know? They might be the new government. We can represent an approved corporation."

I felt like I was living in a parallel universe. I could only put Morgan's behavior down to stubbornness. Perhaps he didn't like installing himself as a local king, only for someone else to turn up and tell him what he should be doing.

Morgan gestured at Harris after somebody knocked on the door. He sprang to the entrance and held a hushed conversation with a person outside.

"Update me," Morgan said.

"Alpha-two have picked up Harry's brother and one other. They're waiting for orientation."

"Both birds?"

"One bird, one dog," Harris said.

"Process the bird; put the dog in quarantine."

For the first time, my mask of calmness slipped, and I returned his glare. "'Dog in quarantine'? You've got to be kidding me! Quit with the stupid games and listen. It might just save your community."

"It's house rules. We've had all kinds of problems—"

"Dogs and birds? You're mad. I've told you about what's coming. We've got three days, probably less," I said.

"Am I missing something here?" Morgan said. "You claim to have traveled around but don't have trust issues with people who were on the ground last week?"

The silly naming convention threw me, but he did have a point.

"No, I'm just saying—"

"You're a bird, Harry. It could be worse. We let a dog straight in two days ago. He was fine for a day—"

"Then he killed a bird," HR said. "We won't be making that mistake again."

"What exactly is quarantine?" I asked.

"We've decided to keep dogs locked up for two days," Chip, the security guy said. "We've got one due for release this afternoon."

"Rick's been fine—I can vouch for him."

Morgan took off his glasses and groaned. "If this place is going to work, we need to follow procedures. No exceptions. We'll quickly lose trust if people find out we let in another stray without a quarantine period."

"It's for the best," HR said.

Chip looked at the form and frowned. "You're one hundred percent sure about this? A ship, possibly a destroyer?"

"I'm guessing about the type, but one is heading over," I said. "How many men do you have?"

"What's this about a cattle prod to the head?" Morgan said.

"You can avoid the effects of an activation, probably. But what use is that if we're surrounded by a powerful force?"

"What kind of strength are we facing?" Chip said.

"I've already said I don't know. But the longer we wait, the more powerful it will become. The local GA team is shit scared of their Headquarters. That alone should tell you something."

"If the bulk of the main force isn't here yet, what do you know about the local team?" Chip asked.

"Not the most capable. Maybe forty or fifty. Conventional small arms. Run by a man who seems to be more intent on personal revenge. How many men and women do you have?"

I didn't say that I had similar motivations for Anthony. The overall goal of stopping GA had to take priority, but I wanted to put a bullet in his brain for killing Brett. Jerry would have to answer to Jack, and that wasn't going to be pretty.

"Forty in my security team. Enough to take out the local threat," Chip replied.

"If they are a threat," Morgan said.

"Look around you for God's sake," I said. "We've got an opportunity to stop activations happening in the short term. After that, we take the fight to them on a wider scale."

Looking at expressions across the table, I felt like I was winning everyone around, apart from Morgan. He glanced to either side of him and gave them a disapproving look before returning his focus back to me. "We've started to build something here. What have you done?"

"Given you information that could save the lives of *the company*. We need to hit them in forty-eight hours. Are you with me or not?"

"If we deal with this group, avoid any future events . . ." the director of logistics began.

"He's right," Chip said. "We can take a team—"

"Stop," Morgan said, slapping his hands against the table. "The company will not be making any rash decisions. I need time to think this through."

The room fell silent, apart from the secretary's pen scribbling on her pad. I took a deep breath and composed myself. At least Jack and Rick were safe.

Morgan hummed for a moment. I got the impression he enjoyed making others feel uncomfortable. "You can be part of Chip's team, along with your brother. I'll decide about the dog after evaluating his orientation form tomorrow."

"You mean Rick?" I said. "If you lock him up, we go."

"That's just great. Run away, give up the chance of making a difference."

As Morgan said it, Chip looked at me and gave an affirmative nod. I took it as a sign that at least he accepted our story and would act.

"You haven't got long to decide, Morgan," I said. "I suggest we reconnoiter tonight and hit them tomorrow night."

Morgan dismissed me with a derisive wave of his hand.

"Harris will show you around. I'll speak to you later," Chip said.

"Just remember," I said, "every minute we waste is another minute their Headquarters will get closer."

The management team gathered around Morgan, who whispered to them and pointed at the form. Harris led me out of the room.

A few yards along the corridor, the boardroom door banged open behind us.

"Wait a second." Chip said. "Give both of them the orientation. Keep Rick in the suite for a day. Morgan won't notice."

"The suite?" I said.

"I'll show you. It's fine," Harris said.

"I'll talk with you both later," Chip said. "I believe you, Harry. I'll start preparing my men for a mission tonight."

Heading back to the orientation room, Harris spoke into his radio. "Bring the two new arrivals for processing."

"Both?" a response crackled.

"Yeah, the dog's already been quarantined externally."

"Roger that."

"Don't you feel embarrassed using the animal names?" I asked.

He looked sheepishly away. "Didn't take long to stick. They're all different, the dogs—"

"It's like *Animal Farm* around here. I take it the management team are pigs?"

"What?"

I sighed. "Forget it."

Back in the orientation room, I found Jack gazing through the window. Moments later, a man armed with a rifle escorted Rick through the door. Harris sat behind his desk.

Harris placed a form on the desk and nodded at the bench. "Please, take a seat."

Jack and I exchanged glances and nodded. It didn't need to be stated that we were pleased to see each other alive and to be reunited, although I hoped Jack had his patient head on for what was about to come.

Harris proceeded to interview Jack and Rick with the same set of questions. After five minutes, the director of HR entered the room. She interrupted occasionally, cross-referencing my story with that of the other two. Appearing satisfied, she took the forms, instructing Harris to place us in a bunk suite.

"I almost didn't believe it," Harris said after she left the room, "until I spoke to the three of you. My team captured a man dressed in black yesterday, snooping around the practice courts. We interrogated him, and he gave us a similar story about activations. One of the guys lost his shit and shot him."

"Why didn't you report it up the chain?" Jack said.

"We passed him off as crazy, but in the back of my mind, I thought there was something to it. Chip will convince Morgan. He's probably worried that the threat might spread panic."

"It's not our intention to destabilize the whole place," I said. "The shocks can limit activation exposure, but GA won't stand idly by while you build up a community."

"It's a black-and-white decision," Jack said. "Kill or be killed."

Harris stood and slung a rifle over his shoulder. "I'll give you the guided tour. Get you settled in before we head out tonight."

"We're heading out?" Rick asked.

"I think they got our message," I said. "I suggested a reconnaissance tonight and attack tomorrow. We haven't got any other sensible options."

Harris led us downstairs to an inner concourse where food outlets, souvenir shops, and bathrooms previously serviced tennis fans.

"The place is split into an inner and an outer ring. This is the boundary," Harris said, pointing along the concourse. "Our team patrols this area and the immediate vicinity. Two groups of nineteen, each with a team leader, eight-hour shifts."

"So one team gets sixteen hours off a day?" Jack said.

"We don't take time off unless we're sleeping. End up doing stuff like this. I finished my patrol this morning. A couple of us watch the kennels."

"You've got dogs here?"

"I'll tell you about it later, Jack," I said.

"Nineteen doesn't seem like a lot," Rick said.

"We ring the outer concourse. You can see the men to your left and right. It's worked so far. More numbers would obviously be great."

Harris led us in a wide, internal circle around the stadium. Guards stationed evenly around the complex nodded a silent greeting as we passed them.

"Locker room's through there. Come back when we've finished. Logistics will give you some food and equipment."

Steam wafted out of a pair of open doors, and my mouth watered at the smell of frying onions. "That's the kitchen, run by logistics too. Food was rough for the first couple of days, but they make a good stew. There's a hot meal every evening."

"Who scavenges? Your team?" Rick asked.

"That's part of the logistics team's role. They cook, gather food, blankets—general stuff, you know?"

"Sounds like they've got a harder job," Jack said.

Harris raised his eyebrows. "You reckon?"

"Any others about?" I asked.

"We're over a hundred in total and growing every day. The rest clean, have admin jobs. There are a few kids—"

"Haven't seen any alive since . . ." I trailed off, not wanting to mention the incident close to Bernie's apartment, when Jack had shot a girl who tried to kill us.

"Funny thing," Harris said. "We found a small group. Didn't reveal much during orientation."

After completing a circuit, he led us back up the stairs. "This is the inner ring. At first we designated it a weapon-free zone, until that dog went crazy the other day."

"What's with dogs? Someone called Rick one," Jack said.

"During the activation, if you were on a plane, you're a bird. Ground: dog," I said.

Jack frowned. "Eh?"

"Didn't take them long to start discriminating," Rick said.

"It's not like that," Harris said. "I'm sure you're smart enough to understand the risks. This way; I'll get you armed."

Weapons neatly lay across the carpet of a small meeting room. Three rows of rifles and two of handguns. Our two cattle prods were propped in the corner. Harris picked up an AR-15 and two loaded mags and passed them to me.

"Why not give us ours back?" Jack said.

"We're trying to standardize the weapons across the security team. Interchangeable—"

"We had AR-15s, Harris," I said.

"You won't be complaining then?"

He passed a rifle to Jack and Rick.

"You okay with that, Rick?" Jack asked.

"Sure, I'll use it to shoot birds," he said without a hint of a smile.

"I'd leave out the wisecracks if I were you," Harris said. "They'll only land you in serious trouble. People have lost their loved ones. You catch them at the wrong time . . ."

We followed Harris up another flight of stairs to a wider internal corridor. Windows on the outer wall gave an elevated view of our surroundings. The mower continued to buzz around the golf course. *A wasted resource,* I thought. Clearing the parking lot was a good idea. It provided fewer obstacles for intruders to hide behind.

"There're ninety luxury suites," Harris said. "At first we had one each. A couple of days ago, we moved to a sharing system."

"Morgan didn't waste time getting this place organized," I said.

Harris nodded. "There are a couple of camp beds and a couch. No electricity—we boil water on camping stoves; don't know what might be floating in the supply."

He led us through a door, revealing a tidy furnished area that wouldn't have looked out of place as an IKEA showroom. A bulky brown suede couch and two matching armchairs were positioned adjacent to each other on large circular red rug. Thick white duvets covered both bunk beds, partially obscuring dark wood cupboards of a kitchenette.

"Nice place," Jack said.

"Nice? It's awesome compared to the last few days," Rick said.

Jack didn't waste any time checking out the kitchenette cupboards and drawers. I slid open a glass door and stood in a seated balcony area outside.

The suites ran around the midsection of the stadium; a couple of people sat on the balconies around us. The rest of the place looked neat and tidy, as if I had tickets for the U.S. Open and was one of the first to arrive. A woman swept the green surface surrounding the blue tennis court. She stopped and waved. I returned the friendly gesture.

Harris sat next to me on one of the padded folding seats. "Impressive, huh?"

"Amazing place. Who decided to come here?"

"Morgan. He likes to think big. Yesterday at the parade, he told us that we were the new founding fathers."

"He holds a parade?"

"Motivational speeches, corporate bullshit."

"Got to admit, I thought we'd be better off in the country," I said.

"Same here. Between you and me, I'm not Morgan's biggest fan. But you've got to give him some credit."

"Are people happy here?"

"Still early days, but yeah, we've got a chance. That's more than I expected last week. Your news, though . . ."

"Put a monkey wrench in the works?" I finished.

He sighed and checked his watch. "I'll leave you boys to it. Don't forget to visit the locker room. You'll need candles for tonight."

"Cheers, mate," I said.

We returned inside. Rick relaxed on the couch with his feet up, flicking through a glossy magazine. Jack stabbed a knife into a can of olives.

Harris paused at the entrance and turned. "I'm glad you've come."

He closed the door behind him. I felt satisfied that we now had the required manpower to take out Genesis Alliance.

———

Jack tossed an olive into his mouth, squirmed, and spat it back into his hand.

"What was the story with Morgan?" he asked.

"I met his management team. He's the only one that didn't totally believe our story."

"Why doesn't that surprise me?"

"I'm seeing our new boss, Chip, later. He runs security and will help us strike GA."

Rick lowered the magazine. "How many can they commit to the fight?"

"If they have any sense, they'll all join us," Jack said.

"Let's grab some supplies," I said. "We need to start thinking about ways to attack."

Hundreds of cardboard boxes, five piles of clothing, and at least twenty baskets full of kitchenware gave the locker room a scruffy claustrophobic feel. Two women were in the process of taking an inventory, checking the contents of boxes and then writing on pads.

"Get what you need," the closest said without looking up, giving me the impression that we were getting in the way of the task at hand.

I rummaged through the clutter and selected candles, a lighter, cargo pants, a T-shirt, and a clean set of undies and socks. In the food area, I threw cans of stew, vegetables, a camping stove, water, and instant coffee into an Aldi "bag for life." In our current climate, the boast on the side of the bag seemed ironic. With arms full of supplies, we headed back.

"How easy was that?" Jack asked as we reached the luxury suite level. "Makes me realize we've got something else to save."

I liked his thinking. Pockets of survivors around the world would be banding together like this. Hopefully, a few of them were already destroying their local GA teams. We already had something to fight for, but Flushing Meadows cemented it.

"Are you thinking of staying here after and not sailing away?" Rick said.

"It's possible I—"

A small boy burst around the corner and crashed into Jack's legs. He dropped his supplies and only just managed to maintain his balance by thrusting his hand against the wall.

Jack picked up his supplies. The boy cowered away from him. A woman with spiky blonde hair and piercing blue eyes, wearing a gray tracksuit, jogged around the corner.

She rushed over. "I'm so sorry. I've told him a hundred times not to run in the corridors."

"No need to apologize," I said. "Jack's been hit harder than that before, by far bigger people."

She knelt by the whimpering boy. "What happened? Are you all right?"

"It's okay," Jack said. "Accidents happen."

"He doesn't listen like the others," she said to us, but her words were meant for the boy's ears.

"You look after the kids?" I asked.

"We've got five here, all different ages. I used to be a teacher, so they put me in charge."

"You guys really do have things worked out," Rick said. "If you need help, just ask."

"Hey, I've just been talking to Pam. Are you the people who showed up today?"

"Who's Pam?" I asked.

"She runs HR. Told me about another event in three days and that you know how to avoid it."

"Cattle prod to the head—it's not pretty," Jack said. "Our plan is to stop it before that."

The woman nervously laughed while studying Jack's serious face. She seemed to see something in him and rested her hand on his shoulder. "We've all been through a lot. If you know a way, I'd like to help the little guys first."

"I'll head over later. Where are you staying?" Jack asked.

"We'll be in Room 72. I'm Lisa, by the way."

She grabbed the boy's hand and continued down the corridor. We returned to our suite.

Rick nudged his shoulder against Jack's. "I think she likes you."

Jack scowled and quickened his pace. "Probably the last thing on her mind. You reckon people are thinking about that?"

"No, but . . ."

I changed into the blue cargo pants and plain black T-shirt, and relaxed on the balcony seat. An occasional armed patrol prowled across the court, looking around, taking different routes back through the stands. I managed to doze for a couple of hours until just before eight in the evening, when the sun set below the stadium and the temperature dropped.

I returned inside. Rick snored on the bottom bunk, Jack had stripped his rifle and scrubbed the working parts.

"This one's filthy," he said. "Better check yours."

"I'm off to the boardroom, see if I can find Chip," I said. "If they're heading to Hart Island tonight. I want to be part of the patrol."

"Want me to come?" Jack said.

"Don't want to confuse him. I'll go on my own, see if they've decided on anything."

I went via the orientation room to see if Harris could help me locate Chip; the door was locked. I carried on toward the boardroom, but stopped when I heard raised voices from behind a door.

A male and woman argued; I could only just make out the words.

"Just tell him," the woman said.

"No, we'll go. I'd rather split," the man said.

"They took us in."

"You saw how the prick threatened me."

Note quite the paradise we'd been shown. I edged closer to the door in order to listen. A floorboard creaked under my foot. The conversation stopped.

I carefully stepped away and continued to the boardroom. When I arrived outside I opened the door without knocking, not expecting to find anyone. Morgan and Chip's eyes shot to the entrance.

"We knock on closed doors," Chip said.

"Sorry mate, didn't realize," I said.

"Come in, sit down," Morgan said in a friendlier tone than he'd had when previously addressing me. "We were just about to send for you."

I sat in my previous position and waited two minutes for them to finish their discussion. Morgan leaned back in his chair and cracked his knuckles.

"I'll make sure the security's sorted. Ten in the morning, okay?" Chip said to him.

"Good man. Best of luck tonight," Morgan said and turned to me. "We've had the chance to discuss your tale. May I be blunt?"

"Please do," I said.

"Chip's volunteered to work with you on this proposed protection method tomorrow afternoon. As impossible as I . . . *we* think the activation is, there's a question of responsibility. We owe it to our staff to treat your accusations with a degree of respect and don't want to be behind the eight ball."

"Can you repeat that in English?" I said.

"I don't want you disrupting the company," Morgan said. "You've seen how far we've come? You are going out with Chip and Harris tonight on a scouting mission. Tomorrow night, if we confirm your story, Chip has agreed to lead an assault. That's my final word."

Morgan's final word was the same as my initial suggestion. I wasn't going to argue, though. We had gotten what we came for. I imagined Jack repeatedly stamping on Jerry's face and suppressed a smile.

"Harry. You okay with that?" Chip asked.

"I'm more than just okay," I said. "It's the smart move. Count us in."

"Excellent, we'll leave it at that," Morgan said. "You look like you could do with forty winks. Get yourself back to the suite."

"I'll drop by in the early hours," Chip said. "Be ready."

"Count on it," I rose from the chair. "Until the early hours, Chip."

———

I found our suite door unlocked. Candles on a central table provided ambient light against the gloom outside. Jack and Rick were nowhere to be seen. I pulled on a sweater, made a cup of coffee, and sat gazing at the star studded sky. Morgan had organized everything extremely well, and he'd come to the right conclusion. But, even if we beat GA tomorrow, he needed to think about strengthening his defenses.

I decided to discuss security arrangements with Chip tomorrow morning. As it stood, the Arthur Ashe stadium presented an easy target for Genesis Alliance. I felt sure that tomorrow would only be the start of our fight.

Rick broke my concentration by flopping down on a seat next to me. "All okay, Harry?"

"Fine. I'm set for a scouting mission in a few hours. They're starting to cattle prod tomorrow. Where's Jack?"

"He went over to Lisa's room. Probably helping you with the harder part of the task. What time are we going?"

"You're not going. It's me and two of the company." Rick frowned. I cut him off before he had chance to protest. "Did he get the prod from the weapons room?"

"I think so, said he wanted to sort them out first."

I returned my gaze to the sky. Typical Jack, wanting to help the most vulnerable first. I knew he would be annoyed at not being invited along for the mission, and I think I could have insisted he come along, but he deserved a break.

Rick hit the hay and I read a motorcycle magazine on the couch for an hour. At ten in the evening, I blew out the candles. Jack quietly entered the room an hour or two later and headed straight for bed. I considered telling him about Chip's plan, but drifted off.

———

Somebody thumped on the door. I immediately sprang from the couch, grabbed my rifle, and swung the door open. A flashlight beamed in my face.

"Wakey, wakey. Harry," Chip said.

The light winked off. I checked my watch. One in the morning. My eyes slowly adjusted to the dark. Chip's stocky silhouette stood in front of me.

Jack groaned and pulled his duvet to one side. "What's going on?"

He propped himself up by his elbows and squinted toward the door.

"I'm just nipping out for an hour or two," I said. "Nothing for you to worry about."

"Need me to come?"

"No. Just a routine thing around here I agreed to help with. Get some sleep. I'll be back soon."

Why should both of us suffer when we'd finally found a place to get a safe night's rest? I planned to catch up on sleep in the early afternoon before our main assault. I slung my rifle and fastened my bootlaces.

"Harry, come on," Chip said.

Harris waited outside, dressed in black, his face smeared in cam cream. Chip was also dressed in black and took out a cam stick. He painted diagonal green stripes across his face and passed it to me. I rubbed the greasy end across my cheeks, nose, and forehead.

"What's the plan, Chip?" I asked.

"We're heading to the eastern edge of Little Bay. If there's lights on Hart Island, we might be able to pick them out."

He shined his flashlight on a laminated map. It looked like a sixteen-mile round trip, and even then, the island looked too far away.

"That's gonna take us all night," I said.

Chip smiled and placed the map inside his jacket pocket. "We've got a fully charged golf cart outside. Nice silent mode of transport with a range of thirty miles."

"I've patrolled that way," Harris said. "We've got a relatively clear route. Should be back in three hours."

"And if we don't see anything?" I said.

"We attack anyway," Chip said. "I'll tell Morgan that I identified the enemy force."

"Okay, let's do it," I said, pleased that at least one man in the leadership team recognized the threat and was prepared to act without solid evidence. Morgan was a corporate thinker; Chip had a better head for our current situation.

Harris led us through dark corridors, eventually down a staircase and back to the main entrance.

A guard opened the glass door. "Good luck, guys."

I mumbled thanks as I passed him. A white four-seater golf cart, with the number twenty-one plastered on the front and side, waited outside.

"Harris, you take the back seat and cover our rear. You ride with me, Harry, and cover our right flank."

He didn't waste any time starting the cart, and soon we hummed our way along the moonlit Whitestone Expressway, cutting a path between the shadows of carnage.

I aimed at gaps in the debris and listened for any suspicious sounds. After an hour of trundling along without facing any threats, Chip veered onto the Cross Island Parkway, taking us directly to Little Bay. I had to hand it to him: He'd picked a perfect form of transport. The cart sneaked through gaps impossible for a car to get through and quietly moved at a nice speed.

"It's not all that bad you know," Chip said.

"What isn't?"

"The company. Sure, Morgan's an asshole, but we've got hope. There are some good people back at the stadium. A community of survivors that come together to provide mutual protection and a possible future."

I remained focused on the parkway. "If we don't squash GA, there is no future."

"That's why I took your story so seriously. We're a green shoot of recovery. Anyone who tries to stamp on us has to be eliminated."

"I wish it were a story, Chip. We need a good plan and plenty of numbers if we want to take these fuckers out."

The cart jumped in the air and landed with a crash. I looked back. A chrome exhaust pipe settled on the road surface.

"Careful where you go, Chip," Harris said.

"I can't avoid everything. Just keep your eyes peeled."

After twenty more uneventful minutes, Chip stopped the cart. "It's five minutes on foot from here to Willet's Point. We'll travel in extended line. I'll take the front, Harris—you cover our rear. If we get split, we meet back here. Shoot first, ask questions later. Let's move."

He jumped out of the cart and headed down a road, scanning to the front with his rifle. I liked his no-nonsense style, and as I followed, glancing from side to side, rifle shouldered, I felt part of a small but slick formation.

"Are you going to stay after we take them out?" Harris asked from behind.

"Are you?" I said.

"I like it. Once you meet more of the people, I think you will too. Where else is there to go?"

I thought for a moment and decided he might be right. Morgan seemed the only blocker. But what community didn't have at least one difficult person?

"Don't you get pissed off with Morgan?" I asked.

"Nah, he's all right once you get to know him. Behind that silly exterior, he means well. He listens and generally goes along with our advice. You just need to make him think he's making the decisions."

Chip turned back. "Quit yammering. You'll have plenty of time to talk once we're back."

I guessed he meant talking and understood his point, although it felt like I'd just been dressed down by a schoolteacher.

Chip continued down a moonlit tree-lined street, through a small wooded area to an old stone fortification. He knelt next to a black cannon, the type used a couple of centuries ago, ripped open a kidney pouch on his webbing, and pulled out a pair of binoculars.

I stooped on the other side of the cannon and trained my rifle behind Harris. He crept alongside me.

"You take the left arc, I'll cover the right," Harris said.

In my peripheral vision, Chip shuffled to a gap in the rampart and planted the binoculars against his eyes. He scanned across the bay, stopped, and adjusted the lenses.

"Harry, come here." I edged backward. He passed me the binoculars. "Look straight ahead. You'll see a faint light in the distance. That's Hart Island. That's our confirmation."

It didn't seem obvious at first as I searched the darkness. Eventually I picked up a dark landmass with a small yellow glow at the left edge.

"I take it you don't believe in coincidences, Chip?"

He shook his head. "No. I'll brief Morgan when we return and we'll attack this time tomorrow. We've got a busy day of preparation ahead. Better get back and grab a couple of hours sleep."

He stuffed the binoculars back in his webbing and headed off. People like Chip were perfect for taking down Genesis Alliance.

———

After returning to the stadium, just before five, I tried to sleep but found it impossible while thoughts of our upcoming fight raced through my mind. I decided to grab a cup of coffee and brief the other two when they woke.

The hissing camping stove, heating a pot of bubbling water, must have woken Jack. He threw his duvet to one side. "I'll have one too. Time is it?"

"Just past six."

Rick groaned and rubbed his face. "I'll have one if you're making."

"Where did you go?" Jack asked.

"Had a little trip out with Chip. We've confirmed GA's location. How'd it go last night?"

"A few tears, but I think they've been dealt with. Lisa says there's a big meeting planned today. Morgan sent out a note last night saying he needs to address the company."

"We're attacking tonight," I said. "He probably wants to brief everyone."

Jack's eyes lit up. "I knew they had to go for it. Are we leading the assault?"

I guessed he wanted to reach Jerry first, if he wasn't still stalking us in another part of the country. Treating the kids last night would have stiffened his resolve too. If Jack thinks there's something worth fighting for, there's no turning him back.

"I'm meeting Chip again in a couple of hours. I'll let him know we want to be in the vanguard."

After sipping his coffee, Rick hopped into jeans and made us porridge and hotdogs. Not an ideal breakfast, but we were still assimilating into stadium life.

We sat on the balcony in the murky dawn light. Soft light glowed from a few of the luxury suites opposite. Somebody slid open a door and lit a cigarette. We discussed potential ways of raiding Hart Island. Rick likened it to the D-Day landings. I liked the idea of attacking from two different angles, with a cutoff group at the opposite end to mow down any fleeing goons. Jack favored a simple right flanking maneuver.

The late spring sun quickly rose above the stadium, bathing our side in glorious warmth and light. At seven o clock, Chip entered the room without knocking. He'd scrubbed himself clean and dressed in combats. I wouldn't fancy facing such a mean-looking bugger.

"Harry, twenty minutes in my office, if you don't mind?"

"No worries." I turned to Rick and Jack. "I'll brief you when I get back."

I followed him a short distance to a large room, more like a lounge than an office, with modern art on the walls and red leather bucket chairs spread around small white tables. We sat opposite each other. Chip tossed me a bottle of water.

"I need as much information about Genesis Alliance as possible," he said. "Take it from the top."

"You've seen the report," I said. "What else do you need to know?"

Chip shifted forward in his seat. "I want more details, potential weak spots, types of weapons. We can't afford too many casualties, especially with more enemy coming our way."

I told the story again, from landing in New York to arriving at Flushing Meadows, concentrating on the parts with the goons around Monroe and Ohio. Chip didn't interrupt and scribbled notes.

"Sounds like we're matched in terms of weapons," Chip said. "Tell me again about the device you found."

"No markings, about six feet, very heavy. The convoy had a couple."

"Alien?"

The thought seemed ridiculous. If aliens had planned this attack, I doubted that they would have employed the fools from

Monroe to act as an operational arm. I pushed the thoughts to one side. Second-guessing imaginary aliens wouldn't help any of us.

"No, I'm sure of that. Brett told me he was recruited to work on the system."

"What did he say about neutralizing?"

"It can be done with an EMP device—"

"Nanobots?"

"Pardon?" I said, not recognizing the word.

"Are they using nanobots? Do you know?"

"No idea. The cattle prod is a rough workaround solution. You have to do it several times, but the guy in Ohio—"

"Forget about him, what else did Brett say? Specifically."

"The activations make us act in a certain way. The one that has already occurred was the first 'event,' as you call it. He said another's coming. The notebook confirmed the date as Tuesday. He estimated the main force might be here tomorrow. Everything seems to line up."

"Not everyone acts the same way. You've seen it yourself. Did Brett expand on that?"

"We didn't get into technical detail. That's not really Jack's or my area of expertise."

Chip nodded. "Do you know their reasons? Ultimate aim?"

"We won't know the full story unless someone at the top of Genesis Alliance tells us. That isn't likely. I don't even think Monroe GA knows the full story. There's a guy who runs the thing called Henry Fairfax. Ever heard of him?"

"Nope. The GA big dogs are based in the UK?"

"That's the way it looks. They've somehow invented or acquired the technology to create the event. According to one of their local leaders in Monroe, the next stage is a cleanup operation. I didn't trust him an inch."

"We need to know more, the full extent of what we're facing. I'll make taking a hostage one of our priorities tonight."

"Have you thought about a plan yet? We want to lead the assault. There are some scores that need settling."

Chip stopped scribbling and looked up. "We've all got scores to settle, Harry, but I'll think about your request."

"We've just been discussing options for the attack—"

He held up his hand, stopping me in mid-flow. "Bring Jack along to our planning meeting. After Morgan's made his speech, we're going to prepare a few boats and go over our options."

"Are we taking your full team?" I asked.

"We don't want to compromise stadium security, but this is our main priority. Forty will have to do." He snapped his notebook shut and stuffed it in his breast pocket. "See you in a couple of hours at Morgan's meeting."

"I'll sit this one out."

"Show your face. Don't antagonize him."

I left Chip's office without answering.

———

Just before eleven, after managing to snooze for two hours, I sat with Jack and Rick, watching the empty court while taking them through my mission and conversation with Chip. People filed into the lower part of the stadium, taking up seats close to the umpire's chair.

Rick waved us over to an opposite suite. A man in a green T-shirt replied in kind. "I spoke to the guys in the kitchen this morning. There are a lot of happy people here."

"What do you mean, 'happy'?" I asked, thinking it was an odd choice for a word to describe our current situation.

"Imagine your problems disappearing overnight: debt, boring job, no sense of purpose or importance. There're a lot of reasons why some are feeling they've gotten a new start in life."

Jack grunted. "A new start in life for the cost of billions of others. I don't get it."

"You know what I'm talking about," Rick said. "They can't change the past, but they can make their own future."

I considered Rick's comments and could see his reasoning. An electrician would be like a movie star, the new celebrity in our sparse world. All our histories had been wiped, records expunged; the only currency now would be transferable skills and the ability to work with others. Ultimately, though, without an army or law enforcement, strength would take control of any new organization, weapons, and numbers.

A small ripple of applause grabbed my attention. Morgan strolled onto the court, flanked by Chip and another man dressed in full combats, perhaps one of his team leaders.

Morgan climbed the umpire's chair and raised a megaphone to his mouth. "Welcome, fellow company members. I'm sure, like me, you were looking forward to the wine tasting tonight. I'm afraid it's been cancelled."

A quiet murmur echoed around the stadium. He continued, "I will try to be brief, as we have a lot of work to do. You have worked tremendously hard since we came together. Some of you I have grown to know well. Others have recently joined us, but only by integrating and working together can we be strong."

"Do you think he'll mention GA?" Jack asked.

I shrugged. "We'll see."

"Everybody here is integral to our survival," Morgan said, sweeping his hand around the stadium. "Your past does not matter. What's important is the part of our jigsaw puzzle you can fill. Our fledgling community can keep you all safe; work with us, share with us, and grow with us. I can't promise that things will return to the way they were. All of that is gone. However, with hard work and organization we can ensure that no one is hungry, cold, or living in fear."

Rick rolled his eyes. "This guy loves himself."

"I've started a research and development team. They're looking at other sites outside the city. We'll evaluate farming and producing our own food sources, and build long-term sustainability for future generations. In short, we've all achieved incredible progress in a short space of time. There is still an incredible amount of work to do."

He paused, raised his chin, and looked around the stadium. "This brings me to our most important item. We are facing a threat to our very existence. Currently, on Hart Island a force is planning another event, and our capture or destruction. Chip is building a team for an assault tonight. We will defeat them and stop them in their tracks. I'm sure you have questions, so please consult your team leaders. But let me say this." He raised a clenched fist. "Together and only together, we will survive. Thank you."

A quiet ripple of applause followed. Two people raised their hands. Morgan climbed down the steps of the umpire's chair and tossed the megaphone to Chip. He mingled with a group sitting in the front row. Chip and the suit stood behind him. Members of Chip's team approached him, no doubt full of questions about tonight's activities.

The atmosphere around the court seemed purposeful. People busily chatted in the glorious sunshine. Chip shot a glance to me and gestured to a side entrance. He probably wanted to start planning and organizing our supplies immediately. I certainly did.

"You know, this isn't—" Jack said.

He gaped at me.

The stadium jolted, like a mini-earthquake had hit. A shock wave ran through my body.

8

I unslung my rifle. "Jesus Christ, no. It can't be."

"Is this it?" Jack asked.

Rick didn't appear to understand our sudden fright. I looked at the group below. Some ducked behind their chairs; others stood in a huddle in frantic conversation. I noticed Chip standing on baseline, hands on hips, gazing skyward.

I held my breath.

Like an alarm clock breaking sleep, four more jolts pulsed through the stadium in rhythmic succession.

"Get down!" I shouted.

I scrambled behind my seat and aimed toward the court.

Roars, screams, and cries echoed around the stadium, followed by multiple gunshots. An "every man for himself" fight broke out by the net. People fired at each other from close range.

A man pinned a woman to the ground, grit his teeth and clamped his hands around her neck. Another stamped on a smaller man's head, jumping in the air to provide extra force. A woman fired a pistol at the back of his head. He collapsed lifelessly to the ground. She pressed the weapon against her temple, pulled the trigger, and fell on top of him.

A man with a blood-soaked knife picked up the woman's pistol and fired into his own mouth.

I looked across the stadium at a previously populated balcony. Two people struggled with each other among the seats.

Others backed away, through the entrances to the court. A woman leaned over her balcony and sprayed the court with automatic fire.

A window shattered to our right, possibly three suites along. The stadium crackled with gunfire and echoed with screams.

A round ricocheted off the metal rail in front of our balcony.

"Inside!" I shouted.

I following Jack and Rick, slammed the door, locked it, and closed the curtains. Rick sprinted to the suite entrance and secured the latch. Thankfully, our procedure on him had worked. The activation was supposed to have occurred on Tuesday, and we had believed it was to process survivors. This looked like a repeat of the first, and we were right in the midst of it.

"This is fucked," Rick said. "Exactly like what happened last Friday."

Jack knelt and peered around a curtain. "That's our bloody plan up in smoke."

"We need to get the hell out of here," I said. "Too many hiding places for killers."

I'd only had a tiny glimpse of what had happened en masse last Friday, but it had been chilling enough. I guessed that with HQ breathing down the neck of the local goons, they'd sent out the second activation as soon as they could, although this appeared to be against their plan. It smelled of Anthony and Jerry.

"Lisa and the kids," Jack said. "I'm going to their suite. They need our help."

Rick tried to grab him as he ran for the door. "You're mad. We can't go charging around."

Jack wriggled free of his grasp and unlocked our door. "It's nine doors down. I'm not leaving them."

I could see Rick's point, but we had to take some responsibility. Jack had neutralized Lisa's group, and I could tell he'd quickly built a rapport with her. I hadn't seen them at the parade, so they might be in their suite.

On current evidence, it seemed unlikely that any others had carried out our procedure. If we wanted to rescue them, we had to move.

"Let's do it," I said. "We go in all-round defensive formation. Any sign of trouble, shoot."

"I'll take us straight there," Jack said. "Don't worry about that."

Rick took a deep breath and moved to the door. "Okay, guys, I'm in."

I opened it slightly and listened. Hearing no footsteps, I peeped out in both directions. "Clear."

Jack edged past me, crouching, and aimed along the curving corridor. I dodged to the left, covering the opposite direction. Rick stepped between us.

Because of the circular nature of the structure, we could see no more than thirty yards in either direction.

I waved Jack and Rick away. "I'll cover the rear—go."

Shuffling backward, I tried to keep pace with Jack and Rick.

Behind me, I heard faint knocking, not like the distant gunfire, but more like knuckles on wood. A hand pressed against my back.

"Wait," Rick said.

"Someone there?" I asked.

"Knocking on Lisa's door," Jack said.

"Come out, Lisa. Everything's fine," a male voice shouted.

"Fuck this," Jack said.

He ran forward. Two shots split the air, and a scream blasted along the corridor.

"Clear," Jack said. He ran to Lisa's door and knocked three times. "It's me, Jack."

Rick and I crouched on either side of him, protecting the flanks. The man's legs twitched. One shot had entered just above his left eye.

"Are you sure?" she cried from behind the door.

Jack leaned against it. "Open up. We know what's going on."

"Are you sure? Are you sure?" she kept repeating hysterically.

"Just open the bloody door. We've come to save you."

After a brief pause, the lock clicked and the door creaked open.

"Come on guys—get in," Jack said.

Rick backed into the room. I followed, closed the door, and locked it.

Five children, all around seven years old, huddled in the kitchenette area. Lisa looked terrified. She pulled at Jack's sleeve. "Is it all happening again? Oh my God, is it?"

"If we stay calm, we'll get out of this," Jack said.

Tears streamed down her cheeks. "Who was outside? Did they come to kill us?"

"Probably," I said. "You might see a bit more of it until we get clear."

"We can't move from here. It's not safe for the kids."

"It's not safe to stay here, Lisa," Jack said. "We need to find a safe place to hide."

"People won't find us here; we can keep quiet," she said.

"If I wanted to find and kill someone, I'd look in the suites," Rick said.

"We can wait here for half an hour," I said. "Give them time to wipe each other out."

"Get the kids ready to move in thirty minutes," Jack said.

I heard a faint banging noise and put my fingers to my lips.

Somebody knocked on a suite door along the corridor and shouted. Then again, closer.

"Keep quiet—they're not lingering," I said.

Lisa sat among the kids and gave each one a reassuring rub on the arm. Jack, Rick, and I lined up behind a couch and watched the door.

Someone knocked on the next door along. Footsteps echoed outside. I took a deep breath.

"Come out—I know you're in there," Chip said. "Parade in five minutes."

"He's screwed," Jack said.

I'd quickly grown to like Chip after finding him a warm man of integrity and action. GA had turned us into mortal enemies. I hoped he would move along and meet a swift end.

He banged on our suite's door.

"Come out! I know you're—"

One of the children screamed.

"Open it," Chip said. "I'll give you five seconds."

The door shuddered three times. I imagined him outside, thrusting his large frame against it. I aimed at the center.

Two gunshots rang out. Wood splintered inward around the lock. The door boomed open and thudded against the wall. Chip stood in the open entrance and held his gun forward in a two-handed grip. The children screamed.

I pumped four rounds into his torso. A hot shell case from Rick's rifle bounced off my cheek. Chip's arms fell by his side. He jerked as the rounds slammed into his body, and fell flat on his back.

Lisa cupped her cheeks and gasped. I felt a lump in my throat but had to stay vigilant to the situation at hand. With the door broken, we were even more exposed.

"We need to get clear of the stadium," I said. "It's too dangerous."

"Won't it be like this everywhere?" Lisa asked.

"The main concentration of people is here," Jack said. "We'll protect you, Lisa. Staying here is suicide."

"I'll scout the way ahead," I said. "Jack, you stay with Lisa and the children. Rick, bring up the rear."

"Roger that," Rick said.

The kids surrounded Lisa, and she gave them a pep talk.

I checked the corridor in both directions and headed for a fire exit between our two suites. Somebody screamed on a lower level. Lisa and the kids linked hands and formed a chain. I depressed the metal exit bar and shoved the door open. A shaft of late morning sunshine flooded into the corridor.

I scanned the immediate area outside the stadium while descending the concrete steps. The parking lot was deserted, and the golf course showed no signs of the madness inside.

The kids and Lisa stood against the wall of a brick building, perhaps a former security office. Rick and Jack joined me, and together we surrounded them in a defensive formation. A seagull obliviously flapped overhead as screams echoed from the stadium.

"Take us back to the marina, Rick," I said, thinking water might be our safest place.

He nodded and led the way around the stadium, toward Flushing Bay.

Forty yards later, Rick crouched and pulled his rifle into his shoulder.

Jack and I knelt in front of the kids. Multiple footsteps slapped against the ground, heading in our direction.

Harris and three of his team, all with packs strapped to their backs, bolted out of an entrance tunnel.

"Stop or I fire!" Jack shouted.

Harris skidded to a halt, swallowed hard, and rested his hands on his knees. "Thank God, it's you."

"Get over here," I said.

The group joined us by the wall. Two of them swept the surrounding area through their sights.

"We took your advice—shock to the head," Harris said, trying to catch his breath. "Doesn't look like many others did."

"They probably didn't even know about it," Jack said.

"How'd you get away?" Rick asked.

"When the killing started, we headed for the nearest exit and ended up in the locker room."

"The logistics women were strangling each other," one of the men said in a French accent.

"We left them to it," Harris said. "Hid in my suite till it died down. What happened to Chip?"

"We shot him," Jack said.

"Did he turn?"

"Didn't have a choice. It was him or us," Rick said.

Harris sighed. "Let's get the fuck out of here. Any ideas?"

"We came here in a cruiser, docked at Flushing Bay," I said. "It's not far from here."

"What have you got in those backpacks?" Jack said.

"Emergency supplies. We grabbed what we could from the suite. Figured it could be a long few days," Harris said.

"We share. Not a problem," French said.

"You up for a boat trip?" I asked.

Harris nodded. "Sure, let's get those kids to safety."

"You four flank the kids; Rick and Jack can bring up the rear. Let's move."

A ground-level emergency exit banged open. A man in a chef's apron staggered out of the door, holding a carving knife. He looked in the opposite direction. I raised my rifle. He slowly turned around. Our eyes met. He raised his knife and sprinted forward.

Before I had a chance to fire, multiple gunshots zipped through him, checking his run and peppering his dirty white apron with red spots. He dropped to his knees and weakly threw the knife in our general direction, before crashing face first on the road.

French drew a Glock from his hip holster, stood over the chef, and fired into the back of his head. I found his action chilling. The chef had already cooked his last stew.

"No pissing about— *move!*" I shouted.

We headed out toward Citi Field, the quickest route to our cruiser.

Harris, his men, and Lisa carried the children. Jack and Rick shuffled backward, covering our rear. I felt we were becoming too strung out, so we stopped below a concrete bridge to regroup.

"It's alright, guys," I said to the children. "We're taking you somewhere safe. Who wants to go on a boat?"

The closest sniffed, wiped brown hair away from her face, and nodded. The landscape opened out to our right, where Citi Field dominated the skyline. I kept us between the trees at the side of the road, and we trudged through the long grass surrounding them.

A vehicle engine roared. I gestured downward and ducked behind a tree. Moments later, a black Range Rover with tinted windows tore past us, heading for the stadium. A surge of anger ran through me. I wanted to spray the Rover with rounds but didn't want to compromise the kids. Although the second activation had killed our plans for Hart Island, we still had to fight back.

Jack crawled to my side. "Got to be them."

"Reckon they're after the community or us?" I asked. "We shouldn't put everyone at risk."

"Might be Anthony or Jerry," Jack said. "Let's drop this lot off and find out."

Rick nudged in between us. "Are we coming back for those fuckers?"

"You read my mind," I said. "I'm sick of running."

I looked along the line and caught Harris's attention. "Can you handle a boat?"

"Sailed one a few years ago on Lake Windermere. I'll be all right."

"No sailing involved," Rick said. "You'll be fine."

"Take your guys and protect Lisa and the kids," I said.

"Where you going?"

"We'll come for you when the dust settles," I said. "Keep within earshot of the launch point."

A burst of automatic fire echoed in the distance.

Our group moved again in a formation similar to a World War II shipping convoy across the Atlantic Ocean. Those of us who were armed led, flanked, and protected the rear of our precious cargo: Lisa and the kids. We crossed the dry dock to our tethered boat.

Harris's men ushered the kids into the cabin. Jack and I took up defensive positions, facing the city. Rick took Harris to the front of the cockpit to give him an overview of the controls.

"Do you think they've been watching us?" Jack asked.

"You mean GA? I don't believe in coincidences. That Rover was nearly on top of us."

"So much for bloody laborers," Jack said. "Looks to me like they're trying to catch anyone who survived the first activation."

"Either Brett was lying, which I doubt, or they've gone off-plan again."

The second activation led me to a few uncomfortable conclusions. Genesis Alliance had managed to get the backup base on Hart Island functional, ahead of schedule. I'd stupidly hoped that their Headquarters would turn up, kill the local goons, and leave us in peace. We had killers to deal with again, and I wondered if the global population would shrink to an unrecoverable level. Finally, if Martina had knowingly used the launch codes and was neck deep in GA, the chances of Lea being alive were slim. Jerry and Anthony wouldn't take her along for the ride.

"Where are you going?" Harris asked.

"To find that black Range Rover," Jack said.

"Why risk it?"

"We can't stay out of their way forever," I said. "Time to get on the front foot."

"I come with you," French said.

"You need to guard Lisa and the kids," I replied. "If we don't start protecting what's left, there's going to be nothing to fight for."

Rick hopped off the boat. "They're ready to go. What's our plan?"

I narrowed my eyes. "We'll get some ammo from the stadium and teach those assholes a lesson."

———

We said quick good-byes and watched the boat plow away from the pontoon, into open water.

With a smaller group, we made quicker progress. I led us through a large parking lot to the left of Citi Field, ready for a fight.

"Look out for the fresh ones," I said to Rick as we passed two decomposing bodies. "One played dead at the airport and killed a good woman."

The state of the bodies littering our alternative route suggested they were victims of the first activation. I stopped fifty yards short of the tennis center. A black Rover was parked outside the main entrance.

A single gunshot rang out from somewhere inside the stadium.

"They're still here," Jack said.

"This one's for my brother," Rick said and ran for the concrete stops we'd descended half an hour ago.

His excitable streak came to the fore, and he dashed for the fire exit. I winced as his feet thumped against the concrete steps.

Shouting at him to slow down and proceed with more caution would only further advertise our position.

Our suite was only twenty yards to the right of to the stairwell entrance. Rick eased the door open and slipped inside.

"I'll grab the ammo—give me two minutes," Jack said.

"Be careful, Jack. We've got goons and killers about."

I expected to find the place as we'd left it only hours ago. Somebody had ransacked it. Our bunk beds were pulled over, armchairs lay on their sides, and smashed crockery littered the floor.

"What the fuck?" Rick said.

I shook my head, crept to the window, and surveyed the stadium.

Morgan knelt on the baseline, hands tied behind his back. Two men dressed in black stood over him. Bodies from the second activation lay spread around them. One of the men punched Morgan in the stomach, and he cried in pain. The other yanked his hair back and shouted in his face.

"Are those GA?" Rick asked.

"Dressed in black. Rover outside. I'd put my house on it."

"Whadda we do?"

"As much as I don't like him, he's one of us, and they are the enemy."

One of the men walked to the tennis net and sliced off a length of cord with a knife.

I heard Jack's double knock and gestured to Rick to open the door. Back home, he always knocked twice and burst in, no matter who was around or what I was doing. I didn't mind; my house was his house, and we'd spent hours in that place, drinking cans and watching movies after finishing work. Now, he entered the suite with three full magazines, looked at the mess on the floor, and frowned.

"Two GA and Morgan," I said.

Jack pushed the curtain to one side. "I'll take the one on the left. You two kill the other."

I slid open the balcony door. We crawled out and squatted behind the padded seats. Shouting echoed up from the court. Fist connected with skin.

"Ready?" I asked.

Rick nodded. "You betcha."

I swung my rifle over the seat and aimed at the goon by the net. The three of us fired in unison.

My goon dropped to his knees, clutching his side. I repositioned my aim and fired. My next round punctured the side of his head. I looked to the left. The other sprawled on the surface next to Morgan. Jack fired again to make sure. The man flinched after a round slammed into his guts. His arms fell by his sides.

"Stay alert," I said. "Might be others."

Morgan's battered and swollen face looked in our direction. His shoulders sank, and the noise of his sobs drifted up to our position.

"Players' entrance," Rick said.

By the time I swung my rifle across, he'd already fired. Another goon dropped to the ground.

"We can't go down there," Jack said. "Place could be crawling with them."

"Morgan, get your arse up here," I shouted.

He gingerly rose and headed through the court exit immediately below us.

"Guys, he could be activated," Rick said.

"Something tells me he followed our advice," I said.

A minute later, somebody knocked on the door. I covered Jack and he slowly opened it. Morgan stood outside. He had swelling around both of his eyes and blood across the right cheek of his tanned face. Jack grabbed him by his shirt collar, yanked him inside, and threw him to the couch.

Morgan scowled. "Touch me like that again—"

Jack jabbed a finger toward him. "Why didn't you listen to us?"

"Listen to you? It's all your fault."

I needed to split this pair up and see to it that we remained vigilant. Besides the threat of killers, three dead goons out of radio contact could spell trouble.

"Jack, guard the internal entrance, Rick, keep watch on the court." I turned to Morgan. "What do you mean *our fault?*"

"They asked for you specifically. We were targeted because you were here. If I'd only listened to my conscience when you showed up. I knew you were trouble."

"What did you tell them?" I said.

"That you were here, but they already knew that."

"How did they know?" Jack said.

"They said they'd been watching us since yesterday and caught one of our scavenging teams this morning. What's the difference? They knew."

He bitterly emphasized the last two words. Whether they knew our location or not, I doubted it would have made a difference to the overall plan. He glared at me like he'd found a piece of shit on the bottom of his brown tassel shoes.

"Anything else?" I asked, resisting the urge to slam my rifle in his face.

"Some came on boats. I heard them mention a rendezvous back at the marina."

Jack bolted over and grabbed Morgan's collar. "Which marina? Where?"

"How should I know? Get your hands off me, you asshole."

I ignored his unoriginal insult. I never went for this whole north–south divide. A lot of my friends in the Army lived in the south of England, and I loved vesting London. Greatest city on Earth in my opinion—or it had been.

"You're coming with us, Morgan—grab a rifle," I said and cut loose the bonds behind his back.

He caressed the red marks around his wrist. "Where are we going?"

"The marina at Flushing Bay."

"You've got to be joking!"

"I'm struggling to find anything funny."

———

Morgan guided us to his personal arms store, a formal office like Harris's orientation room. He took a rifle and pistol from a locked cabinet. The rest of us topped up our mags and grabbed a Glock each. I found a small collection of tasers and slipped one into my back pocket.

For the second time, we headed back toward the marina, this time moving between the trees that lined Shea Road, keeping Citi Field to our right. Our pace quickened after an extended rattle of gunfire to our front. I ran under Northern Boulevard, stopping a hundred yards short of the launch point, and scanned the secured boats.

"We can't just go running in there," Morgan said.

"They didn't all come on boats," I said. "We saw a black Range Rover earlier."

Footsteps thumped along the ground. Two men dressed in black jogged along the Flushing Promenade toward the marina.

Both checked their stride to a slow walk within fifty yards of the marina and shouldered their rifles.

Rick dropped to the prone firing position and adjusted his sights. "I can take them from this range."

I dropped next to him and remembered the marksmanship principles taught to me in the Army: No snatching. Relax. Make every shot count.

The goons collapsed after being hit by our collective broadside. One must have instinctively pulled his trigger as he went down and wildly sprayed bullets into the clear blue sky.

I felt we were making progress. Five of them dead in the space of an hour. I checked my watch to see how much natural light we had left. Quarter past three in the afternoon. A good few hours. After receiving a knock to my confidence earlier today, I felt it building again.

"Everybody down!" Jack shouted.

I spun around. Thirty yards away, a man with a pistol ducked behind a tree.

"Drop your weapon and come out with your hands up," I said.

"I'm here to help you. I heard the gunshots," a voice called back.

"Who are you?" Jack asked.

He thrust out a spread hand. "I was at Flushing Meadows with you. Saw what you did back there."

"Do you know me?" Morgan asked.

He peered around the tree and focused on Morgan. "'Course I do."

"Come out where I can see you," Morgan said. "I interviewed every member of the company. I never forget a face."

"Wait," I said and turned to him. "You're not calling the shots anymore."

"You seem to be forgetting that I got off the same plane as you and led a group to a supermarket before taking over an entire stadium. What have you done besides fuck things up?"

I was about to reply when the man edged from behind the tree. He held his pistol in the air. Something about him didn't look right. He looked like he hadn't washed for days, and his neutral expression unnerved me.

"Whatever's going down," he said. "I think you could use an extra pair of hands."

Jack circled around his side. "Drop your gun."

"Not sure I recognize you," Morgan said. "Did you work in logistics?"

The man continued toward Morgan and passed Rick, who leaned against a tree. He quickly lowered his gun and fired into the side of Rick's head. A thin spray of blood speckled my face. I instinctively raised my rifle and pulled the trigger. Jack fired too and the man toppled backward by the force of the impacts.

Rick slumped against the tree trunk. The man lay a few yards away, with small chunks of blood, brain, and skull sprayed beyond him. Morgan clutched his rifle to his chest and looked back and forth from me to Jack.

"You fucking idiot!" Jack said.

I pulled Rick over. His bloodshot eyes stared vacantly to the sky.

"How was I to know?" Morgan asked.

"Because you got off the same plane as us," Jack said.

Jack lunged toward Morgan. I grabbed his arm. "There's nothing we can do here. Let's get to the marina, but it's our way now. Morgan, you got that?"

Jack shook his head toward the marina.

I made a visual sweep of the area before deciding to head for a boat. "We need to stay mobile. After all that shooting, everyone in the area knows exactly where we are."

We moved with stealth toward the marina. Jack led the way, followed by Morgan, who thankfully kept quiet. He did have experience leading groups after the first activation. I'd never doubted his organizational skills or fondness for giving orders. The success at Flushing Meadows in such a relatively short period of time was impressive. I would still trade a hundred Morgans for one Rick, who'd had a heart of gold. I felt his loss deeply.

Jack quickened his pace as we reached the deserted marina, and headed for a small silver powerboat. I could understand his concern and hoped Harris would be capable of dealing with any GA threat.

"What if the hostiles find us?" Morgan said.

"What do you think?" I said. "Shoot the buggers."

We couldn't find a key after searching the boat, so we continued along the marina. Jack had an air of panic about him. His head darted in all directions as he ransacked his way through a white cruiser, throwing around any loose object he could get his hands on.

Morgan discovered a six-berth cruiser, with a pair of maggot-infested corpses entangled in a strange embrace on the back decking. Holding my breath, I fumbled through their pockets, searching for any keys.

Morgan burst through the cabin doors and rattled a bunch. "On the table inside."

Jack and I rolled the corpses overboard and released the ropes from the mooring. Morgan sat in the elevated driver's seat and inserted the key. The engine spluttered a few times and rumbled into life.

"I had one of these for a week on Lake Geneva," Morgan said.

"Shut the fuck up and head for the river," Jack said. "Keep an eye out for Harris's boat."

Morgan shook his head and pushed the throttle. Our boat cut through the glinting dark water, away from the jetty. He steered between a couple of stray pleasure boats toward the entrance. I turned to watch how quickly our wake vanished.

Morgan's withholding of our information on how to avoid activation had probably cost a lot of lives. Yet here he was, talking about a bloody holiday in Switzerland.

"Why weren't you affected by the second activation?" I said.

"The what? Not sure what you mean?" he asked, avoiding eye contact.

"You used the cattle prod, didn't you?" Jack said.

Morgan ignored us and navigated around a stray blue passenger ferry. Several decomposing bodies hung from the railing on the top deck. Three windows on the lower deck were smashed and stained with dry blood.

"He used one," I said to Jack, but I made sure Morgan could hear. "I saw a cattle prod in his private weapons store. He believed us all along. He just didn't want it to affect his new community, controlling the information like some kind of tinpot dictator."

Morgan's left eye twitched. He steered hard right. Our boat scraped against the hull of a yellow water taxi. A flock of seagulls burst into the air from its deck. I ducked and they flapped inches over my head.

Once clear of the main clutter around the Bay's entrance, Jack and I took up positions at either side of the cockpit and aimed at everything we passed. Any vessel could hold a GA ambush or an attack point for freshly created killers.

Jack shouted across Morgan to me. "He helped himself first before warning anyone else about the danger. Selfish prick."

"Stop talking about me as if I'm not here," Morgan said.

"Tell us how you managed to avoid being activated then?"

"Okay, okay. I used a cattle prod. I didn't know if you were telling the truth or not. It sounded so far-fetched that I thought it might have had an element of truth."

"Element of truth?" I said, struggling to control my anger. "Rick's dead because of you. Choose your words carefully."

"I was going to make an announcement about the prodding and had already drafted a memo to all personnel. Information like this could have caused widespread panic and requires a process map for successful implementation. Did you consider that?"

"Fucking process map?" Jack said incredulously.

"You sound like a politician," I said. "They deserved to know about it. The only goal is survival. You should have realized that and not tried to maintain your own position."

He sighed and ran a hand through his hair. I decided not to press him further. His decision must be weighing heavily on his conscience. Not that he'd admit that to us.

We passed Rikers Island on our left and entered the main part of East River. The smashed remains of the Bronx-Whitestone suspension bridge lay directly ahead. The middle section was collapsed in the water, and stray cables rocked in the wind.

Jack pointed to his right. "Over there. Four hundred yards away."

Morgan increased the power, and we sped for what appeared to be our old boat. A recognizable thick blue stripe ran along its side.

I shielded my eyes from the sun and peered across the water. "Can't see anyone on board."

As we plowed nearer, I noticed the boat slightly listing to one side; the windows were shattered and a number of black holes peppered the hull and cabin wall. Morgan brought us alongside the stricken craft and our starboard brushed against its port.

Harris and two other men lay on the sun deck. He had two visible bullet wounds on his left cheek and forehead.

I rushed down from the cockpit, grabbed a boat hook, and pulled the vessels tightly together.

"Harry, can you see Lisa and the kids?" Jack asked.

He gulped and bowed his head.

I jumped across to *Candy Cane*'s deck and entered the open cabin doors. The scene of slaughter didn't need sharing, and I immediately returned to the sun deck.

Jack crouched to jump onboard.

I shook my head. "Don't. It's too late."

"Everyone?"

My silence told Jack everything he needed. He let out a loud roar that echoed across the water. I pushed our boat free and watched *Candy Cane* slowly bob away.

———

"Who was onboard?" Morgan asked.

"Men, women, and children," Jack said. "People from Flushing Meadows. We thought they'd be safe on the water . . ."

He trailed off and gazed into the distance. I hoped the murders wouldn't tip him over the edge again. We were under no illusions about the evil that we faced, but if we wanted to hit them hard, we had to be calculated about it. Lisa and the kids were another addition to the long list of those who needed to be avenged. I would remember these people after our job was done. At the moment, they supplied irresistible motivation.

"Why did they do it?" Morgan said.

"Look around for Christ's sake." Jack swept his arm in the direction of the city, where plumes of smoke rose from the tall buildings, and sporadic gunfire crackled. "That's probably other survivor groups, killing each other."

Morgan hands trembled on the wheel. He turned to me. "What do we do now?"

"Survive and fight," I said. "GA has cars, boats, planes, plenty of manpower, communications, weapons, and the activation devices. But if we're going to have a shootout, I'd rather it be on dry land, where we can have the element of surprise."

"Don't forget HQ," Jack said. "This lot is only the tip of the iceberg. We've got something bigger and uglier coming, and they might show up tomorrow."

"Let's find a safe place to work out how to tackle this," I said and turned to Morgan. "Take us back in."

He gave me a single firm nod and increased the throttle. We sped back in silence to Flushing Bay. Morgan cut the engine close to our starting point, leaving the cruiser to drift toward the mooring.

I found it difficult not to feel intimidated by our current situation. We had threats coming from everywhere. Morgan couldn't yet be trusted. I needed a way of defusing the potential confrontation between him and Jack, which would be sooner rather than later.

If we were going to hit GA, we needed every available resource. At the moment, though, we needed some kind of safety and familiarity, and I knew the answer.

"We're going to an apartment in Elmhurst to figure out our next moves," I said. "We know the area and left a few supplies there."

"We're going to Bernie's?" Jack asked.

"Yep. You okay with that, Morgan?"

"That's fine—lead the way," Morgan said.

The insincerity in his voice grated on me, but he had little option unless he wanted to go it alone. Morgan knew Jack and I had survived in a small group, and a person like him usually went with the strongest chance of success.

We still held an advantage over GA. Their activations couldn't affect us, and we knew the location of the local team. Their time had come.

"It's four miles from here," I said. "The sooner we get there, the quicker we can plan our attack."

"Stay alert, Morgan," Jack said.

Morgan sneered and headed for the nearest vehicle.

We searched Citi Field's parking lot. Car batteries and engines were still functional, but we faced the usual problem: A lot of them had disease-ridden bodies inside.

A rotting face pressed against the glass of a dark blue Volvo's passenger window. Saliva gathered in my mouth. As the decomposition took hold, the face had slid downward, leaving a horrible trail of human grease above it. The receding skin and lips had exposed yellow teeth and red gums that made the face appear to be either screaming or laughing.

Finally, I found a usable but filthy Lincoln. I started the car and headed south toward Elmhurst. I knew the way from here and picked up the Long Island Expressway, retracing our original route out of the city.

Jack turned to Morgan in the back seat when we passed Aldi. "Why were you so rude when we met you here?"

Morgan ignored him and stared out of the window. I could slice the tension between the two of them with a knife. I hoped Jack wasn't planning on making him his next target.

It now seemed strangely natural to be driving on the right-hand side of the road through stationary traffic, weaving and bumping through routes cleared by others since the first activation. We merged onto Queens Boulevard, which had more than just a feeling of déjà vu about it.

I stopped alongside the vehicle we'd taken to the Queensboro Bridge only a week ago. We made our way toward Bernie's apartment block on foot from here. The neighborhood looked exactly the same. A clutter of two-story houses with wooden façades, mixed with larger apartment blocks, along streets lined with overhead cables. I avoided taking the route that took us past the little girl. Jack didn't need any extra stress. None of us did.

Bernie's street had noticeably lost its sheen. Weeds pushed through cracks in the paving; rubbish littered the road surface and drifted around in the light breeze. The smell in Queens had an increasingly suffocating effect. I dreaded to think what it was like in Manhattan.

I carried out a visual check of the immediate vicinity of Bernie's apartment block before we entered the building. Jack lifted Bernie's doormat and grabbed the key.

"Was he the fat guy with you last Monday?" Morgan asked.

"Watch your tongue," Jack snapped.

"GA killed him," I said. "I'm heading up to the roof first to scan for black Rovers."

"Good idea," Jack said and barged past Morgan. "I'm not staying down here on my own with him."

Morgan puffed his cheeks and spun toward the stairs.

I decided to check the roof first, because we would lose natural light in two hours, around half seven in the evening, damaging any chances of reasonable reconnaissance.

As I passed the fifth floor, an apartment door creaked. I froze on the staircase, turned, and put my finger to my lips.

Jack crept to my side and craned his neck around the corridor. "An open door. Cover me."

Six apartments were on this floor. I followed him to the closest. He kicked its door fully open and aimed inside. A smear of blood ran from the hall into a living area.

"Stay on guard outside, Morgan," I said. "We're going in."

Two fresh bodies lay on the fake wooden laminate floor, surrounded by dried pools of blood. One had a knife in her limp hand; both had multiple stab wounds.

Empty cans were piled in the corner of the open-plan living area. Bottled water, chocolate, and some fruit-flavored tea bags sat on the kitchen counter. I pulled a black plastic chair from under the glass dining table, rested my right boot on it, and retied my shoelace.

Jack gazed at the corpses and titled his head to one side. "Might have been hiding here last week."

"Come on, let's grab the stuff and get to the roof," I said, not wanting to dwell on their history or fate.

We filled the remaining empty spaces of our packs with water and chocolate.

"What did you find in there?" Morgan asked me.

"Two dead—"

I spun and knelt by the door. The noise of slow, deliberate steps echoed from the staircase. Ascending toward us.

"Think we were followed?" Morgan whispered.

"Maybe," I said and jerked my rifle to the left. "Get inside."

After backing into the entrance, I lay in the prone position and closed the door ajar, leaving a crack to observe and aim outside. Jack crouched over me. Morgan paced around the lounge area, rubbing his temples.

"Morgan, keep bloody still," Jack said over his shoulder.

The footsteps reached our level, and a man, dressed only in a pair of shorts, carried on trudging upward. His bloodstained arms dangled by his sides, and something glinted in his right hand. Possibly a knife. A door slammed on the floor above us.

"You see that, Jack?" I asked.

"Just another madman. We should leave him to it."

"Was it one of my company?" Morgan asked.

"No idea," I said. "But I don't want to find out."

A faint noise of a door opening sounded overhead.

"Was he armed?" Morgan said.

"Had a knife or something like that."

Morgan tried to shuffle past Jack and me into the narrow hallway. "I'm not staying in the same building as a lunatic. Get out of my way."

I grabbed Morgan's shirt collar. "Wait a minute. He might be coming back down."

"The rules have changed again," Jack said. "We take no risks."

Morgan scowled at me. "I'll give you five seconds to take your hand off my shirt."

"Cast your mind back a few hours," I said. "You know the consequence of not working as a team."

"What do you know about teamwork?"

Morgan ripped himself away from my grip and strode purposefully toward the staircase. He stopped five yards short and looked down his sights.

Footsteps descended. The man in shorts appeared, carrying a small hacksaw. He seemed in a trance, unaware of our presence.

"Freeze! Put your hands up," Morgan said.

The man stopped and looked at Morgan as if he'd just told him he'd slaughtered all of his family.

"Hands up or I'll shoot. You've got five seconds."

"Bloody hell," Jack said and raised his rifle. "What's he got us into?"

The man shuffled toward Morgan. "Do you hear the voices?"

"Voices? What voices?"

The man lunged forward and grabbed the muzzle of Morgan's rifle. They spun as the man fought to gain control of the weapon.

A shot split the air.

The man staggered back. His back thumped against the magnolia-painted wall. He clutched the center of his chest. Blood ran through his fingers and dripped to the gray vinyl floor.

Morgan swung his rifle butt into the side of the man's head. The man collapsed and groaned, revealing a red patch on the wall behind him. His right leg kicked spasmodically before his body relaxed.

"You're such a tit!" Jack yelled at Morgan. "Every man and his dog will be coming here now."

"Really?" he said with a smug look of triumph. "Didn't you hear other gunshots on our way here? If you're not prepared to act, I will."

"You could have just let him go down the stairs," I said.

"I'm going to find out what he was doing."

Morgan turned and headed for the staircase. Jack raised his eyebrows and immediately followed. As soon as we locked ourselves in Bernie's apartment, I needed a serious word with this annoying liability.

On the next level, Morgan made for an open apartment door. He stood to the side of it with his back against the wall and spun to face the entrance with his rifle stretched in front him, a textbook clichéd move. I assumed his clearance training came from the TV. He cupped his nose with his left hand and entered.

"Jesus Christ," I heard him say.

The filthy living area buzzed with flies. Severed heads lined an eight-row bookcase in lines of five. A stack of seven more leaned against it, like a grisly totem pole. Various bloodstained implements lay around: a bread knife, bolt cutters, and a coil of metal wire. In the kitchen area, three blackened heads hung like ugly lanterns from each rotor blade of the ceiling fan.

Jack covered his mouth and immediately walked out.

"Do you still think we should have kept him alive?" Morgan said.

I shook my head and left the apartment, finding it impossible to comprehend the reason for such a grotesque collection. We'd witnessed some random and strange behavior, but this was the most calculated and horrific yet. I remembered the headless corpses in Elyria. The first activation had really screwed some people's minds. If this was the real GA plan, its leaders were even more twisted than I'd thought.

"Back to Bernie's," Jack said.

"Yep, I've lost my appetite for surveillance," I said.

At this point, after everything that had happened today, I reckoned we could all do with being in a safe place to take a mental break and plan for our future.

We descended to Bernie's old apartment. I took the key out of my pocket and opened the door. The familiar place looked welcoming in our frazzled state. I stepped inside and my foot slipped on a piece of paper. It hadn't been here when we'd left last Monday. I leaned down and picked it up. Morgan bumped me from behind.

"Are we going in?" he asked.

"There's a note," I said. "Delivered after we headed to Monroe."

I took the paper to the couch, sat down, and squinted at the untidy handwriting.

Jack secured the door and rushed over. "What does it say?"

"Same time, same place. My heart will go on."

"That's the song you played in the parking lot, wasn't it? Celine Dion?" Jack asked.

My pulse quickened. This could be the kind of boost we needed. "It's Lea. She must have put it here in the last two days. There's no other explanation."

Morgan tore the note from my hand. "Who's Lea?"

"Do you think she means the Queensboro Bridge at eleven a.m.?" Jack asked.

We'd arranged on Twitter to meet Lea a week ago at the Queensboro Bridge. She hadn't shown because of the presence of a killer, but later fell into our trap at the parking lot. Jack's theory made sense. Lea might have inside information for us if she'd managed to meet up with Martina.

"We should go tomorrow morning, hide somewhere and stake it out," I said.

"It's worth the risk. She might be able to help us—"

"I need to be involved in this," Morgan said, his voice rising over Jack's. "Who is she, and how did she know you would be here?"

"We came here before escaping the first time," Jack said. "She went missing in Monroe."

I smiled at the thought of her being here and trying to contact us, but wondered exactly what she'd done to stay alive.

———

At eight in the evening, Jack lit three of the half-melted candles on the table, providing us with gloomy light. He sat on the couch opposite Morgan. I checked the cupboards, remembering we'd left a few cans behind. After preparing three bowls of cold baked beans, I sat with the others.

Jack and Morgan immediately spooned beans into their mouths.

"She wanted to make her own way and try to find her partner," I said.

"I'd have thought the chances of that were pretty slim," Morgan said with his mouth still full of chewed beans. Once a corporate ass, always a corporate ass. Being a corporate ass doesn't instantly grant you good table manners, though. He could still be an officious buffoon and chew with a half-filled mouth.

"Not when you consider that they both worked for Genesis Alliance, and the partner was the niece of the head guy up there."

He clanked his spoon in the bowl and placed it on the table. "You were with someone from Genesis Alliance?"

"She wasn't really one of them," Jack said. "She had a job as an admin assistant or something, sorting out shipping and payments."

"You know they want to find you. They'll be using her as bait."

"She's not like that," I said. "Lea's pretty smart and doesn't take any shit. She went back because of her partner, Martina. She won't go along with GA."

"Suit yourselves, but don't expect me to come."

"Fine by me—you can stay here," Jack said. He threw his bowl in the sink and headed for the bedroom. "I'm going to sleep. Wake me when it's my watch."

Jack had probably turned in early to avoid a growing temptation to use Morgan's face as a punching bag.

I spent the evening cleaning my rifle, checking the magazines, and thinking about the morning plan. Morgan fidgeted for an hour before reading *Moby Dick*, which he'd found next to the telephone.

He kept peering over the book at me, humming to himself and clicking his tongue.

"Are you going to sleep?" he eventually asked.

"I will when Jack gets up. We like to keep watch."

He drummed his fingers against the arm of the couch and sucked his teeth.

I swear he was trying to piss me off on purpose by invading the silence with his incessant noises.

"Will you stop that?" I asked.

He smiled at me and put down the book. "Sorry. Can you give me any more info on Genesis Alliance?"

"Not much more than what we've already told you. They're on Hart Island and are obviously still operating. Their Headquarters is coming after the locals messed up. Don't know what they have planned, but we need to try and beat them to the control unit."

"You're not going to beat them by sitting in here cleaning weapons."

I put down a working part and glared at him. "If we find Lea, she might be able to help. We'll work something out tomorrow. I've got no intention of sitting around."

"You said they have a tech team and that Headquarters is in the UK, right?"

"So what?"

"Sounds like they're organized."

I shrugged and continued to clean my rifle. It felt like he was being flippant with me.

He continued to read and glanced over the book every few minutes. I wasn't sure if he wanted to say something or offer his advice on what to do, but I thought it prudent to ignore him. The mere presence of him got on my nerves, and he had a funny way of making a room feel small.

My temper bubbled to the snapping point over the next three hours as he continued to fidget and make noises. Thankfully, Jack poked his head out of the bedroom. "Harry, want to get your head down? Get yourself four hours before we head off."

I sighed with relief. "Cheers. I've cleaned your rifle—twice."

He gave me a knowing smile, and I headed for the bedroom.

I didn't need a second invitation to get out of the living area, but I expected him to send Jack into a rage. I tossed and turned for a few hours, gaining restless sleep, mixed with thoughts about the dead children on the boat, Lisa, Chip, Harris, and Rick. We'd lost a lot of good people over the last day, but Lea's note had given me hope.

———

The apartment door slammed shut. I scrambled up and headed into the living area.

Jack sat on the couch reading a book. "He's gone."

"Morgan? Gone where?"

"He was being an annoying bastard all night. I kept telling him to shut up. He said he couldn't take it anymore and left."

"Did he say where he was going?"

"Said he was getting a boat or something. To be honest, I'm glad he's gone."

I had mixed feelings about Morgan leaving. I realized that if he'd stayed with us, it wouldn't have taken long for an explosive situation to happen. But we were a man down, and that was something we couldn't really afford at the moment.

Morning sunshine seeped through the metal blinds near the top of the wall. We finished off two cans of beef stew from the cupboard and washed ourselves in the sink. Bernie and Linda's twentieth anniversary porcelain carriage clock chimed from its shelf. Nine o'clock on Monday morning.

Our understanding of the killers had changed since our last excursion to Queensboro Bridge. People suffering aftereffects were less predictable, but still highly dangerous. Above everything, the shadow of Genesis Alliance loomed, and could grow even larger today if their ship docked at Boston.

We decided against taking a car. Things were quiet around us, and we didn't want to draw any unwanted attention. We hugged a concrete railway bridge that ran along the center of the Queens Boulevard, staying away from the stores that lined either side of the road. Only the ones containing food had been looted. In the distance, Manhattan stretched into the sky. The faraway noises that had punctuated the silence yesterday evening had died down. I only heard two distant gunshots as we approached the Queensboro Bridge.

We arrived with an hour to spare. I found a car with black tinted windows, pulled out its two inhabitants, and observed the area around us from the front seat. A large flock of birds flew across the broken Manhattan skyline, through tunnels of smoke rising from the ruined buildings. Lack of maintenance and violent acts must have triggered the fires.

A city dying in front of my eyes, along with its inhabitants.

9

For the next hour, the only sign of life was a couple of dogs. The first skulked over the bridge, stopped to lick the face of a corpse, then ran as if startled by something. The other trotted around in the distance for a few minutes before disappearing down a side street. At least the twisted minds of Genesis Alliance hadn't made animals part of their program.

"Would've helped if she put a date on that note," Jack said.

"I've been thinking about it. We left Lea in Monroe and pretty much came straight here."

"We could always come back tomorrow if she doesn't show."

Something moved in the rearview mirror. I slipped between the front seats and scanned the area.

"Problem?" Jack asked.

"Dunno. Might be."

Moments later, a woman darted from behind one car to another, moving in our direction.

"Problem," I said. "And she's coming this way."

"She seen us?"

She crouched by the side of an SUV, paused, and advanced to the cover of a red and white ambulance with FDNY plastered on the side. Nobody would ever forget the bravery of New York's firemen after the previous terrorist attack on this great city.

The woman reached a position within twenty yards, but she wasn't concentrating on our vehicle. She pressed herself against the side of cars and kept advancing, clasping a carving knife in her right hand. We aimed our rifles and tracked her movement. She glanced around and continued along the bridge, stalking her prey.

Before the activation, I'd disliked tinted windows and thought they were used by show-offs and wannabe gangsters. Today, they helped us avoid a dangerous confrontation.

"How many do you think are still about?" Jack said.

"Not many. The second activation'll probably mop out most of the survivors."

A single gunshot rang out. The woman's head snapped back, and she dropped to the ground. A woman stood in front of her, dressed in black with her hair in a tight black ponytail and her gun extended forward. Lea.

Jack went to pull open the door.

I grabbed his arm. "Not so fast. Let's make sure she's on her own first. Look at her clothes."

Lea advanced to within thirty yards and looked around before ducking into an abandoned gold Lexus. We waited for ten minutes but saw no other signs of movement.

"It's eleven," Jack said. "Let's go."

I slipped out, crept to the Lexus, and gently tapped on the back window.

She sprang out and pointed her pistol at me in one movement before lowering it to her side. I resisted the urge to hug her but couldn't hold back my smile.

"Put the rifle down, Jack," she said over my shoulder.

"Let's get out of here," I said, "before any interested parties turn up to check out the source of your shot."

She returned my smile. "No 'Hello, how are you?'"

"That woman you shot walked right past us," Jack said. "Might be others around here."

"Okay, I know a place. We've got lots to talk about and very little time."

"We could always go back to Bernie's apartment," I said. "Like the good old days."

She smiled again, although this time it looked false. "They know about that place. It was compromised just before I left this morning."

Jack raised his eyebrows. "What? How?"

"We can talk while we walk. Come on."

This was the Lea I loved. Abrupt and to the point. She headed across Queens Boulevard. Jack and I flanked her and covered each side.

"How did you know we'd go back there?" I asked. "And why has it been compromised?"

"I didn't know. I posted the note yesterday and planned on coming here for the next few days. You said you were headed back to New York, and I thought you might return to Bernie's apartment. Where else do you know to go around here?"

"That was a bit of a long shot," Jack said. "Although it's our nearest thing to home, I suppose."

"You're more predictable than you think, Jack."

He frowned, but I knew what she meant. I would have done the same thing in her shoes.

"What's with the black gear?" I said. "You back with Genesis Alliance?"

"It's complicated. I have my life thanks to Martina. I had to make compromises." She quickened her pace and headed for a side street. "GA have boots on the ground here, and we need to be careful."

"We know about their boots on the ground, boats in the water, and planes in the air," Jack said, anger rising in his voice. "Why has Bernie's apartment been compromised?"

"Early this morning, just before I set off, Morgan arrived on Hart Island in a small boat. He told the guard he wanted to talk to the boss and was taken to see Anthony."

"That bastard. I knew it," Jack said.

The revelation didn't surprise me either. Morgan probably thought he could persuade his way in with the dominant force and worm his way to the top. I should have suspected after his questions a few hours ago.

"Anthony's the boss?" I said. "I thought he broke away to track us down?"

"Anthony runs most of it through radio comms. He's got a real hard-on for you—"

"Hold on; back up a minute," Jack said. "What exactly did Morgan tell him?"

"He didn't have time to say much."

"Why?"

"Morgan told Anthony that you two were in an apartment in Elmhurst and gave Bernie's address. He said that he'd lead them back and make sure you were in when they arrived."

"That sneaky bastard! What else did he say?" Jack asked.

"Nothing else. Anthony called him a treacherous piece of shit, dragged him to the shore by his ear, and blew out his brains. They dumped him in the sea."

"Anthony got that one right," I said.

Jack grunted. "Serves him right."

Lea dropped to one knee and swept her pistol across the street. A tin can bounced off the curb and rolled in front of us.

She rose to her feet and shook her head. "I left straight away to find you. Anthony was preparing his boat when I left on mine."

"Did Anthony come on a boat yesterday?" I asked.

"When the second activation hit, he took a squad to Flushing Bay. His plan was to have a quick scout around the stadium. Ever since he found out that they're in deep shit with Headquarters, he's become more erratic and doesn't give a shit about their plan."

Lea doubled back and led us along 43rd Avenue. Drab brick industrial units and garages were packed together on either side of the road.

"What's the story with HQ?" I said. "We hear they're coming, but that's about it."

"Headquarters wants to meet the whole team today in Boston. Anthony told them on Saturday that he moved the control unit to Massachusetts. He's doing it to buy some time in his hunt for you. A lot of people are getting nervous about lying to HQ. He executed a guy yesterday morning who asked to leave."

"Why don't they kill him if he's risking their lives?"

"Claims he can smooth it all over once HQ shows up, and they'll understand him stamping out a local issue."

"We met a techy guy in Monroe who told us they were a nasty bunch. He reckoned the local team was for it," I said.

"I heard about, Brett. Anthony said you killed him in Ohio."

"That lying piece of shit," Jack said. "He shot Brett."

Lea let out a deep sigh and shuddered. "Doesn't surprise me. A group of survivors attacked Hart Island two nights ago. They failed, but our techy guys reported it. HQ is nervous about tech falling into civilian hands and are furious that they got so close."

"Why don't the techs tell HQ they're still on Hart Island?"

"They don't need to. As soon as they sent out the second activation, Headquarters would pick up device activity on their network. Anthony doesn't know it."

"Christ," I said. "Sounds like it's all falling apart. I'm surprised it hasn't descended into full-scale mutiny."

"Trust me, it's close. If I ran GA, I'd be kicking their asses too."

"What about you?" Jack said. "Anthony and Jerry just let you tag along? I find that hard to believe."

"I'm safe as long as I'm with Martina. She's memorized the launch codes. If they touch me, they get no activations."

The information came at me in an overwhelming flood. But it sounded good. Others had attacked the GA team, and Anthony had plunged the local team in even deeper shit. HQ still provided the unknown, but at least they weren't coming for us, not at the moment.

At the end of 47th, we headed for a small industrial structure with two silver columns protruding from the top. Manhattan stood directly behind it, separated only by the river. Quite a spectacular view for such a dull building. I was surprised that hotels, housing companies, and leisure complexes hadn't taken over these kinds of spots. It happened everywhere in Manchester city center.

"This way. I saw it from the bridge, and it looked quiet," Lea said.

Lea squeezed through a gap in the chain-link fence and headed toward a series of small brick buildings. She walked between two of them and leaned against the wall.

I glanced around. We were obscured from any view unless somebody entered the complex.

"I'll guard one way, you the other," Jack said to me.

I trained my rifle back toward the road. "What happened after you left us in Monroe?"

In my peripheral vision, Lea lowered her gun, lit a cigarette, and took a deep drag.

"When I split from you guys, I dodged the patrols and headed for Martina's house."

"We heard a shot," Jack said.

"I think they found someone else. I don't know. She lives by the airport on the other side of town. I went to her yard and waited. Where did you go?"

"We lay in a pit of rotting bodies," Jack said.

I wondered if a day would go by where I didn't think of that experience. I was sure it would haunt me for the rest of my life.

"Gross. No wonder they couldn't find you. I heard all hell breaking loose in the town and wondered if you'd come back to get me. I figured you knew why I slipped away without telling you."

"We worked it out," I said. "I might have done the same thing if this idiot was hiding out in Monroe."

Jack laughed sarcastically. Lea continued, "It had gotten dark, and I heard a vehicle approach the house. They dropped Martina off and sped away. When she went through to the kitchen, I knocked on the window, giving her the fright of her life."

"I'm surprised she didn't shoot you after what happened with Ron," I said.

"She was angry and upset. We had a fight in the kitchen but quickly made up."

"A physical fight?" Jack asked.

"Mostly shoving and screaming—it wasn't pretty. Anyway, I told her about our journey from New York, and she began to understand the situation. Although I did tell her I tried to stop you from killing Ron, but you wouldn't listen."

"Fine by me," I said. "You did what was needed to survive. It's understandable. Does she want us dead?"

"She did at first, but we've got bigger things to think about. I'll get to that part. Martina uses the codes to keep us both safe. Anthony and Jerry are both furious that they didn't have time to get them from Ron."

"I'm glad. Pair of assholes," Jack said.

"I'm surprised they just didn't torture them out of her," I said.

Lea took another drag of her cigarette and blew smoke out of the corner of her mouth.

"I worried about that, but she's memorized them and said she'd rather die than give up our safety. There are plenty who don't like Anthony and Jerry. Most of the GA guys I've spoken to have been forced into the organization in one way or another."

"Why don't they rise up and kill them?" Jack asked.

"Nobody knows who to trust locally, and Headquarters holds family members and loved ones hostage."

"Brett told us about that," I said.

"On our way down to New York, one of the guys called Anthony a prick. Not to his face, but he managed to hear about it. He sliced his throat in front of the convoy. That had a funny way of keeping things quiet."

I thought about how good it would be to teach Anthony a lesson. Not a quick bullet to the head—he deserved something far more slow and painful.

"What happened when you met Jerry and Anthony?" Jack asked.

"Jerry keeps his distance and is always sneering. He's constantly asking questions about you. Apparently, he's like an expert hunter."

"He's not much of an expert. We're still here, aren't we?" I asked.

"And now he knows it. Man, he's neurotic. Wanted to know your habits, what food you like, what you said before I left you, where you're from. He recorded every last little detail in a notebook. HQ has taken a back seat in his mind. If GA suspends him, I get the feeling that you'll become his life."

"Suspend him?" I asked, confused about the choice of words. "Wouldn't they just kill him?"

She shrugged and had another drag. "They're losing men every day. Anthony thinks Headquarters can't afford to kill their own staff."

"But he can?" Jack asked. "You know he cut a woman's throat in Monroe and blamed it on us?"

"I heard about her. Poor woman. There's a rumor that he took a boat out to South Bass Island and killed two GA members for raising a false alarm about you."

"No, that was us," I said. "Although you don't have to spread that around."

"Honestly? None of the other guys I've spoken to give a shit about you. It's only those two, and I think you know why."

"What did they expect us to do?" Jack said. "Bring them a picnic hamper?"

Lea shook her head. "Jerry's been kissing Martina's ass because she holds the power with the launch codes. He boasted to me yesterday about digging up Bernie's corpse as a message for you."

"Did you tell Martina?"

"She doesn't care about Bernie or you. She might not want you dead anymore, but that's as far as it goes."

"Did he tell you he booby-trapped it?" I said.

"No, what did he do?"

"He wedged a knife through a grenade pin and stuck it in Bernie's body. The poor bugger got blown to pieces.

Lea screwed up her face and cursed under her breath. I had a hard time believing that she just went along with GA. I could see her motivation in terms of Martina, but it all seemed bizarre with Anthony and Jerry involved. I suspected Lea wasn't reading them correctly. There had to be more to their motivations and actions involving her.

"How much sway does Martina have?" Jack asked.

"She sits on a council with Jerry and Anthony. They speak at ten every morning, whether that's face to face or over a radio."

"Jesus, a council? She's in this right up to her neck," I said. "You sure you know what you're doing?"

"She's kept me alive, hasn't she?"

"We would've kept you alive," Jack said.

She dropped her smoke and crushed it with her boot. "If only things were so simple, Jack."

"What about HQ?" I asked. "Do you have any idea what's coming?"

"Everyone's guessing at the moment. Jerry reckons they'll have their hands full in the UK. I'm not so sure. The tech guys speak to their people over there and are terrified about their arrival."

"Haven't some already arrived?" Jack said. "Two jumbos landed a hundred and fifty miles north of here the other day."

Her eyes widened. Not by much, but I noticed and thought her reaction curious. "Surprised by the revelation, Lea?"

"I heard their ship is arriving tomorrow. Nobody mentioned anything about a plane."

"Seems like we're not getting the full story," Jack said. "How many are on Hart Island at the moment?"

"The Ops team number about forty. I don't know exactly. I know five of them didn't make it back yesterday."

"We took them out," I said. "Three of them to save Judas Morgan."

"He told us they got into a big firefight with the local defense force on the water; said that's how he lost his men."

"That's bullshit," Jack said. He dropped his guard and turned to face Lea. "That so-called 'defense force' was a boat full of kids and a woman."

Lea looked nervous, and I started to question whether we should continue this meeting. I didn't give a rat's cock about her time on the road with GA; I only wanted to know how we could destroy them.

"What was the second activation all about? I thought they were supposed to be processing people," Jack said.

"They are, but not here."

"What do you mean?"

"When Anthony caught one of the scavenging teams from the stadium and confirmed you were around, he ordered the device in Manhattan to be programmed with the same instructions as the previous activation. So it's only localized in this area."

"The rest of the country is being processed?" I asked.

"The official second activation was launched nationwide in all other areas. One of the guys mentioned a team in Virginia."

"That's still going off plan, right?" Jack said.

"Right. I heard Anthony debating it with Jerry and Martina. Jerry said they could slit your throats when you came in for processing. Martina knows I want you alive, so she proposed that we just leave you to rot in the city; then GA could sweep you up when the situation was back under control."

"But Anthony went for Plan C: Take us out with a local activation, and come in after to make sure the job was done?" I asked.

"He's not letting this one go. I'd bet you a million dollars that he's breaking down Bernie's door at the moment."

"What about the tech team?" Jack said.

"A guy on the other end of the sat comm knew they'd configured Manhattan for a first activation. He told them to move down to a safe house outside Atlantic City . . ."

"They're going today?" I asked.

"They might have already gone. I think they're nervous about traveling through New York, but they're heading out tonight."

"You're not mentioning Martina much. What did she say about all of this?"

"Martina went along with it and supplied the launch codes. She asked to be left alone when she punched in the sequence. She had to do it; it keeps me alive."

"Doesn't she realize the number of people who have died because of the activations?" Jack said. "If she's against this thing, why didn't she run?"

"And have Anthony tracking us? No way. Besides, we've come up with another idea."

I'd been waiting for the point of this whole story. As interesting as it was, we weren't standing here for a casual conversation. I knew Lea had found us for a reason, but I didn't know why.

"Come on, Lea, what's the plan?" I asked.

She didn't reply and rubbed her face. I considered her loyalty.

"We're not stupid," Jack said. "You're in bed with these fuckers. What do you want?"

"This is where you two come in. We've thought of a way to end this."

"We had a way until this morning. And who is *we*?"

Lea paced around and stopped in front of me. "Martina and me. We all want the same thing. I've told you how fragmented this whole thing is. We've got an opportunity."

"So where do we come in?" I asked. "I take it Martina doesn't know you're here?"

"She does, actually. We've got a small window to bring down the local operation, with your help."

At last she got down to brass tacks. I'm sure she didn't take us for fools. Any kind of reveal like this usually led to consequences.

"Cut to the chase. Why are you really here?" I asked.

"We'll only be free if we eliminate Jerry, Anthony, and the control unit."

"When you say *we*," I said, "I take it you mean you and Martina?"

"Fuck off, Harry. I mean *all* of us. I'm giving you an opportunity to wipe out the leaders of the local team. Are you in?"

"What kind of opportunity are you talking about?"

"Tonight. Anthony likes to send night patrols out to check for anyone sneaking about in the local area. We'll probably only have to deal with Anthony, Jerry, and a few guards. I'm sure you two can handle that."

"And Martina?" Jack said.

"She's going to keep them busy in the control room. I'll pick you up at City Island, just to the right of Pelham Cemetery, at ten. It'll be dark by then . . ."

"Sounds like you've got this all planned out," I said. "Forgive me for being skeptical, but you're in with a bunch of toads."

Lea placed her hand on my shoulder and looked me in the eye. "It's our chance. They won't see us coming. Come in black clothes. You'll be on top of them before they know what's happening. I'm a familiar face, remember?"

"Yeah, but we're not," Jack said.

"Just walk behind me. Whoever it is won't be able to tell in the dark. Anthony likes to have two guards stationed outside the control room, but I've seen them all go out on patrol."

"And if the patrol doesn't go out?" I said.

"We do it tomorrow, or the day after. They won't be staying on the island for too long. HQ will figure out Anthony's bullshit."

"What's Martina doing once we're on the island?" Jack said. "I can hardly remember what she looks like from that picture."

I could tell he had the same reservations as me. This was the second time he'd asked about Lea's partner. Her plan all seemed a little too convenient.

"Don't worry about her. She'll join in as soon as we attack." Lea slipped a creased photograph out of a wallet and handed it to Jack. "You take out the guards and move inside for Jerry and Anthony. They'll be in the control room with Martina. Blow the control unit, and we get the hell out of there before the patrol comes back."

"Brett said it was in a tough protective casing," I said.

"Martina's going to get a tech to take off a side panel. She's thought about everything."

I had nagging doubts about her plan, but the opportunity to kill Anthony and Jerry had a strong appeal.

"You're sure Anthony and Jerry will be there?" Jack asked.

I knew he would jump at the opportunity to have a crack at them. Perhaps that's what they wanted? To lure us in by using Lea. I dismissed it as being too intricate for their brutal brains.

"Harry, are you in?" Lea asked.

"You haven't exactly given us a lot of details. We show up at a dock tonight, you pick us up, and we kill Jerry and Anthony. Is that it?"

"That's the bottom line."

"I'm in," Jack said.

His instant decision didn't come as a huge surprise. Jack always thought with his heart rather than his head. With our previous plan screwed and a larger enemy force on the horizon, I had to agree with him. We were neutralized and could run away, wash our hands of this thing, but I wanted revenge.

"Count us in," I said. "Nine hours to get ready and up to City Island."

"You need explosives to blow up the control unit."

"Leave that to us," Jack said.

It all seemed too easy. Lea turning up and serving up two of our mortal enemies on a plate. Perhaps I was being too cynical, but who could blame me?

"Are you sure about Martina?" I said. "She's been an important part of the operation for years and obviously knows Anthony and Jerry."

"I've been with her every day since I split with you guys. I know her; she's serious about it."

"What about HQ?" Jack said. "Are we just doing their job for them? Do we need to really do this?"

"You know there's nothing guaranteed in this world."

"If your HQ doesn't show up," I said, "we'll end the local team tonight."

The final words stirred something inside of me. From a hopeless situation a few hours ago, we had been handed a new lease on life.

Lea smiled. "Thanks, guys. I knew if I reached out, you'd be able to help."

"What about afterward?" Jack asked.

"We're planning to move south, down to Florida."

"Living in fear?" I said. "Lea, I want to survive too, but we've seen enough shit recently to give us another purpose. If we want any kind of a society, we need to take the fight to GA on a grander scale."

"Do you think it's possible to get away from these people?" Jack added.

She checked her gun and started to walk away. "We can talk about this if we pull it off tonight. I need to get back. See you at ten?"

"We'll be at City Island dock," Jack said. "Make sure you are."

"One last thing, Lea," I asked. "Why are some people acting so weird? I mean, way beyond the weirdness of killers?"

She looked over her shoulder. "There are all kinds of aftereffects, apparently. One of the techs said there's been a high error ratio in the software. Don't ask me to explain."

With that, she jogged away and disappeared from view, back toward the factory entrance.

"I'm looking forward to this," Jack said. "We've got a chance to settle a few scores here."

"Can't say I'm that convinced," I said. "We can go with it for now, but something tells me this isn't as straightforward as she's telling us."

"What about Morgan?" Jack asked. "I knew we couldn't trust him, but I didn't expect him to go running to GA."

"Doesn't surprise me. Let's hold off the celebrations until we get this thing done."

I could understand Jack's excitement, but Lea seemed hesitant, and her association with Genesis Alliance over the last few days deeply concerned me. From what she'd said, they were also in disarray, and desperate people do desperate things. I remembered the picture of Martina with Anthony from his house in Hermitage, and that she had the launch codes. What did we really know about her motives?

We moved away from the factory. I slipped into the Ravel Hotel back on Queens Boulevard and took a local map from the reception desk. A man and woman lay next to a pair of suitcases in the lobby, surrounded by shattered glass.

The most sensible route to Flushing Meadows, avoiding Elmhurst, was cutting through Astoria, past La Guardia airport, straight to the stadium. The main routes were mostly cluttered with vehicles, giving us plenty of cover and places to hide if we noticed anything unusual.

An elevated steel structure ran above us on 31st Street, supporting a railway track. We walked under it, and I noticed it needed maintenance and repainting. Without protection, the steel would corrode and fail. I wondered how long the city had left before it started to collapse. Bursts of automatic gunfire rattled in the distance for around a minute.

"Do you think that's GA at Bernie's?" Jack asked.

"Could be any number of things. We'll have to be careful at the stadium. I wouldn't be surprised if they decided to go back to find out what happened to their guys."

We reached Tribora Plaza and headed in an easterly direction, soon joining the Grand Central Parkway. On our right, we passed St. Michael's Cemetery; loving headstones formed neat rows. On the road outside, the dead lay scattered around in random formations. The juxtaposition changed from death and life to respectful and profane.

A short distance along the parkway we passed La Guardia Airport. Two planes were parked at angles on the runway; both had their slides deployed. Lea had arrived on one of them from Detroit. The terminal building windows glinted in the midday sun. We left JFK burning to the ground.

"Down," Jack said.

He crisply indicated to our front. I crouched and looked under and around the vehicles to see if I could spot any hidden killers. In the Army, we were taught not to point, but to use a flat hand when indicating direction. I had slipped out of the habit long ago, but Jack often did it.

A cat hopped onto a car's hood around fifty yards ahead of us and licked its paw. I lowered my rifle and continued forward, swept around a bend to the right, then crossed back on to Shea Road and stopped short of Flushing Meadows.

I leaned against a tree, took a package of Reese's Peanut Butter Cups out of my backpack, and tossed one to Jack. Its black paper tray fluttered to the grass, but he caught the important part and stuffed it in his mouth.

"Straight in and out of here," I said. "I hate the idea that GA have been all over this place in the last couple of days."

"If they came by boat and they're now in Elmhurst, maybe we can ambush them. Take half of the crew out early."

"Let's follow Lea's plan. We want them sweating about their Headquarters. Let's not give them a sniff that we're planning to strike Hart Island."

Due to Morgan's cleanup operation around the stadium, there were limited hiding places for killers and goons. Most corpses from the second activation were recognizable. As much as his death had stirred little emotion inside me, I still had grudging respect for his work here. We followed the same route we had before: through the fire door, up the stairs, and straight to the storeroom.

I grabbed the grenades and stuffed half of them into the top of my pack. Jack cleared some space in his, putting in chocolate and water, and placed more grenades into his bag. They looked like the British fragmentation type, with a pin and a timer.

I grabbed a pair of binoculars and two fully loaded Glocks, and dropped the cattle prod.

"A couple of those goons on the court looked roughly our size," Jack said. "Saves us a shopping trip. I'd rather get to our pickup point early."

"Sounds good to me," I said.

After observing the arena from our corporate suite, we headed down to the playing area. The three GA corpses still lay in the positions where they'd fallen, among members of the company. I judged the corpse by the net as the closest fit to me. Rigor mortis had set in, and I couldn't maneuver the clothes from his stiff body. Using my knee as a brace on his chest, I snapped his arms over his head and freed the sweater. The cargo pants came off more easily, and I swapped my clothes. I grimaced when I pulled the sweater over my head. This man had a serious body odor problem. I rubbed my fingers across a light-blue embroidered GA logo across my left breast. I couldn't understand the point of branding their uniforms if they were the only formal group left on Earth.

Jack squeezed his finger through a small bullet hole in his sweater. "These should do the trick."

"I'd put on a Newcastle United shirt if it meant a chance to kill Anthony," I said.

Jack smiled. "Come on, Harry. Don't exaggerate."

Newcastle United were the rivals of our football team, Sunderland, and such an action would previously have been seen as sacrilege. I would never get to feel the pure adrenalin rush of the ball smashing in the back of Newcastle's net again. Too bad; it was better than any commercially available drug.

Getting to City Island unseen in broad daylight looked impossible by car. The island had a single road leading to it, which posed obvious problems. We'd easily be seen if anyone watched the route or indeed used it at the same time we approached. City Island shielded Eastchester Bay from Hart Island; the obvious solution was to take a small boat across Eastchester Bay under the cover of darkness, but we'd have to move quickly to make our meeting time. The plan was to head just north of Throgs Neck Bridge and find a suitable vessel. We'd land on the west side of City Island and make the short journey across the place on foot to the boatyard next to the cemetery.

Confident we had a workable solution and time to implement it, we took a pair of mountain bikes from the locker room and headed off.

Robert F. Kennedy Bridge ended up being an impassable mangled mess. The railway crossing to our right still stood, so we crossed through a park, carried the bikes along the tracks, and rejoined our planned route on the Bruckner Expressway, which led very close to an ideal coastal launch point. I needn't explain the state of the roads. The carnage was standard fare.

As we passed through Soundview, two explosions boomed in the distance, followed slowly by a rising cloud of thin black smoke from the Queens area.

"I hope that's GA," Jack said.

"Why's that?"

"Because it means they're miles away from us."

Jack's conduct and general mood had continually improved since we'd left Monroe. I think something clicked inside of him after spending hours in the pit. It focused rather than disturbed him, and he had that old look of steely resolve in his eye. Determination had overridden his worrisome temper. I shared his optimism.

I recalled the importance of the Allied victory at the Battle of El Alamein, when Sir Winston Churchill said, "Before Alamein we never had a victory. After Alamein we never had a defeat."

I was hoping we'd be able to say the same thing about Hart Island and Genesis Alliance. The war would be far from over, but it could be a crucial first victory and a turning point. Without the threat of GA locally, we could gather an army and continue fighting. I believed Headquarters was only here to deal with the Monroe goons' incompetence. They wouldn't stay forever.

A lone voice repeatedly shouted from a park on our left as we passed Schuylerville. I couldn't see anyone in the long swaying grass and didn't feel the need to investigate. We knew from Lea that other areas had had a different kind of second activation. New York would be a poor recruiting ground in the future, but we'd have our revenge for that tonight.

We exited the parkway, past a tired old sports field on our right, and headed down Ampere Avenue. An Italian restaurant had a smashed front window, and a moldy flap of pizza hung from a jagged shard. A red brick church had "Save Our Souls" painted on its open green door, and six of the houses were burnt to blackened block shells.

A sparkling bay greeted us at the end of the road. Water lapped the hulls of twenty boats, secured to moorings in the marina. I felt confident we'd get one working and gazed over the water to the houses dotting the coastline of City Island.

I peddled to the marina entrance and propped the bike against a car. My thighs felt stiff from the exertion, but in a good way. Exercise has a positive effect on me. I'd heard it had to do with endorphins being released in the body. They sounded like sea creatures to me.

Jack made his way to a sleek white Sunseeker with a corpse slumped over the stern. I scanned five ubiquitous wood-clabbered houses overlooking the boats. Satisfied there were no signs of immediate danger inland, I fished out the binoculars and surveyed the bay.

The boat's engine rumbled into life, and water bubbled from the back of it.

"We're in business," Jack called.

I hopped onto the wooden decking at the back. "Clear out here. So far, so good."

Inside, the Sunseeker felt luxurious. It had a small recreational area with white leather seats and polished chestnut tables and cupboards. We avoided the temptation of a stocked mini bar, although I slipped two whiskey miniatures into my pocket for a post-operation drink. A small internal staircase led to a raised cockpit. From here, through slightly pink-tinted windows, we had a good view of our evening route.

During the last hours of daylight, only a single vehicle flicked in and out of vision along the route, heading onto the island.

———

At eight in the evening, when darkness enveloped the bay, Jack fired up the engine, and we drifted away from the marina. I'd taken a compass bearing that would lead us to the center of the western shoreline, which looked to be a mixture of pontoons that lined a long beach. We planned to ground on the sand.

Jack increased the throttle as we broke into the free water, and the Sunseeker cut through dark shadows of vessels at anchor. He kept a steady course and headed for the black silhouette of City Island. After ten minutes, with the island looming large, our hull crunched against land and slid to an abrupt halt several yards short of the shore. Without hesitating, we left the cockpit, jumped from the side of the boat into waist-deep water, and waded to dry land, with our rifles above our heads.

I led us straight to Bay Street, past the dark shapes of previously expensive large properties.

A figure moved to our front.

"Cover," I whispered.

We ducked into a front garden and hid behind two large tropical trees.

A woman stumbled between two houses in a nightgown.

She shuffled stiffly in our direction, holding her arms rigidly by her side, palms open and fingers spread. She closed in on our position. Moonlight reflected off her pale face, staring vacantly ahead.

A dark stain splashed across the front of her nightgown, which stuck to her stomach. Probably blood. She moaned and wailed in low tones.

We edged around the trees as she made her way past us. When she reached the end of the road, she turned around and started making her way back up the street. I checked my watch. We still had twenty minutes.

"Cut across to another street," I whispered. "It's like a grid system here, so we won't get lost in the dark."

"Looks like she's on another planet."

"Just another one of GA's victims."

The woman shuffled past us again, up the street and back between the two houses from where she'd first appeared.

"It's like she's walking a circuit," Jack said.

"Perhaps it's all she knows. I'm not waiting for her to come back."

He nodded and we moved purposefully down William Avenue and turned right on Tier Street in the direction of the boatyard. Within five minutes, we arrived. Adrenalin pulsed through my veins at the thought of our imminent attack and facing Anthony and Jerry again.

"Last chance for a weapons check," Jack said.

I quietly tested the working parts of my rifle, took the Glocks out of my pack, and handed one to Jack. "Hopefully, we won't be needing these."

The moment had finally arrived.

10

We had two hundred and forty rifle rounds between us and planned to take single aimed shots unless things got out of hand. The Army had taught us to make every shot count, to only spray if you could afford to or if the situation was desperate at close quarters and there was no other way. I felt confident in our ability to fire under pressure and calculated that we had more than enough ammo, if Lea's numbers were correct.

"We'll rendezvous at the pontoon on Hart Island if we get split. Our secondary RV will be the boat we arrived on, okay?"

"Got that. What if one of us . . ." Jack trailed off.

"If one of us gets wasted, I've got a feeling we're both screwed."

"I'd hunt GA until my final breath."

I admired his sentiment and would probably do the same thing, but we didn't need our minds clouded by depressing thoughts. I preferred to think of our mission as the starting gun for the destruction of Genesis Alliance.

"Let's not think about it just yet. Anthony seemed capable. We take him first if we can."

"He's my number-one target. Don't worry about that."

I looked over to Hart Island and noticed a dim light.

"Still no sign of their HQ," I said. "Reckon it was a scare story to keep them in line?"

"I think it's way more than that," Jack said.

We waited between two dry-docked vessels. Jack rapidly tapped his right boot on the ground, a sign of his nerves and excitement. After fifteen minutes, the buzzing noise of an engine drifted over the water.

"Here we go," I said.

A small boat split the moonlit waters, coming from the direction of Hart Island, leaving a disappearing white trail behind it. Its engines whined in reverse, and it stopped at the end of a long wooden pontoon.

A single figure jumped off the boat, quickly secured it with a thick rope, and walked toward the yard.

"It's her," Jack said as Lea got closer.

I stepped from between the boats. She flinched and reached toward her hip holster.

"Weren't expecting to see us?" I said.

"I didn't expect you to be waving flags," she said. "You can't be too careful."

"Are we good to go?" Jack asked.

"We're good to go, but we need to hurry. There's only one guard on the island. Jerry, Anthony, and Martina are in the control room. They're preparing a presentation for Headquarters."

"A presentation?" Jack repeated.

"They're coming up with ways to justify the delayed activation and the Manhattan device configuration. Anthony's made up quite a back-story for you two. HQ got in touch with them this afternoon. They're heading this way and might be here in a couple of hours."

"No time to hang around then—straight in and out," I said. "Where's the guard?"

"He's outside the control room. We'll be able to walk right up."

"Are you sure? You left on your own but return with two people?" Jack said.

"Who will they expect it to be? You casually walk right up, in the dark. Before they realize"—she made a two-fingered pistol gesture with her right hand—"Paw!"

"What excuse did you use to get away?" I asked.

I still had a gnawing doubt at how easy this seemed to be. The potential prize helped to quell it—and the fact that we had someone on the inside helping us.

"I told Martina that I needed some sleep. Anthony and Jerry didn't question it. Martina backed me up."

"Where did the others go? We didn't see any big patrols go out," Jack said.

"Twenty left from the other side of the island an hour ago."

"Do you know when they're coming back?" I asked.

"Not until tomorrow morning." She flashed me a wicked smile. "You'll love this: they're actually scouting Elmhurst, looking for you."

"That's sweet," Jack said. "While they're looking for us we'll be taking out their base."

"There's something else I need to clear with you guys before we go over."

"Clear with us?" I said and stepped closer to her. "Why don't I like the sound of this?"

She sighed and looked away. "Martina started getting cold feet this afternoon."

"Spit it out," Jack said.

"You know there's nothing any of us can do against Genesis Alliance, and the world's fucked, right?"

"Go on," I said.

She bowed her head. "What if we ran the U.S. operation of GA with Martina?"

"You've got to be kidding!" Jack said.

"Just think about it for a minute. We could make a difference. People wouldn't have to be processed. We'd give them a chance to build a community together. We need to make sure what's left of the population can try to rebuild."

"Jesus, Lea," I said, barely believing her suggestion, especially at this last stage. "Listen to yourself. You sound like Ron."

"I don't sound anything like Ron. I'm being serious," she snapped.

"You sound exactly like him," Jack said.

"This is her, isn't it?" I said. "She doesn't want to let go of power, with those launch codes. Has she even considered what is going to happen for not following HQ's orders?"

Lea paused for a moment and looked to the sky. "I told her it was a stupid idea, but she wanted to back out."

"You really surprise me sometimes," I said. "You had the guts to go back to GA, knowing you could be killed, and found a window of opportunity to take them out. Now you're asking us to replace them? What did you think we'd say?"

"I told her you wouldn't go along with it."

"We're destroying that control unit, whether she likes it or not."

"We could pretend to go along with their plans while neutralizing as many people as possible," she said.

"Bollocks to that," Jack said, his voice rising, probably along with his blood pressure. "I'm going over there to kill Anthony and Jerry. This isn't a negotiation. Bigger boys are coming our way, and we need to move."

"There's no arguments over Anthony and Jerry. It's what happens after that."

"There's no arguments from our side," I said. "Do you expect us to leave that thing intact so GA can carry on terrorizing? Do I need to remind you about Bernie? Or everyone out there?"

"I can't believe you've come out with this shit," Jack said.

Both Jack and I knew how poor leadership and muddled planning without clearly defined objectives could lead to disastrous consequences. Any other lover of military history would know the same things. The centuries were stuffed with examples.

Lea paced around the yard with her hands on her head. Jack and I leaned against a boat and glared at her. Once we were taken to Hart Island, nothing would stop us from smashing up the control unit if we had the opportunity. If she didn't take us, I decided, we were going anyway. This was too good an opportunity to miss.

Genesis Alliance was a large, powerful organization. Did she seriously think they'd let a large section of their operation free to do as they pleased, helping out survivors that they tried to kill? The Lea I knew would see straight through her partner's cyanide-tipped olive branch.

When dictators in rogue states are deposed or die, it's very rare that something better takes their place. We were all supposed to fall into line and salute the Arab Spring, but I knew deep down that armed men in pickup trucks rarely formed a cohesive democracy, especially when it was won with blood.

Lea finally stopped in front of us. "How about a compromise? We make the place safe, and the four of us discuss our options?"

Jack looked at me and shook his head.

"No," I said. "I'm not standing around debating the impossible. You said HQ is on the way. We're going now, with or without you."

She took a step back and raised her eyebrows. "Without me?"

"You don't have to take part," Jack said, "but I'm not missing this opportunity."

"We're sticking with the original plan," I said. "Do you seriously expect us to back out?"

She shook her head. "I can't believe I even asked you. I had to try for Martina. She's gonna be pissed."

"I don't give a fuck what she thinks," I said, no longer able to mask my irritation.

"Leave it. I'm sorry, okay?"

"Are we good to go?" Jack asked. "She won't be causing us any problems?"

"None of us have too many choices anymore. I'll deal with Martina."

———

Lea's boat slapped over the waves toward distant Hart Island. Jack and I crouched in the back and covered ourselves with a tarpaulin. We needed speed and direct force to overwhelm Anthony and Jerry before they could form any defensive positions. My heart thumped against my chest when Lea decreased the speed and steered to the left side of the island.

I pulled the tarpaulin to one side and looked out at it.

"That's the light on the dock," she shouted over the spray pounding the side of the hull. "We'll be there in two minutes."

I instinctively checked my rifle again and patted the magazines in my thigh pocket. A dim light on the center of the island illuminated a square brick building around three hundred yards to the left of the dock.

"Is that the control room?" I asked.

"It's just a short walk through a field. We'll be there in no time."

Lea cut the engine, and we bumped into the side of the pontoon. Jack grabbed a support with both hands and held the boat steady against the wooden structure. Lea secured the rope, and we thumped onto the planks.

She motioned us forward with her gun. "Martina's gonna stay out of view of the window, to give you clear shots."

I wondered if it might be best to shoot Martina. Lea's feelings were the only thing stopping me from putting a bullet in her partner's head.

She strode off the pontoon onto a grass field. A well-trod path cut directly through it to the gloomy building; the rest of the overgrown field swayed gently in the sea breeze. Dark shadows of trees surrounded most of the shore.

She turned back and whispered, "They're still here. Can you—"

Bright light flooded the area, and people screamed from all directions.

I immediately dropped to the prone position and raised my head.

Two large halogen lights shone straight down the path, lighting up the area all around us. I crawled into the long grass. Jack did the same in my peripheral vision. Lea froze and raised her arms in surrender. The screaming voices closed in on my position.

I squinted against the lights but couldn't see a thing.

"Drop your weapons and stand up."

"Put your hands in the air, now."

"You've got five seconds."

"You're surrounded! You're not getting out of here alive unless you do what we say."

The last shout sent a shockwave through my body. I thought about spraying the immediate vicinity, and I'm sure Jack did too, but it would be a death mission. We'd been caught in a professional ambush. They knew our exact location and we'd be taking potshots at muzzle flashes, all zeroed in on our position.

I looked at Lea. Her shocked expression was clearly visible in the artificial lighting. "I didn't know, I . . . I . . ."

A man shouted, "Five . . . four . . . three . . ."

I stood up with my hands in the air. Jack followed and glanced across at me. "We're dead meat—should have gone out in a blaze of glory."

"We'd have been cut to ribbons in two seconds—"

Before I could finish my sentence, I felt a heavy blow slam into my back, and I staggered forward onto my knees. Strong arms forced me down. Multiple hands pinned me to the ground. My pack straps were sliced, and it was ripped off my back; my arms were pulled behind me, and my wrists were secured with a zipping noise, crushing them together. Hands searched every one of my pockets and emptied the contents.

"He's clean," the knife-wielding man said.

"This one too," another voice said.

Somebody grabbed a fistful of my hair and pulled me to my feet. Jack stood close by with his hands tied. A guard led Lea at gunpoint toward the building. Two men grabbed my arms and frogmarched me behind her.

They stopped ten yards short of the building. One of the guards kicked me in the calf.

"On your fucking knees, now," he said.

Saliva sprayed against my ear, and he kicked me in the back of the knee. I dropped to my knees.

A goon punched Jack in the stomach, and he crumpled to the grass. I couldn't believe our hope had been ripped away in seconds, and I was under no illusion what they had in store for us. A quick death.

A tall, slim woman appeared in the doorway. Thin lips with peroxided blonde hair. I recognized her as Martina from the picture we'd recovered at Anthony's house. She gave me a look of contempt.

"Why?" Lea said. "How could you do this to me?"

"I did this for your own good," she replied in a chillingly calm voice. "HQ is coming, and we had to stamp out any threat. I'm choosing the right side for us."

"You said you wanted out, and—" Lea said.

"Listen to her, Lea," I said. "You've got a chance to get out of this."

Jack and I didn't, but at least she had a chance. I didn't want her to waste it by falling on her sword.

A guard slapped me over the head. "Be quiet, asshole."

Martina smiled. "Oh, how sweet. Look, he's defending you."

"You've betrayed me. We had plans," Lea said.

I looked across to Jack. The guard twisted my head forward.

Martina walked past Lea and glowered at us. "I couldn't let them get away with killing Ron. Which one of them was it?"

"Sorry, guys, I didn't know, sorry . . ." Lea said. A tear rolled down her cheek as she turned to face Martina. "You said you'd have done the same in their position."

"I would, but he was my uncle, your boss. You'll come to realize that I'm right."

Martina jabbed her fingernail into my forehead and twisted it. "Was it this one?"

"It was me, and he deserved it," Jack said.

She spun toward him and slapped him across the face. "Kill this one. They can have fun with the other one."

"No—no you can't!" Lea shouted.

"She's right, not yet," a familiar voice said.

Anthony stood by the building's door, holding a cardboard box. He looked even more like Larry David in this light. "I've got business with these two, and it's going to be a long, long night."

Jerry pushed past him. "Well, look what we've got here. You're gonna regret the day our paths crossed."

Anthony dropped the cardboard box. He didn't have the same jocularly spiteful demeanor as Jerry. He narrowed his eyes and stared at me with a stone-faced expression.

"Just get it over with. We need to finish the presentation," Martina said.

"I've invested a lot of time in getting my hands on these two," Anthony said. "There's gonna be no rushing."

"Martina," Lea pleaded, "tell them you won't give them launch codes. You can't let them do this!"

Martina looked indifferent and shrugged. "Sorry, it's out of my hands. Come inside and we can talk."

"I'm staying out here. With Harry and Jack."

Anthony nodded at a guard. He shoved Lea forward with his rifle muzzle. She staggered into the building, and the door closed behind them. Muffled shouts and screams came from behind the door.

Jerry knelt in front of me, grabbed my sweater with both hands, and head-butted me on the bridge of my nose. Stars flashed in front of my eyes, and sharp, searing pain shot through my head.

He stood and cracked his knuckles. "That's just the start of it."

Anthony gestured to a guard. "Put them against the wall while we get prepared."

Two goons grabbed me under each armpit and threw me against the side of the structure, near the end of its wall, away from the entrance. Jack bounced down next to me. Two guards stood in front of us, pointing AR-15s at our heads.

Anthony crouched in front of Jack. "Remember what you did to me in my garage?"

Jack spat in his face.

He fished a handkerchief from his breast pocket and wiped his cheek, before thrusting his rifle butt into the side of Jack's face.

"And you . . ." He turned to me. "In the Second World War, the Japanese would use a torture technique involving the forced ingestion of water. Let's see how you like that."

"How's your house, Anthony?" I said.

He shook his head. "You really are a piece of work."

I refused to beg for mercy from either of these two; it wouldn't change their minds.

255

Jerry nudged in front of Anthony. "Did you go back to Montgomery?"

"We did. You need to start looking for a new home," I said.

He advanced toward me, but Anthony held him back. "Take it easy. They need to feel everything . . ."

They both walked out of sight. I tried to make eye contact with the guard. He looked away.

"Look, mate, let me go—you can't agree with this," I said.

"You're not getting out of here. Your brother isn't either. These two have made us walk through walls to get hold of you. I'll be glad when it's all over."

"What kind of bloke are you?" Jack said.

"I'm just a guy trying to survive. Now do me a favor and shut the fuck up."

The shouting continued between Lea and Martina inside the building. Our chances of help from anywhere seemed nonexistent. Two men carried a large wooden table from around the side of the building and positioned it in front of us. Then they placed on it a drum of rope, bolt cutters, and a roll of masking tape.

Jerry returned, slipped a knife out of his belt, and cut lengths of rope from the drum. "You're first, Jack. Don't think I've forgotten about you."

"You'll never forget me after you see the state of your house," Jack said.

Jerry shook his head. "You stupid fuck. I can choose a better place."

The building door creaked open, and Martina leaned out. "Anthony, get over here."

"He's getting ready in the pump room," Jerry said.

"Jerry said he's going to slit your throat after he gets the launch codes from HQ," I said to Martina.

Anything was worth a shot at this stage. Although they'd probably see straight through my weak attempt to drive a wedge between them.

"You're pathetic," she said. "Come on, Lea; let's talk to Anthony."

Lea's face looked puffy and white as she followed Martina. It surprised me that she didn't even look at us.

"What are you going to talk about?" Jerry called after her. "You're not letting these two go—that's not part of our agreement."

"You'll get your fun," she said. "Come with us if you want."

He pointed his knife at me. "I'm not letting them out of my sight."

Jerry walked over to two guards who stood by the halogen lights. I could hear parts of his conversation. Something about being ready for when HQ arrived, and no more fuck-ups from here.

"This is it then," Jack said. "Got any last minute brainwaves?"

"Our only hope is Lea, but what chance does she have persuading Anthony out of this? We should have backed out when she started coming out with that nonsense at the boatyard."

"It was worth a shot. She didn't know—" he replied.

Jerry stomped over to Jack and kicked him in the chest. "Who gave you permission to talk?"

Jack rolled onto his side and coughed. Jerry returned to the other two goons.

Raised voices came from the back of the building. Maybe Lea making a final plea for our lives. I would even settle for a severe beating, although that was probably already part of Anthony's plan.

"Are you okay?" I asked.

Jack hauled himself up and looked at Jerry, who repeatedly glanced in our direction.

Jack leaned toward me. "There are a couple of lights in the sky. Have a look over my shoulder when you get a chance."

A low buzzing noise drifted across the breeze. The GA guys all looked upward.

"Over there," one shouted and pointed high to his left.

Two separate lights grew brighter in the dark sky, and the buzzing gradually increased to a recognizable sound of helicopters.

Jerry ran past us and called down the side of the building, "There are a couple of choppers approaching. It might be Headquarters."

I detected both panic and excitement in his voice.

"It might be hostile. How do we know?" one of the goons asked.

Jerry turned back to him. "Coming directly to Hart Island? Don't be stupid."

He shouted in the general direction of the guards around the field and building. "Call everyone in, and look sharp."

The goons gathered in the artificial light at front of the building.

Jerry ran back to the side of the building. "Anthony, Anthony . . ."

"I'll be two minutes—just be patient," he replied, out of our sight.

"What are you doing? We've got two choppers coming in," Jerry said.

"Martina's using the launch codes as leverage again."

"Fuck her; we might get them from these guys coming in."

"Keep your voice down. She's not the problem. You know what the issue is . . ."

"Just shoot her. We'll get them how I originally wanted," Jerry said.

"You know we've just about managed to pull things back into shape. Don't do anything rash. Wait until the time's right. You need to muster the troops and greet the choppers. We need to look well organized if they're to believe our story."

"What about Harry and Jack?"

"We'll deal with them when HQ has gone," Anthony said far too eagerly. "Just roll out the red carpet, right?"

Jerry looked down at us. "We waited long enough, I suppose. A couple more hours won't hurt."

The moon cast Anthony's shadow along the grass. "Just bide your time, listen to everything they say, and keep your answers vague."

"Got it. I'll get everyone organized at the front," Jerry said and looked into the sky at the now clearly visible helicopters.

He organized the assembled goons on the field into three lines of ten, and stood in front of them like a second-rate drill sergeant.

One of the choppers thumped through the night sky, making a low-level pass of the island. It turned in a wide arc and hovered for a few moments over the field before slowly descending and bumping on the ground seventy yards away.

It looked like a large black Sea King. The blades slowly spun to a halt and relaxed.

A side door rumbled open. Ten armed men streamed out and lined up in the field, crouching with weapons aimed forward.

The local GA team exchanged whispers. All eyes were on the new arrivals, who held their position.

Two minutes later, another Sea King slowly dropped to the field. Four people sprang out, folded out some steps, and formed a guard. A silver-haired man in a cream suit, carrying a clipboard, descended the steps and looked around.

He walked toward Jerry. The armed guards edged forward, keeping a few yards behind him in an extended line across the field.

"Identify yourselves," he called out in a northern English accent.

"I'm Jerry Caisley, Genesis Alliance Regional Coordinator for New York Three in North America," he said with an air of confidence.

The man frowned at his clipboard and ran his finger along it. He continued forward across the flattened grass. His squad also advanced, stopping twenty yards short of Jerry.

The engines of the second helicopter whined to a halt.

"Are you in charge?" Cream Suit asked.

Jerry nodded. "Yes, sir."

"Are these all of your men?"

"Yes, there are others, but—"

The man raised his hand, stopping Jerry in his tracks. "Are these all of your men?"

Jerry nodded again. "Don't worry about the two by the wall; they're dead men."

I noticed Jack immediately close his eyes; I followed suit. I didn't like the look of this one bit. It seemed a strange and aggressive way to introduce themsleves.

"Which ones are from the tech team?"

"They're not here," Jerry said.

"Then go and get them."

"I can't. They were ordered to Atlantic City by Headquarters."

"Sorry, my mistake. When did they leave?"

"Today."

The man folded his clipboard under his arm. "Okay, relax, everyone, but stay where you are. I'm an Operations Director from the other side of the pond. I'm going around all of our sites, checking resources and compiling progress reports from the local teams. As you're aware, we've faced some issues, so I want to focus our efforts into the right areas. Please form a single line. I'm going to come along and ask your name and a few short questions."

"Get moving then—you heard the man," Jerry shouted.

I squinted half an eye open and watched the man moving along the line, shaking hands with people and having brief conversations while writing on the clipboard. After talking to the last man, he tucked the clipboard under his arm again and walked back in front of the local team.

"Gentlemen, thank you for your time. It's been invaluable."

He turned to walk away.

"Is that it?" Jerry asked. "What do we do next?

Cream suit raised his right hand. "Fire!"

The field lit up with muzzle flashes. Deafening bursts of automatic fire ripped through the men and women lined up in front of the building. Rounds thumped against the wall and shattered windows to our right.

I tensed and watched the local goons being ripped apart through my half-closed eyes. None had time to go for their weapons; the attack happened too quickly and unexpectedly for them to react. The man held up his arm again and the firing ceased.

He reached inside his jacket and pulled out a silver revolver and waved it in the direction of the massacre.

They searched around the bodies, two of whom were finished off with a close-range shot to the head. I heard Jerry groan.

Cream Suit stood over him. "Why? Because it's been a total fuck-up over here from start to finish. A destroyed control unit, a late activation, repeating the first activation in New York."

Jerry raised a quivering, bloodstained hand toward him and let out a mumbled cry. Cream Suit shook his head, lowered his revolver, and fired directly in Jerry's face.

He walked toward the entrance of the building and looked inside. I closed my eyes and hoped he assumed we were dead. I wasn't about to start negotiating with him or his team, and lay as still as possible.

"It's in here," he shouted. "Remember, take out the processors, but don't mess it up. We just need to leave it unworkable for anyone who finds it, and easy to put back together if we decide to send another team."

I squinted an eye open again. Two men entered the building with large plastic briefcases.

"I hear they might be sending the California team here," one of them said.

"Won't be for at least a couple of months. They're too busy at the moment."

Cream Suit leaned against the exterior wall and lit a cigarette. Drilling noises came from inside. In a matter of minutes, both men left the building. One carried three large circuit boards; the other, a hard drive.

One of the assault team approached Cream Suit. "Want us to sweep the island, sir?"

"Don't worry about it. We've done what's needed. Let's get the hell out of here and back to the ship."

He tossed his cigarette to his side. It landed inches from my face, and smoke drifted up my nostrils. I strained to keep still and suppressed a cough.

"Everybody out!" a voice shouted.

Propellers started to spin, and the engines noise increased. The group boarded the helicopters and weren't wasting any time. The first rose slowly into the sky, closely followed by the second Sea King. They both inclined forward and thumped away.

"Let's get the fuck out of here," I said.

I used the wall to lever myself up, picked up the bolt cutters from the table, and threw myself into the long grass, acutely aware that three people remained alive at the back of the building.

Jack landed next to me. "Make for the trees."

We staggered up and ran thirty yards to a small wooded area on our left. Close to the sound of water lapping against the shore.

I ducked behind a tree.

"Turn around and I'll cut you free," I said.

Jack spun and held out his arms. I snapped the cutters' teeth through the tie.

He stretched his arms and grabbed the cutters.

The tie flipped off painful wrists. I rubbed them and looked back at the scene or carnage. Relief washed over me, but we weren't safe yet.

"We've got two options," I said. "Pick up a rifle and finish it, or head for the boat."

"We finish it—and save Lea."

I sprinted the short distance back across the small field and knelt by a corpse. He had entry wounds in his nose and forehead, the final one perhaps being the "coup de grace" delivered by one of his own organization. I pulled an AR-15 from underneath him, checked the magazine, and reloaded.

A shot split the air. Jack flew back.

In my peripheral vision, I noticed a figure at the corner of the building.

A muzzle flashed and a tracer round zipped over my shoulder. I swept the rifle around and fired five shots.

Anthony screamed and fell into the light, clutching his chest.

"Jack, are you alright?" I shouted.

"I'll live," he groaned and rolled onto his front.

Anthony tried to raise himself with one hand and gurgled, "Bastards."

We both fired repeatedly. One of the rounds smacked into Anthony's temple. He lurched forward and flopped face first to the dirt. Jack fired again and struck him in the top of the head. His body didn't move.

I scrambled over to him but kept half an eye on the building. "Are you okay? Let me have a look."

Jack lay on his side and pulled his trousers down a few inches with his thumb. He had a small entry wound a couple of inches from his hipbone.

"Lea," I shouted. "Come out—it's clear."

Moments later, the two women appeared from behind the building. They both gaped at Anthony as they passed him.

I pointed my rifle at Martina. "You. Throw your weapon on the ground. The one in your holster."

She slowly took out the pistol and dropped it in the grass.

"That's right. Now come closer," I ordered.

She had some serious questions to answer. Lea had her weapon back, but I felt sure she wouldn't use it against us. Even if Jack killed her partner.

"She was forced to do it," Lea said. "She's just been telling me about it."

"Oh, I bet she has," Jack said. He grimaced and used his rifle to haul himself to his feet. "She nearly got us all killed."

Lea stepped in front of Martina. "It's Morgan's fault. He told Anthony everything."

"Bullshit," I said. "We hadn't even met you by then. All he knew about was the note."

"When I left to meet you, to discuss our plan, they threatened her with all kinds of crazy shit. You know what they were like; she had to come clean to save my life."

"Anthony let you leave the island?" Jack said. "Straight after finding out you were coming to try and meet us?"

"He wanted to know what Martina knew about it and to see if she would sanction my execution."

"Come off it. You know that's rubbish," I said. "If they wanted us so badly, they could have just followed you to the Queensboro Bridge."

Jack jabbed his rifle at Martina. "Can't she speak for herself?"

"It's true. We've all got what we wanted, in a roundabout way. I'm sorry about before. It was all part of the act. I had to be convincing."

Martina looked and sounded insincere. Perhaps that was her way, but she took us both for fools if she expected us to swallow her crap.

"You seem to be forgetting that you wanted me killed first," Jack said.

She half-closed her eyes and looked at Lea.

"You can't blame them for being like this," Lea said.

"She sold us down the river, and you know it," I said.

"By the way, Martina," Jack said. "Jerry and Anthony were going to kill you as soon as they got the launch codes."

"Do you think I don't know that?" she asked. "I've still got them, though, and that's a big bargaining chip."

"What do you think just happened?"

I edged sideways and placed Martina firmly in my sights. "They took parts of the control unit, so it can't be used. There's another team coming over . . ."

"I can negotiate with them," Martina said.

It annoyed me that she thought she could simply talk her way out of this. I wasn't sure how anyone could like this woman, especially Lea. "This isn't a stupid game, you know? They're bringing in another team from California. It's over for you, Martina."

Lea tugged at her arm. "It's a fresh start. We can forget about this whole thing."

Martina scowled at me. "It's not over until I say it's over. I've been Henry Fairfax's eyes and ears on the ground. He'll have me back in the blink of an eye."

I stared at her over my sights, not quite believing what she'd just said.

Lea's eyes widened, and she leaned away from Martina. "You never told me this. I thought you said Ron kept most of it secret from you. Tell me you're just saying this to—"

"I was only trying to protect you," Martina said. "Ron was the front. Do you really think I kept going to South America when I kept returning without a hint of a tan?"

Jack winced and raised his rifle. "How much more evidence do you need, Lea?"

Lea cupped her cheeks. "Oh my God. You scheming bitch."

"Watch your tongue," Martina said. "Fairfax wouldn't kill the person who helped him plan this whole thing. I sent him e-mails while you made me meatloaf. Do you know how stupid that makes you look?"

Lea silently shook her head, stepped away from Martina, and walked over to my side. It had a symbolic feeling, like she'd finally made her choice and taken her foot out of one camp. Who could blame her after Martina's revelations? Although I suspected some of them weren't true. I decided we should leave her on the island to stew in her own juice. A quick death was far too good for this bitter woman.

My mind already raced with bigger things than her. The immediate threat was replaced with breathing space. But we caught a glimpse of what loomed on the horizon if we didn't act.

Martina dived to her right and grabbed the pistol from the grass. She swung it around in our direction. Before I could pull the trigger, Lea fired two rounds. Martina jerked twice as the bullets hit her chest in quick succession. Her arms fell limply by her sides.

Lea slowly lowered her gun and bowed her head.

"It was her or us," Jack said. "I was going to do it anyway."

Good old Jack, as subtle as a brick, but I agreed with the sentiment.

Martina coughed. Lea ran to her side, knelt, and held her hand. Martina wheezed heavily and stared at the clear night sky. Blood soaked the front of her vest.

"Why did you do it?" Lea cried in anguish. "Why did you have to ruin it all?"

Martina fixed her gaze on Lea and squeezed her eyes closed. In a final act of spite, she spat blood into Lea's face. Her head flopped to the left, she exhaled, and her eyes glazed over.

Lea sprang to her feet and wiped her right cheek. "I've been fooling myself, right up until the end. I'm sorry."

"You've got nothing to apologize for. She left you with no choice," I said.

Lea covered her face with her hands and sobbed. Jack and I backed off to give her a minute. Martina's betrayal ran even deeper than I'd ever imagined. It must've cut Lea to the bone.

"Let's get off this island and somewhere safe," I said. "You're better off without her."

And I genuinely believed it. Martina had been a poisonous influence on Lea, and it had nearly cost us our lives. We could now focus as a single-minded group.

Jack put his arm around me for support, and I helped him back toward the boat. Lea joined him at his other side, and he folded his other arm around her. We shuffled along together and reached the landing.

Jack slumped into the back of the boat, and Lea took the controls. I stood looking down at them and felt a strong sense of determination.

"What's the plan?" Jack asked.

"We can't go on fighting Genesis Alliance in open warfare," I said. "They're too strong for three of us. But we can't ignore them. They need to be ground into the dirt."

"What do we do?" Lea asked.

"We go over to England and cut the head from the snake's body. We decapitate Genesis Alliance. Are you in?"

They both nodded.

The End

ACKNOWLEDGMENTS

Paul Lucas from Janklow & Nesbit, for his advice, support, and the fantastic job he did of finding us such a great publisher in 47North.

Emilie Marneur and Sana Chebaro from the Amazon UK team, who have guided us through every step and have been a pleasure to work with.

Jennifer Gaynor, our excellent structural editor.

Jill M. Pellarin, our equally as good copy editor.

Harry Dewulf for his creative input.

Mike Meredith, David Spell, and Jean Dunn for your beta reading and support.

Finally, and most importantly, our readers. We've had some great feedback, communication, and encouragement from you in the last twelve months. We wish we could mention you all, and we appreciate the time you have taken to read our book.

ABOUT THE AUTHORS

Photo © 2014 Dawn Cotton

Darren Wearmouth was born in Yorkshire and spent six years in the British Army's Royal Signals Division before pursuing a career in corporate technology. After fifteen years working for telecommunications firms and a startup, he decided to follow his passion for writing. A sportsman, he loves watching and playing football, cricket, and golf. His other hobbies include reading, mountaineering, and socializing. He also has a hidden talent for Italian cooking. He currently resides in Manchester, England.

Marcus Wearmouth was born in Yorkshire and also spent six years in the British Army, serving in the Royal Electronic and Mechanical Engineers. He graduated from Northumbria University with a degree in surveying and now owns a consultancy that specializes in subsidence. Marcus loves spending time with his two wonderful children, Andrew and George. He currently resides in Harrogate, England, and is secretly a very gifted bagpiper.